D1528059

THE HEIDELBERG GHOST

A SWEET HOLIDAY ROMANCE

NICKIE COCHRAN

MOUNTAIN WHISPER PUBLISHING

The Heidelberg Ghost by Nickie Cochran

Published by Mountain Whisper Publishing
Cover by Nickie Cochran
Edited by Frankie Sutton

 Created with Vellum

ACKNOWLEDGMENTS

To my husband Don and my twins Jamey & Danny, who have lived months without seeing their wife and mother during the writing and editing process of this book. Thanks for being so understanding when I sent you off to have a guys' night at the movies, while I was typing away in solitude at home. Not that you didn't have fun…

Also, a special thank you to my daughter, Jessica, who returned to our roots in Eppelheim and Heidelberg after she had earned her undergrad degree in archaeology. She is continuing her education at the University of Heidelberg and involuntarily became my go-to person in anything related to Heidelberg and its history. More than once, she helped me out of a plot-hole with her witty ideas. You rock!

Then, there are my Mama and Papa in Germany who, every time we talked on the phone, had to listen to my ramblings about how my story developed over time. Maybe one day, I will publish a German version of the book, just for you.

Finally, many thanks to my family and friends, who

encouraged me and made me believe in myself. Without you, I would have never experienced the feeling of joy and accomplishment when holding my first book in my hands, ready to share it with the world. You gave me the courage to continue writing, even when things got a little tough.

Thank you all!

~

CHAPTER 1

*T*he airliner hit yet another rough patch of turbulence on its journey across the Atlantic Ocean to Germany. As the jumbo sagged, the water sloshed over the edge of Andrea's cup and left a small puddle on her tray.

So much for a good start, she sighed, then grabbed the used dinner napkin and mopped up the mess in front of her. Andrea hated flying. Traveling hundreds of miles across the ocean made her nervous. What if they crashed, who would rescue her? She envisioned herself swallowing the salty seawater as she fought to stay afloat. Yes, being burned alive, drowning, or getting eaten by sharks definitely ranked high on her list of miserable ways to die. Think positively, Andi, she tried to calm herself. A plane crashing from this altitude would probably kill anyone on impact, so why worry about dying a slow death anyway. Great. So that wasn't really helping.

Another violent jolt and a fast drop in altitude ripped her out of her thoughts and made her stomach lurch.

Andrea felt a wave of nausea coming on. Where's a

barf bag when you really need it? She didn't remember seeing one after take-off, when she rifled through the magazines in her seat pocket. Even though she took some motion sickness pills before the flight, she wouldn't get any peace of mind until she found it. She grabbed her cup of water in one hand and slightly lifted her tray with the other, until the soggy napkin began to slide toward the edge. It must be somewhere! She now held the tray up with her pinkie-finger to free up the other hand. One by one, she pulled the magazines out of the seat pocket. "Come on. You've got to be kidding! It's got to be here." She was tempted to give up hope and call the flight attendant, when she pulled out the last catalog and shook it by its spine. Out fell a brown paper bag onto her lap. Andi let out a sigh of relief. Thank God, I found it! She returned the magazines to the pocket and shoved the baggy up front where it was easy to reach - just in case. Finally, she leaned back into her seat, closed her eyes, and waited for any of three possible things to happen: for the turbulence to stop, for her to draw attention to herself by losing her dinner, or worse, for a wing to break off the plane and to sink like the Titanic after plummeting thousands of feet to earth.

Andi was already half asleep when she heard the screeching of the toddler behind her, followed by the sleepy whine of the kid next to the little girl.

Her eyes flew open; so much for naptime. She did not anticipate the possibility of number four; screaming kids. She turned to peek through the crack between the seats. Apparently, the toddler woke up and with her shrill voice, startled her brother, who couldn't be much older than three. Great, they slept through the turbulence. They'll probably be wide-awake until it's time to land. She normally didn't mind kids much, but today she already felt yucky from the roller-coaster ride she had endured. All she wanted to do was sleep. Gee, and it's only been three hours since take-off.

The embarrassed and tired mom behind her tried to distract the kids, but the cries continued, regardless of how much she bribed them with toys and snacks.

Finally, Andrea couldn't take the noise any longer and pulled her phone out of her pocket. She plugged in the airline headphones, selected her "Music to Relax" song-list and played it in shuffle mode. She smiled, as she now could barely hear the bickering behind her. Yes, only seven hours to go!

A few minutes later, the turbulence subsided, and the pilot turned off the seatbelt lights. Once everyone had a chance to go to the bathroom, the crew instructed the window seat passengers to close the blinds, so everyone could rest for a few hours and then he dimmed the cabin lights.

Andrea closed her window cover and shifted in her seat, trying to get more comfortable. Her stomach had finally settled down. Feeling chilled, she wrapped the thin airline blanket a little tighter around her neck. Much better.

Thanks to the vibrations of the plane and her soothing music, Andrea drifted off to her own thoughts and the life she had left behind in Atlanta. She recalled when her long-time fiancé had decided that he preferred blondes and dumped her right before their planned cruise to the Caribbean. Of course, he took his newly acquired girl-friend with him, instead of her. She now was stuck in a lease of an overpriced apartment, which he talked her into, and then took off on a business trip, leaving her to sign for the place. She couldn't believe how stupid she was for falling for him. Her salary as a legal secretary barely covered the bills, so she took a part-time job working at a coffee shop to keep her head above the water, barely leaving her enough time for her passion - writing. She had already published a paranormal romance book, which brought in a little extra cash each month. Just after her fiancé had left, her publisher begged her for a new novel. Though she didn't feel the least bit romantic, she agreed to write another book by the following summer. What did she get herself into? For now, all she wanted was to move out of the apartment as soon as the lease was up in September. What should she do next; return to Savannah, where she had spent most of her teenage and adult life? Or should she take a chance and return to Germany? After a few weeks of stewing on her decision, she was finally ready to take the leap to sell most of her stuff and return to her hometown of Eppelheim. Susi assured her that she would help her with the job hunt, and in the meantime, Andi had all intentions of knocking out her first draft of her novel. She just didn't know where to start. Maybe once she surrounded herself with rich history and beautiful castles, muse would return. She pondered possible plots for her story and then dozed off.

A few hours later, the pilot's voice crackled over the intercom. "We are now approaching Frankfurt..."

Andrea looked out of the window and marveled at the skyline as they circled the city, waiting for permission to land. She was excited to be back at home. Has Eppelheim, her hometown, changed a lot since she had been there last? Are her friends still there, or did they move on? Does the ice-skating rink still exist? She could not wait to go exploring and taking tons of pictures of all the gems and treasures Heidelberg and the other old cities had to offer.

"...please fasten your seat belts..." the pilot continued, "We're about to land."

The approach was a little rough, but she had been

through worse. At this point, she was just happy to have landed and to be alive. As soon as the plane stood still, she opened the overhead compartment to pull out her carry-on and laptop bag. The young mother with her two little kids was trying to gather all the toys that were strewn on the floor around their seats. The mom had not gotten any rest until six hours into the flight, when the kids finally fell asleep again. Andrea handed her one of the action figures that made it all the way to her seat.

"Thank you so much," the young mom said. "I'm so sorry if we disturbed you. The kids were just so tired, and we were already on a three-hour plane ride before we boarded this one."

Andrea waved her off. "Don't worry. A long trip like this has to be tough on little kids." She sat her bags down on her seat while she was waiting for the line to move. "I am so ready to get off this plane."

"Me, too," the young woman replied and zipped her children's book bags. "Are you ready to see Grandma?" The kids still looked a bit sleepy, but Andrea could see their little faces brighten up.

Finally, the line in front of her began to move.

Yes, Andrea thought, *I'm home. This is the beginning of my new life.*

The first stop after she got off the plane was to go through customs. She was always a little nervous going through there, even though she had nothing to declare and her German passport was still valid. Shrugging off her paranoia, she continued to wait in line for her turn. Maybe she just watched too many movies where innocent people were being held at airports for apparent security reasons. Right, Andrea Morgan, smuggler of international romance novels. She grinned, and then realized it was her turn. Quickly, she composed herself, pushed her bags toward the window, showed the customs officer her passport, and answered his questions. "Well, that's it, Frau," he looked at her passport again "Morgan," he said in German. "Willkommen in Deutschland."

"Danke schön," she replied, and accepted her passport back from the officer.

Andrea took a quick breath of relief, before she slung her laptop bag and purse over her shoulder and grabbed the pull-handle of her carry-on. The wheels of her luggage rhythmically clacked on the tiled floor as she followed the signs toward the reception area.

She was so excited to finally see Susi again. Even though she was exhausted from her long flight, she willed her legs to carry her to the roped off section where she was going to meet her aunt.

The reception hall was busy, and people hugging each other and others looking for their families surrounded her.

She was one of the latter. Where's Susi?

*A*ndrea turned, expecting to see her aunt's familiar face. However, there was no sign of her. The crowd thinned out and she still stood in the reception area, waiting.

That sinking feeling in her gut gave way to a twinge of anxiety. I hope nothing happened to her, she thought, as she remembered how fast people drove on the Autobahn in Germany.

Andi dug her cell phone out of her pocket and dialed Susi's handy. She waited for the call to go through, but there was no sound. She looked at the display. "No service."

Annoyed for not thinking about switching to an international plan, she ended the non-existent call. Nice, her phone was a useless brick in Germany. What now? She thought for a moment and then had an idea.

She looked around and spotted a pay phone. It'd been years since she used a contraption like that. She checked her wallet, but only had American change. She then noticed the credit card slot and then swiped her card to pay for the call. She punched in the numbers and listened for Susi to pick up as the phone rang. After the second beep, a recording answered and told her that the number she had dialed was unavailable at the moment.

"NO FREAKIN' WAY!" Andrea slammed the phone on its hook. Panic set in. She was stuck. Hoping that Susi arrived by now, she looked back to the reception area. Nothing. She picked up the phone again. Maybe she's at home. Again, Andi swiped her card and dialed Susi's home number. The phone rang several times and the answering machine picked up.

"Susi, it's me Andi," she said. "If by any chance you get this message, I'm at the airport. Where are you? I'll get my luggage and wait for you at the reception hall afterward. My phone is not working here, so page me if you can't find me." She hung up the phone, glanced back at the reception area one more time, just in case. No Susi. Her heart sank.

She walked over to the information desk to page Susi and left a message to meet her at baggage claim. She had checked two large suitcases and wanted to pick them up before someone could walk off with them. She grabbed a cart and made her way to the carousel where she already spotted one of her suitcases with the neon green tag dangling from the handle. She could barely lift it, but then reminded herself that her life was stashed in it, so she gave it an extra pull and plopped it on the cart. She waited another ten minutes for her second suitcase, wondering where it could be. The crowd thinned and soon there was no more luggage left.

Andi couldn't believe it. "They lost my suitcase! On a non-stop flight, no less! How in the world did the airline manage to do that?" She grabbed her cart with her stuff and took a walk by the reception hall again to see if Susi was there. "I can't believe this is happening!" She then walked over to customer service to submit a claim for her missing suitcase.

"Frau Morgan," the clerk said, "your suitcase is on another flight from Atlanta and should be here in about three hours. Would you like to wait for it or should we deliver it to you?"

"How in the world did it get left behind?" Andi couldn't believe what she heard. "I checked both suitcases at the same time."

The clerk shook her head. "Sorry, all it says in the system is that it's on the next flight, which will arrive at 2 p.m. Will you wait for it?"

"No, just have it delivered." She had packed most of her important stuff in the carry-on for just that reason. It took another five minutes to fill out her claim paperwork and then she returned to the reception hall. Still, no Susi. Her aunt was always on time. Deep inside, she had a nagging feeling that something happened to Susi. It had already been an hour since she landed.

She walked over to the reception hall and then to the information booth in a last-ditch attempt to page Susi again.

While sitting in the reception area, Andi noticed that she was getting hungry and bought herself a salami sandwich on a roll. She sat down on a bench where she had a good view of the hall. Hmm, she bit into her roll and was in heaven. The creaminess of the salami slices, the cheese, hard-boiled egg, and a dab of yogurt salad dressing mingled perfectly with the crispness of the lettuce leaf and the crunchy bun. She had forgotten how much she missed German sandwiches.

After she enjoyed her first couple of bites, her mind returned to racing about what she was going to do next. She could take a train or a taxi back to Heidelberg, but how would she get inside of the house? Resigned to the fact that she'd just have to wait at the airport, she decided to finish her sandwich, call Susi's cell again and stay put for a while longer. If worse comes to worst, she could still resort to taking the train back.

She had just finished her last bite, when she saw someone running at the other side of the hall. Immediately, her antenna went up, because if someone ran in Atlanta, there was usually a good reason for it.

"Andi! Oh Gott! I'm so sorry!" A blonde woman with glasses came running toward her.

In her daze, it took her a second to realize that it was Susi. Thank God! Andi stood up and rushed toward her, almost tripping over her carry-on. They fell into a tight embrace. Andi leaned back a few inches. "Gosh, it's been so long since I've seen you! You look great!"

"You don't look too bad yourself, considering..."

"Thanks, auntie, for reminding me of my less than perfect relationship," she teased.

"And you, kiddo, stop calling me auntie," Susi countered, "I'm only five years older than you."

Andi couldn't resist any longer. "So, Susi, what in the world happened on the way up here? I tried to reach you for an hour and a half."

"There was a wreck on the Autobahn and traffic was backed up for miles." Susi let go of her and moved toward the cart as she spoke. "I tried to call your phone, but I had no signal where I was."

Andi grabbed the handle of her carry-on and her small bag. "I tried to use my phone, but it's useless here. But you're here now, and I'm so glad that I didn't have to take a train."

Susi's expression turned somber. "Andi, how can I make this up to you?"

"Well, you're already taking me into your house, but I sure could use a soft bed sometime soon."

Susi smiled. "So, what are we waiting for, then? Let's go!"

They walked the long halls to the parking garage, where Susi had parked her small VW Golf.

"I forgot how tight the parking spaces are in Germany. How in the world do you get back in the car?" Andi marveled.

"Let's just put your luggage in the trunk first. Good thing your second suitcase is getting delivered, because I don't know where we would've put it." Susi winked at her, "And there's plenty of room for me to get in. I'm a pro at this. If you want, I can back out of the parking space and let you in, so you don't have to ding someone's door on the first day back. There'll be plenty of opportunity for that in the near future."

"Great," Andi replied, "I can hardly wait for my insurance to go up!"

They finally made their way out of the parking garage, and onto the tangle of roads leading out of the airport.

Andi's eyes grew large as a BMW cut in front of them. "Watch out!"

Susi stomped on her brakes and then honked the horn at the idiot in front of her. "Du Depp," she yelled at him then turned to Andi. "Close call! These city drivers are jerks! They think they own the roads!"

Andi's heart still raced. Just let us get home in one piece, she prayed. She already dreaded the day when she would get her own car and she'd have to brave the German roads herself. "You never cease to amaze me how you can drive in this zoo? It's a miracle you haven't gotten yourself killed yet!"

"Mädel, it's a skill, and I got it," Susi replied. "You'll get used to it. Besides, you lived in Atlanta…"

After a few more almost hits - or skilled misses, as Susi called them, they made it to a highway, and finally, to the Autobahn, where speed doesn't matter except in city limits and dangerous spots. They entered the incredibly short on-ramp of the congested Autobahn.

Andi grabbed her door handle with an iron grip. She looked over her shoulder and saw no gap in traffic to merge into. "Aah, car!" That's all she could manage before she covered her eyes with her hands, preparing for impact.

"Andi, calm down, I'll get us home," Susi said and expertly merged into traffic.

"In an ambulance?"

"No, silly," Susi laughed, "You just relax and let me do the driving."

Andi, still on edge, reluctantly took her aunt's advice and leaned the seat back for a while. She felt another wave of anxiety wash over her as they approached an inter-change, but she relaxed once they were on the Autobahn to Heidelberg.

*A*lmost an hour later, Andi woke up to the wonderful scenery of the Odenwald foothills to her left. Strangely enough, the dark green rolling hills reminded her of the Blue Ridge Mountains north of Atlanta, where she had spent many weekends to get away from the hectic life in the city. In the distance, she spotted the giant, sand-colored quarry of Dossenheim, which stood out from the dark hills like a sore thumb. When she was a kid, she could see it from her house. It still looked as impressive as it did back then. Nostalgia filled her heart. Yes, she was home!

Content, she leaned back into her seat when she realized that she had to go to the bathroom. "Hey, Susi, can we make a quick pit-stop?"

Susi smiled at her. "Sorry, kiddo. We just passed the last gas station before our exit. Can you hang on until we get home in about fifteen minutes?"

Andi considered for a moment. "Sure, it's not that bad."

"Good, but let me know if you can't wait, then I'll pull off at the side of the road for you," Susi said with a smile.

Andi looked at her with big eyes. "Yeah, right! When pigs fly!"

They both laughed, and then Susi turned serious. "Oh, oh! Looks like we have a Stau ahead of us."

Andi tore her eyes from the gorgeous hills and looked ahead. She saw brake lights flashing all the way to the curve. "Great, not a traffic jam! Can we turn around somewhere and go back to the last truck stop?"

"Nope, but we're almost at our exit anyway. We'll look for a bathroom as soon as we get off the Autobahn. I promise."

Minutes passed, and Andi felt the pressure in her bladder build. "Oh God, please, let the traffic move again after the curve!"

Then they stood still.

. . .

"Unbelievable!" Andi did a small version of the pee-pee-dance in her seat. "We've been crawling at snail-speed for the last 20 minutes."

Susi looked at her with a hint of a smile: "The exit is just a little past this curve. Can you make it until then? You know, I can pull over and let you tinkle by the side of the road."

Andi's bladder ached as if it was stretched to its limit. Damn, she shouldn't have drunk that whole bottle of carbonated water she bought at the airport. "I am not peeing in front of all these people! Forget that!"

"Okay, suit yourself then."

Just a few minutes later, they finally made it to the exit and found a fast food restaurant. Susi let her niece out by the door before she looked for a parking space.

As soon as the car came to a stop, Andi ripped the door open and ran to the entrance. She noticed a few stares inside the restaurant, but she didn't care what people thought. She just needed to get to the bathroom. Fast. "There it is!" Andi rushed to the door labeled 'Damen,' closed the door to her stall and danced around until she managed to open the button of her jeans. "Oh my God, I can't believe I almost peed on myself."

"Feel better," Susi asked when Andi got back into the car.

"Much!" Andi buckled her seatbelt. "Let's get home. I'm so done with traveling."

They drove into her hometown of Eppelheim. "Susi, I can't believe how much has changed since I've been gone, yet so much stayed the same. Oh, look, there's my elementary school! And that used to be the store where we got our candy from after school let out! I remember that as if it was yesterday!"

"Isn't it great to come home, kiddo? And speaking of which, here we are!" They drove up to an apricot-painted, two-story brick house with a quaint fenced-in garden visible from the street. "Andi, can you open the small gate for me, so I can get in the driveway?"

"Sure," Andi replied as she got out of the car to let her aunt onto the family property.

Susi helped Andi carry her bags into the house up to the second floor, where Grandma used to live, before she passed away a few years ago. She had fond memories of visiting her Grandma, before her Dad received his orders to return to the States for a few more tours before he finally retired from the Army. Grandma loved baking, so whenever she visited her, they baked wonderful Christmas cookies, birthday cakes, and other fine pastries. Once she moved to the States, she gave up baking. She just couldn't get anything to turn out the same as they did back home.

They sat her suitcases down in the bedroom. "Okay, kiddo, let me know if you need anything," Susi said. "You look beat, why don't you crawl into bed for a bit and we'll catch up later, okay?"

Andi nodded and managed to mumble an "okay" in the midst of a gigantic yawn. "Don't let me sleep past three this afternoon, though. I really want to get on a decent schedule as quickly as possible."

"No problem, I'll wake you up. Now go catch some z's. You look like hell." She winked at Andi and closed the door on her way out.

A few hours later, Andi woke up and looked at her watch. "No, it's two o'clock in the afternoon, that's what? Eight in the morning, Georgia time?" She sighed. It was tempting to stay in bed longer, so she wouldn't be a zombie at dinner, but she also wanted to enjoy being home again. Andi heard Susi clunking around in the kitchen, so she dragged herself out of bed. She felt like a train wreck, but she knew she'd get in the swing of things in no time.

"Ah, I see you have arisen from the dead," Susi said over her shoulder as she was preparing some sandwiches and sliced up some tomatoes and cucumbers for a quick snack for them both.

"Not really, it's my ghost you're seeing. I'm actually still upstairs in bed sleeping my head off."

Susi planted a breadboard, a small cutting board serving as a plate when making sandwiches, in front of her and then a big, round, wooden board in the middle of the table, filled with assorted sliced cheese, deli meat, pâté, etc. On the side, she had a big breadbasket and a plate with the cut-up veggies. "Here's the salt and peppermill, if you need it. But don't fill up too much with all the food. I want to take you to this awesome new Greek restaurant tonight. Are you game?"

"Sure," Andi replied. "I haven't eaten in a decent Greek place for years. I'm way overdue!"

"Awesome. Then we can also talk about what you want to do before you lock yourself into a room writing your new novel."

Andi took a slice of bread, smeared some cream cheese on it, and topped her creation with a few slices of cucumber and a wedge of tomato. "Well, first I have to go job-hunting. Besides, muse is not favoring me lately, anyway."

"I just think you need someone to pull you out of the dumps and inspiration will come. I know a guy, who knows a guy," Susi trailed off.

Andi grabbed her balled up napkin and tossed it at Susi. "I haven't even been here a day and you want to play matchmaker. Instead, I should get you hitched. You know, your biological clock is ticking!"

"Touché, you got me," Susi conceded. "Well, when you're finished, you can get settled while I clean up down here. I'll make reservations for the Greek restaurant for around seven, or is that too early for you?"

Andi did not trust her lack of sleep. "How about we go a little sooner, say sixish, to be on the safe side?"

"Okay, let me call them while you make yourself at home upstairs."

Unpacking her suitcase didn't take long at all. Once she tucked her t-shirts and undies in the dresser and hung her professional clothes and jacket in the wardrobe, she arranged her personal hygiene stuff in the shelf above the toilet by the sink. When she was finished, she sat down on her bed and thought of things to do until dinner. What she really wanted to do was go from place to place and eat all the food she hadn't been able to get in the States, but she didn't want to ruin her dinner. She would have plenty of time to catch up on the European delicacies and dishes that she had missed all these years. Instead, she grabbed a pen and a notepad and began brainstorming ideas for her novel until it was time to go.

They arrived at the Akropolis, Susi's favorite Greek restaurant and settled down in a cozy booth toward the back.

"I like this corner. It's a perfect place to relax after a busy day," Susi explained. "I come here a lot when I'm tired from work and don't want to cook."

Andi touched the flower next to the lit candle, and then picked it up by its little vase to smell it. "Oh, it's real? I thought it was a fake rose."

"You seem pretty giggly, compared to a few hours ago," Susi remarked.

Andi set the vase back on the center of the table. "I'm just happy to be home."

The waiter approached their table and took their order. They decided to get a platter for two with gyros, souvlaki, and lamb chops, so Andi could have a taste of it all.

Susi took a sip of her red wine. "So, what are you planning on doing tomorrow? I'll be at work, since I figured you'd want some time to sleep in and get settled."

"My first priority is to go to the employment office. Hopefully, I'll get a job soon, so I don't have to leach off of you when my money runs out. Then, if the weather holds up, I'd love to go up to see the Heidelberg castle. Maybe if I'm around old stuff, I'll get some inspiration for my novel." Andi's face brightened. "I always felt like the castle was a magical place. As a kid, I imagined being a princess in a fortress like that. Now I know better. You couldn't pay me enough to live in the middle-ages."

Susi looked as if she remembered something wonderful. "Every time I go to the castle, I feel like I'm stepping back in time." She then returned to the present and took Andi's hand into hers. "But don't worry about the money part for now. I'm not exactly poor and I don't mind helping you out while you're getting on your feet. You know, I'm just so glad you're finally home."

Andi shook her head. "No, I want to pull my own weight as soon as possible. I just don't feel right spending your money." She followed her statement up with a hearty yawn. "Sorry, so much for my second wind."

Just then, the waiter arrived with a gigantic platter of food.

"Wow, who is going to eat all this?" Andi moved her glass of seltzer water out of the way.

Susi smiled. "We'll just take the extras home for lunch tomorrow. The portions here are so huge that I never get to finish my plate."

Andi did not have time to respond, because she was already busy with loading her plate with gyros, souvlaki and rice. She picked up a small piece of meat and dipped it into the garlicky yogurt sauce. "Hmmm, we probably need to order more tzatziki before it's all over and done with."

Half an hour later, both women leaned back in their seats with their napkins still in their laps.

"I'm so stuffed," Andi sighed, followed by another yawn. She was tempted to unbutton her jeans, just so she could breathe. "Maybe if I go to sleep right after we get home, I'll be okay to get up in the morning. Jet lag sucks."

"Yes, crawling into bed sounds perfect right about now. I'm ready to go, too. I have to be up early anyway." Susi raised her hand to get the waiter's attention. "Bedienung, check please!"

CHAPTER 2

"*W*atch this, Volker," Markus said in old German as they walked through the princess's bedroom. He casually strolled over to the baron's painting, whistling a tune that had been constantly playing on the radio in the ticketing hut lately.

Volker sighed. "Do we have to play this game again? It is getting kind of old."

Markus stopped in front of the piece of art. "Why? Do you have somewhere else to be? You're just as stuck as I am. Might as well have some fun!" Moving stuff around had become a competitive sport between the two ghostly friends for the last 400 years.

"Well, you have a point there." Volker said, as he casually leaned on the dresser by the window and glared at the picture. "I hate this guy! If it was up to me, I'd throw a black cloth over his devious visage."

"You and me both," Markus replied. "So, are you ready?"

Volker nodded. "Go for it!"

Markus concentrated as he sucked energy from the

electricity in the room, making the lights flicker for a moment. Then, with all his ghostly might, moved the painting, so it hung slightly lopsided on the striped wall. He looked back at Volker, quite happy with his results. "What do you think?"

Volker inspected the change and laughed. "Is that all you got? I can do better than that!" He had plenty of practice over the years and knew that he could beat Markus every time, but that never seemed to discourage his good friend from trying to outdo him.

"Oh really? Let's see it."

Volker strutted toward the painting with a cocky grin on his face. "Step aside for the master of picture-moving." Again, the lights flickered, and this time, almost went completely out as he drew energy from the electrical system in the room. He placed each hand around the painting and moved it the opposite way, so that it hung noticeably crooked to the other side.

Markus's face dropped to a frown. "Show-off," he conceded. "I could have moved it more, but I did not want the entire castle to go dark."

Volker shrugged, satisfied with his work. "Whatever you say." He smiled, threw his arm around Markus's shoulder and squeezed it before letting go again. "We both know who the true master is." They walked over to the window and waited for the next tour to come through, betting on who would notice the prank first, the guide or the tourist. This time, Volker bet his translucent Taler on the next tour guide.

*A*ndi's first priority this morning was to start her job-search. She took the streetcar to the employment office in Heidelberg in hopes of finding something suitable, or anything for that matter. She loved the public transportation system here in Germany, especially the streetcars. The ride was a little rough, but it reminded her of times when she rode it as a kid with her friends to the movie theater or the outdoor pool on the weekends.

She didn't have much luck at the employment office today, but since she was already in Heidelberg, she figured that she was well overdue for some sightseeing. Maybe the job-finding gods would look favorably upon her tomorrow. For the rest of the day, she just wanted to go up to the castle and take an imaginary trip back into history, just as she used to as a young girl.

She finally arrived in downtown Heidelberg and Andi gawked at the ancient Holy Ghost Church that loomed prominently over the market square. Memories of eating an ice-cream cone with her family on a hot, humid summer day at this exact spot flooded her mind. She then realized how much she had missed being home.

Her gaze moved between the roofs of the tall, century old houses surrounding the market square, and caught a glimpse of the majestic ruins of the Heidelberg castle. Immediately, she felt a strange pull toward it.

Just then, her stomach growled unusually loud. A little embarrassed, she looked around to see if someone had noticed, but everyone seemed to be wrapped up in his or her own agenda. Relieved, Andi looked at her watch and realized that it was almost 1 p.m. already. She really wanted to get to the castle, but then she felt another unmistakable hunger pang.

"Dang it!" Torn between the lure of the fortress or starvation, she opted for a quite tasty compromise. She found a Greek take-out window and bought herself a gyros sandwich to go. Hmmm, they don't make them that yummy in the States. She attempted to walk and eat at the same time, but the sandwich's yogurt sauce dripped through the wrapper and made quite a mess. She was almost finished, when a shopper accidentally bumped into her. In horror, she watched as a particular juicy glob dripped on her jacket. "Menno!" She tried to wipe the spot clean with her spare napkin, but it still left a whitish, greasy stain next to her zipper. Oh well, she'd just have to wash it tonight and live with people's stares until then.

Within minutes, she arrived at the Bergbahn station. The English tourist signs called the train a funicular. She figured that this must be a British term, because she never heard of it. To her, it was nothing other than a pulley-operated mountain railway.

Twenty minutes later, she stepped off the crowded funicular. She yawned to pop her ears, and then looked around. The castle was only a short walk away from her stop, so she followed the signs and crowds to her magical fortress.

As she was walking, Andi took some time to take in the scenery. Even though parked cars lined the small mountain street, she admired the old, pinkish sandstone walls and the lush greenery along the way. At the entrance of the castle, she was awestruck by the beauty of the ruins and she wasn't even inside the gates yet.

She walked to the cashier's window. The funicular combo-ticket already covered her admission, but she decided to splurge and so she paid for the grand tour of the castle. The stories and legends of this place always fascinated Andi and she never got tired of them, especially after such a long time away.

During her tour, Andrea enjoyed the tall tales about the witch's bite at the gate, the origin of the foot imprint on the terrace, admired the giant vat, but the single thing that really stood out to her this time, was how thick the walls were constructed. It puzzled her how war and fire could so easily destroy a fortress built so strong.

The tour guide led the group to the interior residential section of the castle, which was well-preserved and decorated with furniture and artifacts from various time periods. "This is the princess' bedroom," the guide continued absentmindedly, as if he was bored. "On the wall next to the bed, you will see a painting of Baron Ludwig von Dossenheim..."

Andi's eyes trailed from the guide's pointed arm to the painting. The first thing she noticed was that it was crooked and tilted her head. She shuddered as she saw the face of the man depicted in it. Ugh, that guy looks creepy! As she stepped up to the masterpiece to get a closer look, there was something eerily compelling about this man. Not only did this baron appear quite pompous, his eyes were beady, and his smile resembled more of a smirk than anything else. She didn't like the man and wouldn't ever want to cross his path, if he were still alive. As she looked to her left, she noticed that the group had moved on. She glanced at the painting one last time and hurried to catch up. On her way toward the door, she passed by a window, where an icy breeze seemed to emanate from. Wow, this place is old, she thought. They need to fix these windows.

She quickly caught up with the group and listened to the tail end of a legend, where a mason was innocently accused of theft, thrown into the prison tower, nicknamed 'seldom empty', and then was cursed by a witch. "The mason is still believed to haunt this castle and to move a few things out of place, on occasion," the tour-guide explained. "Legend has it that he is still looking for the princess' jewelry box and the heirloom ring that it previously contained. Once he reunites these two items, he is released from the curse and can find peace." They entered the next room. "This is the dressing room of the princess...," the guide continued.

Instead of paying attention to the rest of the tour, Andi found her mind drifting back to the legend. How fascinating, a possible ghost? Yeah, right, she thought, but it's intriguing. A mystery, with a touch of paranormal, and I could add a touch of romance. The writer inside of her was beginning to wake up again.

After the tour, she browsed around the gift-shop and purchased a book on the history of the castle. Andi wandered around the grounds a bit longer, imagining herself in medieval times to collect experiences for her story. She took some pictures and soaked up the feeling of being in the moment, or rather the past, shutting out the noises of modern society around her. Andi wondered what the castle looked like when it was still intact. How did people live their day-to-day lives? Too bad that she'd never know. She wasn't even sure if she wanted to know. Times were brutal then. Andi grinned, because she knew, she wouldn't last a day in medieval Heidelberg. Just the thought of giving up modern conveniences, such as cars, microwaves, and the like, made her shudder.

When she had her fill, she took the famous heaven's ladder, over 350 steps that led her back into town. Her mind was still sparking ideas like fireworks when she arrived in the tourist-filled shopping zone. I have to write this stuff down before I forget. I need to find a pen and paper somewhere.

She looked around and only saw cafes and tourist stores, but no place to find something fitting with which to write. Didn't she pass a stationary shop or a bookstore earlier? Following her instincts, she walked back through the busy shopping area, keeping an eye out for the little gem of a shop she was looking for.

Ten minutes later, she spotted the small stationary place. It didn't take her long to find the perfect journal, a cute artsy one with blank pages. Of course, with a pretty journal, one must buy a fancy new pen, which writes in lovely colors, like purple or turquoise. She finally picked a green roller pen, which complemented the bright sunflower cover of the journal.

After Andi paid for her exceptionally cute writing para-phernalia, she sought out a cozy little café, where she could go to work with writing down her ideas. She ordered a tall cup of café latte and couldn't get her thoughts on paper fast enough. Hmmm, what time-period could this play in? What's happening? Who are the main characters? This creepy baron already had earned a spot in her story. Having a rough idea what she wanted to write about, all she needed to do was to do some research about the castle, the time period in which her story took place, and maybe learn more about the local legends. Just thinking about her new project made her giddy all over. Good thing that we have wireless internet in the house, she thought, and waved to the waitress that she was ready to pay her bill.

"So, how's your research coming along," Susi asked one gloomy Saturday morning. It was mid-October and the usual thick fog hung in the air.

Andi cut her toast into strips to dip into her soft-boiled egg. "It's coming along. I tried to read up a little more about the legend of this ghost that's supposed to haunt the castle, but I'm not really learning anything new." She sprinkled a little more salt on the egg and continued: "You work for the city. Don't you know any people who know more about the history of Heidelberg and the castle?"

"Sure, I know a few professors from the University that

come into my office on occasion. Maybe I can introduce you to a few of them and you can ask them questions until the cows come home. Come to think of it, one of my friends, Pete, is a historian and will be at the Irish Pub tonight. He's very passionate about his work and will talk to anyone who shows any kind of interest in old stuff." Susi spread some butter on her breakfast roll, topped it with a few slices of fresh salami, a slice of cheese, and took a big bite.

"Oh, really?" Andi asked surprised. "Why didn't you introduce us before? It sure would've made my research a lot easier."

Susi swallowed her food and took a sip of strawberry tea. "I guess, I forgot."

"You WERE my favorite aunt up until just a moment ago!" Andi giggled.

"Gee thanks, but first of all, I'm your only aunt. Second of all, stop reminding me that I am your aunt. It makes me feel old. And finally, you'll get to meet him tonight anyway." Susi stuck her tongue out at Andi for good measure. "So, do you still feel like going up to the castle for the Halloween party with me next Saturday?" Susi asked, and then took another slow sip of her hot tea.

"Of course, I am. Actually, I've been wracking my brain about what I should dress up as."

Susi shrugged. "Well, I went last year, and a lot of folks dressed as monsters or werewolves in period clothing."

Andi glanced at the ceiling in deep thought. "Maybe I could go as a medieval vampire," she pondered.

Susi put on a bored look. "I hate to disappoint you, but I expected more originality from your creative mind. I think you, and about 30 other ladies, will have the same bright idea." She paused for a moment. "Come to think of it, I need a costume, too."

"You're right. It's a bit predictable." Andi took a bite of her egg-dunked toast. "We need something authentic, yet shocking."

*T*hey spent the entire Saturday in the city shopping for their costumes. It wasn't easy, because Halloween only became popular in Germany a few years before, so it was hit or miss in each store to find something that could be usable as a cool and spooky outfit. Most of the costumes they found were to dress as sexy vampires, monsters, or witches. But what's the fun in dressing up like everyone else anyway? They needed something original to wear.

Susi looked at her watch. It was already past lunchtime and they were still empty-handed. "This is going nowhere. We need a game-plan," she said. "Let's grab a bite to eat and figure out what we really want to dress up as, instead of aimlessly walking around."

"You're right. I'm starving, too. Let's go to the Pizzeria across the street. I can smell pizza from here."

They ordered a huge Pizza Margarita with diced tomatoes and cheese. "I love the pizza here," Andi said while chewing on a slice. "The crust is nice and crunchy and not as doughy, like we have in the States. And here, they just put the right amount of sauce and fresh toppings on it... oh, it's heaven!"

"I'm glad you like your pizza, but we have a mission to accomplish," Susi began. "So, we're going to a Halloween party in an old castle. We need something that goes with the theme."

"Something spooky, or creepy, yet historical," Andi added.

Susi rubbed her forehead with her pizza-free hand. "I'm thinking, rich, poor..."

"Like common folk and royalty," Andi asked. "I'll be the princess."

"No, you'll be my chamber maid," she countered. "I'm older and you are living in my house, so you can be my servant girl."

"Niemals! Never!" Andi exclaimed but couldn't hold back a smile.

They brainstormed for a few more minutes, when Andi suddenly smacked her hands on the table. "Oh, yes! This is it!"

Susi put her finger on her lips. "Pssst, don't tell the whole restaurant," she whispered, looking over her shoulder to see if they disturbed anyone. Indeed, several guests stared at them to see what the commotion was all about. Obviously embarrassed, Susi smiled at the spectators.

"Sorry," Andi said, trying to keep her voice down. "I have the perfect idea of what we'll wear!" She dug her green pen out of her purse. "Here's what we'll do." She described the simple, yet effective costumes and began scribbling a list of things they would need on a fresh napkin.

*I*n the evening, after a nice couple of hours of rest, Andi and Susi sat in the streetcar on the way to town. They had bought a weekend discount ticket, so they could ride back to Eppelheim on the same ticket after they had a few drinks.

They rode all the way to the beginning of the shopping zone of downtown Heidelberg. The fog had lifted late in the morning, and because the sun was shining most of the day, the evening was surprisingly mild for October. They walked about half a mile down the main drag of the pedestrian zone, turned the corner, and walked into a small alley where the pub was located. Susi held the door open for Andi as they entered. "Welcome to my old haunts," she said cheerfully.

Andi looked around the pub. It wasn't too crowded. The typical Irish décor and simple wooden furniture gave the place a rustic feel. The sound of Irish folk music and chatter filled the room. She took a step inside and noticed that the wooden floor creaked. "This place is awesome," she said.

"That's why we come to this little gem every other weekend or so," Susi replied. "Do you see the table in the corner over there? That is our Stammtisch, our special table we reserve for those nights that we hang out." Susi took the lead and headed toward the table with Andi in tow. "Looks like Pete and Belinda are already here."

"Pete, Belinda, this is Andi, my favorite niece," she winked, "who finally came to her senses and returned home to Eppelheim."

Pete, a tall guy in his 40s rose and gave her a big hug. "Hi, Andi. It's good to have you here tonight. Welcome home," he said with an Irish accent.

Susi saw the surprise in Andi's face. "Peter spent a few years in Ireland where he studied cultural anthropology. He researches legends and myths," she explained. "For him, English comes almost as natural as German."

"Oh, now that makes sense," Andi replied.

"And this lovely girl next to Pete is his wife, Belinda, from Ireland," Susi continued as she motioned to the pretty, fair-skinned woman.

"Very nice to meet you, Andi," Belinda also hugged her.

Usually, Andi was a little reserved when she met strangers, but for some odd reason, she liked this pair, even though, they had just met.

Andi and Susi took off their coat and made themselves comfortable at the table. "Get the girls a beer," Peter hollered in English to the pub owner, who was tending the bar.

The owner nodded at him and went back to work.

Pete, being the talker of the bunch, turned to Andi. "So, what brought you back to good old Heidelberg?"

Andi thought about how much she should reveal without boring present company to death. "Well, the short story is that I was at a cross-road with the opportunity to sell my stuff and start a new life. So, here I am. Now all I need is to find a job, so I can buy a car and don't have to rely on Auntie here when my money runs out."

"So what kind of job did you do in the States?" Belinda asked while twisting her long, black hair into a bun.

"I was a legal secretary, but since German law is a lot different, I'm having trouble finding something in that field."

"Did I mention that she's a writer, too," Susi added. "She needed some inspiration for a new book. I daresay she made the right choice by coming back to romantic old Heidelberg."

"Call me curious, but what kind of books do you write, Andi," Pete asked.

"Well, I know it sounds kind of cheesy, but I write paranormal romances."

Pete and Belinda's eyes began to sparkle. "Really," Belinda smiled. "I'd love to read one of your books one day."

"I'll let you borrow my copy," Susi offered.

"That's nice of you, but I rather buy my own and have Andi autograph it for me, no offense." The group laughed.

"So, what brought you back to Germany, Peter?" Andi asked, changing the subject.

"Just call me Pete," he corrected her with a smile. "Well, after spending some magical years studying Irish folklore," his eyes began to twinkle, as if he remembered something special, "I realized that I have just as rich of a history in my own country and started exploring odd stories closer to home and closer to family."

"I would love to hear some of those stories," Andi said, when the owner of the pub approached the table with a tray filled with various beers and ales.

"Here's your beer, young lass," said the man setting the mug on a cardboard coaster. "So, you must be Susi's niece? My name is Shai. Welcome to the Irish Pub, where English is spoken, if you so choose to."

"Thanks, Shai. You have a nice place."

Shai smiled in return.

"Hey, boss, put the beer on my tab, will ya?" Pete asked.

Shai nodded. "Sure thing, Pete. When things die down a bit, I'll hang out with you guys for a while. I gotta get to know our new gal, here." He winked at her, and then walked off to the next table to take some more drink orders.

Andi turned to Pete, "Thanks for the beer. Now I'm all ears. Let's hear some of the interesting folklore from around here. You know, I live for this kind of stuff. I'm all about stories."

Pete chuckled. "So, what would you like to hear? Stories of witches, werewolves, monsters? Got anything particular in mind?"

"Actually, I do," Andi said. "When I took a tour

through the castle the other day, I heard parts of a legend that I found very intriguing." She took a sip of her beer. "Do you know the story about the cursed mason, who is still haunting the castle?"

"Of course, I do. There hasn't been much written about this story, but here is what I know." Pete turned his chair to face her. "Once, there was a baron, named Ludwig von Dossenheim."

"Is that the creepy guy whose painting was hanging in the princess's bedroom?" she interjected.

"Exactly, my dear. As a baron, he was low in station and wanted to marry into higher royalty. The princess was still available to marry, so to make himself more visible to her, he stole her heirloom ring in the jewelry box, which, of course was a bad move on his part. He planted both at the mason's house that day, while the mason was still working at the castle. The next day, some guards searched his house and found the jewelry box with the ring in it. They arrested him and threw him in the prison tower. Somehow, the baron lost the ring on the way back to the castle and only returned the box to the princess. She was very angry with him and made him look for the heirloom. His chances for marrying her now were slim, unless he could redeem himself by bringing her the lost ring.

While the baron was busy turning over every stone between Eppelheim and the castle, the mason became very ill in the horrendous conditions of the prison tower. As he faded away, the princess forced a witch to cast a spell on him that he would only find peace when the wrongs were righted, and the ring was back in its box. The witch had mercy on him and added a spell to free him from his pain. The spirit then rose from his body."

Andi looked at him in awe. "So, what happened to the baron?"

"Legend says that the baron was searching for months, but never found the ring. Then, on one unfortunate winter night, he walked out of the room, which contained a big vat, drunk as a skunk. He slipped on a patch of ice on the steep slope and landed awkwardly, breaking his neck."

"Was the ring ever found?"

"Nope, the ring was gone for good. Also, the jewelry box disappeared again while the princess was out of town visiting her sister. Rumor has it that the baron got wind of the spell and was afraid that if the ring was found and put into the box, the mason would come back from the dead and kill him. Back then, folks were still a bit superstitious. Therefore, he took the box and hid it somewhere, where it could not be found."

"Wow, what a great story," Andi marveled and took another sip of her beer.

"There are more stories where those came from," Pete said, "but let's save those for another time."

They spent the next few hours playing Yahtzee, and after most of his guests had left for the night, Shai came over to join them for a while.

"What a busy night," Shai said as he plopped down on a free chair at the end of the table. "Andi, did you enjoy your evening?"

She tried to stifle a yawn but wasn't very successful at concealing it. "Ugh, sorry about that. Apparently, jet lag is still kicking my butt. To answer your question, yes, I had a great time with my new friends. I have to tell you that I'm totally in love with your place. It's so cozy…"

"Makes you want to go to sleep, right? Not the effect I was trying to accomplish. Sleeping guests don't pay." He patted her on her shoulder. "I'm just kidding. I traveled to Australia once and finally managed to work out a decent sleep schedule by the time I had to leave again."

The five of them bantered around for another half an hour, before they finally took pity on Andi, who almost fell asleep at the table. "See you lovely ladies next week at the Halloween party," Pete yelled, as the two girls hopped on the bus to take them to the streetcar stop.

CHAPTER 3

*E*arly in the evening of the following Saturday, Susi and Andi were at home preparing for the big Halloween party.

"Hand me the potato sack, will ya?" Andi asked.

Susi stood in the bathroom applying her make-up. She tossed the sack over to Andi. "Here you go! This is going to look great! I think you make a wonderful poor girl." Susi giggled. "I can't wait until you put those boils on."

"They look gross, don't they?" Andi slipped the makeshift sack shirt over her head. She wore some brownish leggings underneath and slipped on a pair of Susi's old low-cut Robin Hood boots. She tied a rope around her waist and began to mess up her hair for added effect. "Scoot over! And stop being so stingy with the mirror."

Susi grinned. "With all that mousse, you look like you haven't had a shower in a month. You look great!"

"Gee thanks, Auntie! I like the foliage in your hair. Looks like you had a serious encounter with the leaf pile in the garden," she pointed out. "Where did you get those gems you're wearing?"

Susi lifted up a dark green stone, which was attached to a leather rope. "I got this at the Christmas Market last year. Isn't it gorgeous?"

"It is. All these vials and herbs tied to your belt make you look like a true healer," Andi said. "I don't know about your glasses, though, but I think you very much look like a medieval healer to me - like I would know…," she giggled.

Susi put on the finishing touches of her slightly "dirty" makeup and sprinkled a little lavender oil on her wrists and behind her ears.

"Couldn't you find another essence? Maybe something invigorating, like eucalyptus, and not a calming oil? For God's sake, it's a party!" They both laughed.

"It's all I had, so don't hate me for trying. Besides, Chanel No. 5 wasn't actually fashionably back then. So, lavender it is."

Andi spread some pale make-up over her face and glued the boils, which she had purchased at a theater store, with the special stage make-up adhesive on her face. A bit of earthy-reddish blush on the base of the boils gave them the perfect appearance of inflammation. She finished the job by dabbing some gray eye shadow around the eyes, below the cheekbones, and along her jaw, which made her look even sicklier.

"That is so cool, Andi! You look like you have the pest or some other weird infectious disease. Don't mind me if I keep my distance from you," Susi added. "I don't want to get what you have."

"Good, so my work here is done. Are you ready to go?"

"Yep, just need a jacket and my car keys," Susi called from her room. "I'm not riding in the streetcar like this. We can just take a cab home tonight."

"Awe, you're spoiling all the fun," Andi called down as she ran up the stairs to grab her jacket, as well. "It would give people something to talk about!"

"Not on my account. Sorry, I'm taking the car. Are you coming?"

Andi ran back down the stairs with jacket in hand. "Here I am. Let's go."

*T*wenty minutes later, they arrived at the castle. Since the prime parking spaces were already taken, they had to park the car along the side of the small road winding up the mountain and then walk a short distance. It was already dark and the fog that settled in gave the streetlights an eerie glow. The air was heavy around them and the sounds of the nearby night birds seemed muffled.

"How about that for an appropriate atmosphere?" Andi hooked her arm under Susi's. "Check out the people in front of us. Looks like a medieval vampire couple."

"See, I told you that this place is riddled with undead creatures and ghosts tonight," Susi said, making her point. "You know, I think our costumes are definitely more original and historically accurate than theirs."

"Leave it to you to be a stickler for accuracy!" Andi smiled at Susi.

They continued their walk along the side of the road toward the castle entrance. As they strolled by a large bush, leaves were rustling inside of it and a gigantic bat flew out from it.

Andi let out a scream and jumped backward to avoid a collision with the beast.

"Holy crap! That thing almost got me," Andi screeched as she hid behind her aunt.

Susi laughed. "Good thing that today isn't actually Halloween or that beast would have attached itself to your neck, fed on your blood, and turned you into a vampire."

Andi held her hand against her chest. She could still feel her heart throbbing and her head buzzing from all the adrenaline rushing through her body. "No, it would've turned you into a monster. Why do you think I hid behind you?"

Susi, still laughing, turned around to face her. "You used to hide behind me when you were scared as a kid. I see, that you haven't changed much," she teased her. "The bat is gone. We can keep walking now."

Checking her surroundings for wild creatures and anything that didn't belong, Andi fell into step with Susi. "Fine, but I'm staying on the street-side. You get to deal with the next thing that jumps out of the bushes."

"You little chicken," Susi punched her arm. "A fine paranormal author you are!"

Trying not to fall off the sidewalk, Andi replied, "Just because I write about supernatural stuff, doesn't mean that I have to live it."

Susi giggled.

"What?"

"I just visualized you turning into a vampire bat, sort of like a werewolf transforms once a month," Susi explained, "and when you return to normal, you type away about the mischief you caused as a freaking bat."

"I'm grateful that you're taking my craft so seriously."

Andi wrapped an arm around Susi's waist. "Look, we're almost there."

.   .   .

*A*ndi and Susi walked a few more meters and arrived at the entrance of the castle grounds. They showed their tickets to the guard in front of the gates.

"Hey, look! The witch's bite!" Susi pointed at the knocker attached to a small messenger door within the gigantic wooden gates of the castle entry.

Andi took a closer look at the ring with the famous crack. She had learned during her castle tour that, whoever was able to bite through the huge iron door-knocker ring would be ruler of the castle. Over the years, many royals attempted to break the ring with their teeth, but to no avail, until a witch came along. Allegedly, she bit into the doorknocker so hard, that it cracked and left a tooth mark in the iron. Unfortunately, it wasn't completely bitten through, so, like her predecessors, she also missed out on ruling the castle. "How about it, Susi? Wanna give it a shot?" Andi grinned and motioned toward the courtyard. "All this could be yours!"

"Thanks, but I prefer to keep my day job and my teeth."

Andi shrugged. "Dentists these days can fix anything." She lifted the knocker to inspect it closer. "But seriously, what do you think cracked this ring? I know it wasn't a witch."

"How can you be so sure?" Susi looked at her. "Maybe, the story is true," and winked at her.

"Come on, you really believe that?" Andi looked at Susi as if she was crazy.

"Of course not! I think it cracked naturally over the years. Maybe there was a tiny hole of rust and water got into it, froze, and then cracked. Who knows?"

"Sounds plausible, I guess." Andi shrugged, and they

continued to walk toward the courtyard. "Although, I have to admit that I like the other explanation better."

The castle looked very different at night with the orange spotlights illuminating the buildings. There was still some scaffolding in front of some, due to the reconstruction, but it was minimally intrusive, at least in the dark. To their right, they saw a small covered well. Closer to the center of the courtyard stood a large fountain. Andi remembered throwing pennies in it as a child in hopes that her wish of becoming a princess would come true. Maybe she did not put enough money in it. She smiled. How silly!

They could hear the party music emanating from the ballroom into the courtyard. Following the music, they entered the freshly renovated King's Hall and checked their coats. Along with the vampires and monsters, they walked down the hall toward the ballroom.

"Hey, let's get a picture taken of the two of us dressed up like this." Susi pointed at the photographer's setup near the ballroom door.

"It's too expensive, Susi. These photographers charge an arm and a leg."

"Come on, it'll be fun! Besides, you look stunning with your boils."

Reluctantly, Andi agreed.

"Ah, let me guess," the photographer ventured and pointed at Andi. "You look like you have the plague," then shifted his gaze at Susi, "and you, beautiful woman, are you a witch?"

Susi laughed. "Close, I'm actually supposed to be a healer."

The photographer smiled back at her. "Nevertheless, you ladies look wonderful tonight. Let's get started, shall we?"

He artistically arranged them, stepped back, and changed his mind several times, before he took his first pictures.

"This guy takes his job seriously," Andi whispered in Susi's ear.

Susi smiled, "Let's hope the pictures come out nice, considering the time he takes to get his perfect shots."

When they were finished, the photographer asked them to fill out a contact form and handed Susi a business card. "The pictures should be ready in a few days," he said with a smile. "I will give you a call when they are ready for pick-up at my studio. Have fun at the party!"

"Thanks, I'll make sure that we will," she called over her shoulder as they walked giggling toward the ballroom.

When they were out of earshot, Andi stepped in front of her, walking backwards. "He thinks you're hot!"

Susi blushed. "Come on. He does not."

"Seriously, did you not notice how he looked at you?"

"Let's find a place to sit."

Andi smiled at her aunt. "Nice subject change, but this conversation is not over. You better go talk to him some-time tonight."

Apparently, they arrived a little early and there were still plenty of seats available. The lights in the room were dimmed and the tables had little spooky monster center-pieces with candles on them, giving the room the appro-priate atmosphere. Toward the far end of the ballroom, was a dance floor and a DJ, who played a mix of dance music and spooky Halloween tunes.

Susi looked around. "Do you see Pete and Belinda yet?"

"Nope, I think we're a bit early," Andi suggested.

They sat down at a table with a good view of the door

and ordered some drinks. "Look, there's a werewolf!" Andi nodded toward the furry creature, and then resumed tapping her fingers on the table to the beat of the music.

About ten minutes later, Susi spotted the couple. "Pete, wir sind hier." She waved him over to their table. He wore a leprechaun costume and looked ridiculously funny. Belinda, beautiful as always, was dressed up as a fairy with pointy ears and her hair in a cute ponytail.

"How magical you two look! A match made in Ireland," Susi exclaimed.

"Hello, Pete." Andi stretched out her hand, which he took and drew her into a big hug again.

"Hello to you, too. I'm glad you came. I have a tendency to bore folks to tears when I talk about my stories," he winked at her. "Anyway, this is going to be a fun evening!"

Belinda tapped Andi on the shoulder with her wand. "Maybe as soon as this big oaf of a husband of mine lets you go, I get to say hello to you as well," she said with a nice Irish ring in her voice.

"I love your outfit, Belinda," Susi said as they sat down. "It totally fits your personality."

Pete smiled at his wife. "Yes, she's a devilish little fairy alright," and gave her a quick peck on the cheek.

Belinda blushed. "Your costumes are fabulous, too. A healer and a sick girl. Adorable! I love those pocks that you put on your face, Andi!"

"Thanks, it took us forever to find them in this town. We had to go to a specialty store to get them."

They sat down at the table and a few minutes later, their drinks arrived. Pete held up his glass. "So, I'm here for a Halloween party. To a ghoulishly fun time! Cheers!"

They all raised their glasses, "Cheers!"

· · ·

*A*bout two hours into the party, the DJ took a break and Andi was desperate for some fresh air. She was sweaty from doing the 'Twist' and teaching people how to do the 'Monster Mash.' Her choice of flat-heeled boots for tonight had definitely paid off. Ready to get away from the oven of a room, she excused herself from the table.

"Hi, are you leaving already?" the nice photographer asked her on the way out.

Andi smiled and shook her head. "No, I'm just trying to take a break from all the noise."

The photographer looked like he was going to ask her something. "Yes?"

"Uhm, where is your friend?"

"Oh, you mean Susi? She's in the ballroom with friends. Why?" She watched the color rise in his face.

"Well, uh, no, uh, I'm just wondering, that's all," he managed.

Andi smiled at him. "I'll let her know that you asked for her." With a smile, she patted him on the shoulder and walked off toward the coat check.

The temperature outside had dropped considerably, and the fog grew thicker, which lent the castle an eerie glow. Partygoers assembled in the courtyard to smoke cigarettes and to cool off.

A shudder cursed through Andi's body. "Brrr, it's freezing out here," Andi mumbled and drew her coat closer together to keep the cold out. She walked toward the gate to get away from the crowd. Thanks to the cold, she felt the effects of her few glasses of champagne wear off.

Andi followed a path that led through the Elizabeth Gate; an arch made of stone and adorned with stone-carved vines and sculptures, to one of the gardens on the extensive castle grounds. Andi looked over the stone railings, which usually offered a gorgeous view of the river valley and downtown Heidelberg. Tonight, only the brightest of lights in town shone through the white fog. She looked around for a place to sit and found a bench under a tree. With a few strokes, she wiped a few random leaves off the bench and sat down. She leaned back and took a deep breath, only to cough, when the cold air hit her lungs. The next breath was measured, and she relaxed, simply enjoying a few moments of the much-needed peace and quiet.

Her thoughts drifted toward the active times of the castle. What could life have been like, back when the fortress was still in its prime? She closed her eyes and imagined standing in the courtyard.

The clattering of horses could be heard all around her. She imagined several merchants showing off their wares and many people walking around in their long dresses or colorful uniforms. Occasionally, some common people walked through the masses, but were pushed around or snubbed by the royal family members living in the castle, if they were even acknowledged at all. She couldn't help thinking of someone like her entering the courtyard, covered in boils and sackcloth. With her luck, she would've been run over by an oncoming coach. Times back then were brutal. A cold breeze pulled her out of her dream.

*A*ndi figured that it was time to return to the party, before they sent out a search troop for her. She walked back toward the courtyard, which was empty by now, except for a few hard-core smokers by the door.

As she walked by the scaffolding, a wave of nausea

welled up in her stomach and crept up toward her throat. "Oh no, don't let me get sick," she mumbled. If there is anything in the world she hated most, other than her ex, it was getting nauseous. She didn't really have that much to drink. Odd. Andi continued to walk toward the building when she noticed that the scaffolding began to rattle slightly. Her nausea was not improving, and she felt a touch of vertigo setting in. Well, maybe she did have a few too many drinks after all.

The rattling of the scaffolding continued, and she heard a distinct clunk, as something fell right next to her left foot. First, she thought it was a small rock, but it had a more metallic sound to it. She looked down and saw sparkling light reflecting from the object. "Hmmm, what's that," she wondered, as she bent down to pick it up, which did not help her still queasy stomach. "It's a ring!" She turned around to make use of the bit of orange light she stood next to. It looked like an elaborate costume jewelry ring, except, this one felt a lot heavier than the ones you can buy for $10 in the store. The added weight must be the caked-on mud that's stuck to the ring. She held it a little closer, so she could see some of the detail. She could make out stones in different colors but wasn't sure if some of them were red or blue. Among the shiny ones was what appeared to be cubic zirconia or even diamonds. "How beautiful," she whispered. As she stood in the courtyard, admiring the ring, she made a mental note to turn it into the city's Lost and Found Office on Monday.

The scaffolding had stopped rattling and she realized that she was standing way too close to it. Afraid that it could collapse any minute, she did what any person in their right mind would do and walked away from the massive structure of wood and metal, before it piled on top of her.

Still holding the ring in her hand, she glanced over to

the large money-fountain. A few meters away from it stood
a gorgeous man, dressed in some sort of medieval clothing.
She must have stared at him quite obviously, because the
man looked back at her as if he was surprised. Maybe he's
shy, she thought. Funny that she hadn't noticed him in the
ballroom before. Did he just arrive?

She glanced at the ring one more time, and then slid it
on her ring finger, since she didn't have a zippered pocket
to stow it away safely.

As she looked up again and was about to collect all her
courage to say hello to this handsome stranger, all she saw
was the fountain. No cute guy.

"Damn it! Just my luck," she exclaimed and made her
way back to the party, scratching her face where the boils
were itching.

*a*ndi dropped off her coat at the wardrobe again
and walked back into the crowded ballroom. She
zigzagged her way over to the bar and ordered a mineral
water before joining Pete, Belinda and some other people
who she didn't know at the table.

"What? You switched to water?" Pete asked surprised.
"Are you okay?"

"I was getting a little queasy when I was outside, so I
think I'm cutting myself off for tonight." She gave him an
apologetic grin. "I'm still having a good time, though. I just
don't want to spoil it by getting sick."

"Smart girl," he said and lifted his glass of champagne.
"Cheers!"

As Andi raised her glass of bubbly water, Belinda
noticed her ring. "That's a beautiful piece of jewelry you're
wearing. Funny, I didn't see that on you earlier."

"I found it outside in the courtyard by the scaffolding. Someone must have dropped it." She took a sip. "I'll turn it in Monday. I might as well wear it for the rest of the night, since I don't have any pockets on my sack-clothes."

"Can I see it," Belinda asked.

Andi took off the ring and handed it to her. "Isn't it beautiful?"

Belinda's eyes widened in disbelief as she slipped it on her finger and held it in front of her to admire it. "Gal, this thing is real! And I don't think someone lost it tonight. It has some sort of dry mud or rocks between the gems. Where did you find this again?"

"By the scaffolding, where the city is doing the reconstruction of the building facades," Andrea explained.

"Pete, Pete, look what Andi found outside!" Pete danced in place to 'Hey Baby,' and didn't pay much attention to his wife. "PETER!"

That got his attention. "Yes, my dear?"

"Take a look at this ring. Andi found it by the reconstruction. Do you think what I'm thinking?"

Peter twisted and turned Belinda's hand as he inspected the ring. His jaw fell. "Andi, I think you may have found yourself a genuine treasure. This is a very old ring indeed, from as far as I can tell in the dark."

Andi looked at him surprised. "You're kidding, right? I thought it was some costume jewelry, just a bit heavier than I expected."

"Oh no, girl. This looks like the real deal," Pete announced with a slight slur. "Why don't you and Susi come over for coffee tomorrow and we'll take a closer look at it. I'm intrigued." He released his wife's hand.

Belinda slid the ring off her finger and gave it back to Andi.

Andi shrugged. "Sure, why not? I'm kind of curious myself, and you certainly know more than I do about such things."

Belinda suddenly elbowed her and pointed toward the bar.

Andi almost dropped the ring as she tried to put it back on her finger. "Ouch, what was that for," she asked a little annoyed, rubbing her throbbing arm.

"There's a guy over there checking you out. You're on the market, aren't you?"

Andi shook her head. "Nope, I had my recent share of getting my heart crushed." She carefully scratched one of her itchy boils." So who's looking at me," she said. "I'm curious."

Belinda looked around. "Well, he was ... he was right there close to the bar, dressed up as a medieval craftsman of some sort. He's gone now. Sorry, honey."

"Oh? Maybe I saw that same guy in the courtyard earlier. Did he wear a white shirt, reddish-brown pants, and had dark, medium-long hair?"

"Yep, that's him," Belinda confirmed.

"I think he just got here, which is weird, because the party is over in about an hour."

"Well, since you're not on the market, I guess it doesn't matter anyway," Belinda teased.

"That doesn't mean I can't appreciate a good-looking man," Andi countered.

They both laughed, and Andi grabbed Belinda's hand and dragged her out to the dance floor.

When the clock struck midnight, the party was over, and Andi and Susi took a taxi back home. Susi was a bit on the tipsy side, so Andi made sure that they made it safely into the house, helped Susi get some of the pointy jewelry off her, and removed the fake dirt make-up from her face, before she tucked her into bed.

She then went upstairs, removed the bulky ring from her finger and placed it on the nightstand. She walked into her bathroom and took off her sack clothes. Her face was still bothering her, and she couldn't wait to go to work with peeling off her itchy boils.

Andi looked in the mirror and noticed that her face around the boils was redder than the blush she had applied before they left earlier that evening. She pulled one of the boils off her skin, noticed some swelling and pronounced redness, where the boil was glued on with the special adhesive. "Oh no!"

Frantically, she pulled on the next boil. "No!" Another red welt emerged beneath it. "That can't be!" She quickly removed the other fake boils and applied make-up remover to clean the rest of her face. It stung, but she wanted to make sure that she got all of the adhesive off completely. What remained on her tired face were a dozen red welts. "I can't believe this is happening to me," she exclaimed. After taking a final disgusted look in the mirror, she turned around and climbed in the shower. She hoped that some cool water would reduce the swelling.

A few minutes later, she dried herself off with a big towel and slipped on a comfy nightshirt. She took a few steps toward the sink and glanced at the mirror. Thankfully, some of the general redness disappeared from her face. However, the dots were still as noticeable as before.

"No way," she whispered, wondering what she should do next. She couldn't just run around with polka dots on her face while job-hunting. There had to be a way to make these splotches vanish.

In hopes of finding some antihistamines, she went

downstairs into Susi's kitchen to check her medicine basket. "Of course, what was I thinking," she mumbled, "This is Germany." She'd have to go to a pharmacy to get something like that. "Ugh!" And of course, it's Sunday, when everything is closed. "Great." She just resigned herself to look like a polka-dotted creature for the next few days. Maybe Susi had some homeopathic remedies for cases like this. As Andi walked up the stairs to her bedroom, she had a last glimmer of hope. She remembered that she might have a travel pack of ibuprofen that she brought for her flight.

*a*ndi rummaged through her purse and after emptying the contents, she found her last dose of ibuprofen, ripped the package open and swallowed the pill with a drink of water.

She dozed off in no time. The vision of this gorgeous stranger from the courtyard floated in her mind. What a sight to behold, she thought. Too bad, he walked away before they had a chance to talk to each other. She felt a slight twinge of regret, but why was she thinking about that stranger anyway? The last thing she wanted was another man to break her still mending heart.

Sometime during the night, she woke with the eerie feeling of being watched. How ridiculous. She didn't even believe in monsters in the closet anymore. Andi slowly opened her eyes and turned toward her alarm clock to see how long she had slept.

From the corner of her eye, she saw a man standing by her window. In an instant, she sat up straight in her bed. A soft squeak escaped as she drew in a lung full of air. It wasn't just any man. She saw the same man earlier in the courtyard.

Terrified, she backed against the wall. Is he going to rape me? Shoot me? Atlanta's news reports were full of assaults and murders. Who would have thought that Germany's crime rate was on the rise and she would be a statistic? So this is how it ends, she supposed.

They stared at each other for a moment, until Andi finally managed to utter some words. "Who are you? Why are you stalking me? What are you doing in my room?" Her voice was shaking with fear. "What do you want from me? I don't have much money to give you." She grabbed the ring and held it toward him. "Here, take this! It's worth a lot of money, but please don't hurt me," she pleaded.

"Please, speak German. My English is not good," he said with a somewhat gruff voice and strange dialect, definitely from this area, but something was off.

"Wer bist Du und was machst Du hier," she asked him again. A barrage of crime scenarios flashed through her mind. What's next? Would he pull out a knife and kill her? This would be just her luck - the topper of this year's misfortunes.

"I'm not here to harm you," he continued in his odd German dialect. "I'm surprised you can even see me."

That caught her off guard. "Huh? Why would you say that?"

He sat down on the chair in the corner. "For many centuries, I was invisible to everyone, except for some people in the other world."

Andi couldn't believe what she heard him say and laughed. "Get out! Is this some Halloween prank my aunt put you up to? If so, it isn't working very well so far."

He looked at her puzzled. "Your aunt?"

"Never mind." Andi's heart still raced. Great! Did this guy escape from the local loony bin?

"You may not believe me," he continued, "but a witch

put a spell on me just before I died, and only the person who finds that ring," he pointed at the ring she was holding, "can help to set me free."

Andi couldn't believe it. Some weird schizophrenic psycho was robbing her. She had to keep her cool, convince him to leave the house, and then call the police. "Okay, I'll play along. So, you're some sort of ghost and I'm supposed to help set you free?"

The man nodded while looking dead serious at her face. "Exactly."

"Okay, so let's just say that for some reason I believe you, how am I supposed to help you?" She sat up straighter and waited for his reply.

"There is a jewelry box hidden somewhere in the area. You need to find it..."

Andi interrupted him. "...and put the ring in it?" She grinned. "I know that story. You could've been a little more original than that."

The man looked at her. "You don't believe me?"

"No. Of course not!"

"I beg you, I'm telling the truth and I need your help," he said. "How can I make you believe?"

Andi thought for a moment. "Okay, so if you're a ghost, you look pretty solid to me. Can you walk through a door, then?" Andi asked a little amused. "And when you're through that one," she pointed at her bedroom door, "can you leave and never come back?"

"If it will convince you, I will do it," he replied. "But I will not leave. I need you." He rose from the chair, walked toward her bedroom door and walked right through it, until he disappeared.

Andi's jaw went slack, and she had to remind herself to breathe. A few seconds later, he stepped through the door again and stood in the middle of the room. "Will you help me now?"

"Uh, ah, uh, so the legend is true," she stammered.

"Yes. And the ring that you have found at the castle is the ring that belonged to the Princess Margarete."

"No shit? I'm sorry. That just can't be!" Andi wrapped her covers around herself. She needed something to hold on to. Something that is real, because this had to be a dream. Refusing to wake up and losing the view of this marvelous man with the strange accent, she kept the conversation going. "So, what do you need for me to do?"

He sat down on the chair again. "You are willing to help?"

She relaxed a little. "Sure, just to let you know, though, I'm not willing to go to jail for you, kapiert?"

The ghost smiled at her.

Andi thought she was about to faint. Where has this man been all these years? Why could she not have found the ring years ago? Well, of course, she would've been a kid then, and pretty much of no help. It didn't matter; he was here now.

"Of course, I would never think to put you in any danger, Frau...?"

"Andrea. My name is Andrea, or Andi, if you like." She leaned forward and stretched her hand out to him.

"My name is Volker." He extended his as well.

Andi jumped back as her hand touched, well nothing. "Oh." All she had felt was a slight electric tingle. "I think I have to get used to that. Sorry."

"Worry not; I have to reacquaint myself with the skill of interacting with real people." He grinned a little sheepish. "I see you're very tired. We will talk more tomorrow when you have had some sleep."

"What, you're leaving just like that? I'm not tired!" She

shook her head in confusion. As if, I could go to sleep now. "You scared the hell out of me," she replied.

"And I do apologize for that. I will leave you now and return when you are refreshed. Gute Nacht," he said and faded into the darkness.

"Good night to you, too," she whispered.

CHAPTER 4

*T*he next morning Andi rose from her sleep. What a weird night, she thought. That dream of the handsome German guy almost seemed real. The only reason that she knew that it was all a dream was because he was a ghost. And ghosts only exist in books and movies.

Her body felt like a ton of bricks, but she made herself get out of bed, regardless. Slowly, she shuffled her way to her window and raised the blinds. "Ugh!" This was just too heavy of a dose of sunshine for her liking this morning. Still squinting, she walked over to her nightstand and looked at the ring she had found the night before. At least that part was real. Looking at it closer, she saw some red and blue stones, surrounded by diamonds and mortar. Nice. She'd have to clean it up somehow, but then thought better of it. Knowing for a fact that once she cleaned it up herself, half the jewels would be missing. No, Pete probably would do a much better, less damaging job in restoring this ring to its original beauty.

She sat the ring back on her nightstand and made her way to the bathroom to take a wake-up shower. As she strolled by the mirror, she was slightly startled when she saw her reflection. "Oh great, I forgot about those awesome welts!" The face staring back at her was a little puffy from sleep and still covered with penny-size red polka dots. "Looks like I'll have to wear a veil if I'm going anywhere today," she mumbled as she turned on the shower and waited for the hot water.

Once she was dressed and awake, she walked into her small kitchen and poured herself some cereal and milk. It wasn't exactly the breakfast of champions, but she didn't have the energy to make an omelet.

As she turned around, she nearly jumped out of her skin. Andi inhaled sharply in surprise and held her hand to her chest. "Holy crap," she exclaimed. "It's you!"

Volker grinned and spoke in his old dialect: "Guten Morgen. Have you had a good sleep?"

"Uh, uh..." She couldn't seem to get her mouth to work. He looked stunning in jeans and a white button-down shirt. "Uh, good morning to you, too," she finally managed. Was she still dreaming? "You are real?"

"Of course, I am," he shrugged, "considering my condition." He pretended to pick up a glass of juice and his hand passed right through the glass leaving a trail of clear liquid as it passed.

Andi's jaw dropped. "Wow, cool! Do that again!"

He grinned and repeated the trick. "You are easy to amuse, my lady, aren't you?"

"Well, it keeps my life from getting all too boring."

He looked at her, flashing his slightly crooked teeth at her. "I see you're still affected by your disease."

Andi touched her face and felt the blood rising to her head. How embarrassing. "I think my skin didn't like the stuff I glued my boils on with last night. Now I have to run around like I have the plague."

"Actually, die Pest looks very dissimilar to this," he said with his cute accent, "However; I understand what you mean to say." At least, he had the ambition to look like he was serious, when he corrected her mistake, though, another giggle left his throat. "Apply some tincture of balloon plant and the redness should subside," he offered.

"Thanks," she replied, "but I think I'm fresh out." She couldn't help but stare at him. Something about him was different from the other men she had in her life before. Was it the way he smiled? The way his dark brown hair fell over his shoulders? Or was it the way he talked and made her laugh? Great, she's falling for a ghost! She tore her gaze away from him and poured some milk into her cereal bowl. "Well, if you don't mind, I'm going to sit down and have some breakfast, before I pass out." She didn't mention that it was because of him that she felt a little light-headed.

"No, go ahead, because I cannot help you if you faint from hunger. Nobody will hear or see me." He made a chair appear out of thin air and sat on it to join her at the kitchen table.

Andi looked at him. "Actually, that's not true. My friend, Belinda, saw you last night at the party."

"How could that be," he asked. "For centuries, nobody in this realm has ever seen me. Suddenly, two people can in one night?"

Andi thought for a moment. "Well, I handed the ring to her when she wanted to look at it. I wonder if you and the ring are connected in a way. Maybe, whoever touches it will be able to see you," she ventured.

Volker looked at her. "That may be a good possibility."

"Why don't we try out the theory when Susi wakes up? She will freak out," Andi grinned. "She may be a while, though. I think she had a little too much fun at the Halloween party last night."

"Yes, drinking too much liquor can make one feel rotten in the morning."

Andi grinned. "You say that as if you have some experience in that department."

"Naja, well, there wasn't much other to drink than wine, beer, and the such. Although, I do think, it may be much safer to drink the water these days."

Andi leaned forward and scooped a spoonful of cereal in her mouth. "Not to change the subject, but what did you do since you were, uh, hexed, for the lack of a better term? I'm dying to know." She dropped her spoon back into the bowl and clasped her hand in front of her mouth. "I'm sorry, that came out wrong."

"Des macht nix - it's okay," he said in his dialect. "I was tied to the castle grounds, including the upper castle area, which doesn't exist anymore, until you found the ring. I don't know what my limits are now, but we will know in time."

Andi felt pity welling up inside of her. "You mean to say that you have not left the castle in how long? When did you even live?"

"My day of passing was in the year of 1605," he explained.

Quickly, Andi counted off on her fingers, "that's over 400 years that you've been trapped?"

"Well, I have made long-time friends in the castle, and you just learn to live with the others." Again, the left corner of his mouth twitched into a smile. "What were my enemies going to do to me, kill me?"

"So, do you know anybody famous in… your other world?" Andi simply couldn't resist asking.

Volker thought for a minute. "Let me see, if you took the castle tour, you may have heard about of the court jester Perkeo, Princess Elizabeth, who the Elizabeth gate was named after, and occasionally, Mark Twain pays a visit, even though I have trouble understanding his English."

"That's friggin' awesome! Are they under a spell like you?"

"There are some who are hexed, but many of them just have unfinished business," Volker explained.

"Fascinating!" Andi took mental notes of what he just told her. There is plenty of story material for some upcoming novels, she thought. "Tell me more about your time," she prodded, "if you don't mind."

"I don't see why not." Volker sat up as if he heard something. "But I think you have some sort of beast in your house downstairs."

"What?" Andi looked at him quizzically. "What are you talking about?"

"I think your aunt is awake. Why don't I vanish for a while, and you let me know when you are ready for me to return." As soon as he said these words, he faded into, well, nothing, again.

"But wait…" She hated it when he did that. Andi finished off her cereal, put the bowl in her sink, and then went to investigate where the strange sounds came from.

*A*ndi descended the steps to her aunt's apartment, ready to spring the news of her ghostly visits on Susi. Half way down the stairs, she heard the dreadful sounds of Susi praying to the porcelain God. "She's got to be hating life right now," she sighed and was thankful that it wasn't her. She had her fill of nausea last night in the courtyard, and just the thought of it made her stomach queasy. Andi took the last few steps then continued down the hall.

She knocked at the bathroom door. "Are you okay, Suse?"

"Go away, I'm fine," a muffled voice replied, followed by another horrible noise.

"I'm just making sure you're okay. I'll wait for you in the kitchen," Andi said. "Just yell if you need me."

"Whatever," the voice on the other side of the door croaked. "Just go away!"

Andi turned and walked over to the kitchen, where she started a pot of coffee. A little caffeine will perk her up, she thought. She needed her to feel more like herself again if she was going to introduce Volker to her this morning, or she would never forgive her if his first impression of her would be at her worst. Andi drummed her fingers on the counter as she was watching the coffee percolate. How can she make Susi feel better? She flipped through her mental file of "The-Morning-After" foods that might help ease the unbearable discomfort that Susi was experiencing right now. More alcohol? Nope, that's definitely not the right answer, even though Susi might want a glass of schnapps to get over the shock of seeing a ghost. Andi couldn't help the grin that snuck up on her face. She definitely could have used a drink last night after she saw Volker walk through the door. However, more alcohol was not the answer for Susi's condition, so she scrapped that thought and searched her mind for more suitable options. What has helped her in the past?

She remembered the last time she was dealing with a monster headache and an upset stomach. It was the weekend after her ex had broken up with her and her best friend took her out on the town to celebrate the loss of an arrogant and egotistical asshole, as she had non-affection-ately called him. Andi shuddered when she thought of the jerk and the many years she had wasted, believing that they would spend the rest of their lives together, while he was out making the same promises to his other lady friends. She shook her head to force him out of her mind. Focus Andi! She remembered feeling sick as a dog the next morning and the only thing that made her feel better was… "Yes, this is it!" She opened up the fridge and found half of a dozen eggs. Andi took out three of them and cracked them into a small bowl. Scrambled eggs – the miracle cure for hangovers. She concentrated on the task and began stirring the eggs in a small pan over low heat. Andi smiled. This will fix Susi up again and then she'll be ready to meet Volker – or maybe not. There is only one way to find out.

Susi schlepped herself out of the bathroom into the kitchen a few minutes later.

"You look like hell!" Andi pulled the chair out for Susi. "Hier, setz Dich doch," and motioned her to sit down. "Coffee is coming and I'm making you scrambled eggs and toast."

"I love you to death, kiddo, but my stomach can't handle that right now." Susi sat at the table and rested her forehead on her propped-up hands.

Andi finished cooking the eggs and toast, put the food on a small plate and carried it over to the table. "Come on, eat at least a little," she nudged. She had to get her to put some food in her stomach, so they could do the big reveal. Volker was waiting for them somewhere. Or so she hoped. She couldn't help to doubt herself. What if she actually had been hallucinating the whole time? Susi would try to commit her to the loony bin if she told her story and Volker didn't show up. Volker. Ah, the thought of him alone made her all giddy. "It'll make you feel better. I promise," she coaxed again, the excitement showing in her voice.

"Okay, I don't see why you are so determined to feed me, but I'll have a few bites, just so you will leave me alone to dwell in my misery," she sighed. "Maybe I can hold it down." She stared at her eggs, then took her fork and scooped a small bite full on it. "Thanks for making breakfast for me," then looked up at her for the first time that morning. Susi grinned in surprise, despite her feeling like crap. "Holy hell, what happened to your face?" She tried to stifle a laugh but wasn't very successful.

Andi waved her off. "Oh, it's just a slight allergic reaction to the boil adhesive. You don't happen to have an antihistamine, do you?"

Susi then broke out into a hearty laugh. "Nope, sorry. You look really funny, though."

"Great, you're supposed to be my caring and supportive aunt, but all you do is laugh at me?" She attempted to look hurt.

"I do care, but that doesn't mean I can't poke fun at you." Susi touched her forehead. "Aua, my head is throbbing!"

"There, that's what you get for laughing at me. It's karma," Andi added for good measure. She walked over to the pantry and returned to the table holding a small packet with tablets, trying to decipher the medical writing on it. "I found some painkiller for you, or at least I think that's what it is."

Susi glanced at it and nodded.

Andi then punched out a tablet and handed it to her, then got up and fetched a glass of water. "There you go! Take this, and you should feel better soon."

"God, I hope so!" Susi popped the tablet in her mouth. "You're so nice! When I'm old and shriveled up, will you take care of me?"

Andi smiled and squeezed her shoulder as she walked

by her to grab herself a cup of coffee. "Sure, right now, you're acting like you're not too far from it."

Susi sighed. "Well, I appreciate your help. Thanks, kiddo."

"How about you finish up some of your breakfast, sit for a bit, then take a shower. When you're feeling better, I have something to tell you."

Susi's eyes got big. "You're not getting back together with this loser of your ex, are you?"

Andi propped her hands on her waist. "Oh, hell no! Never, ever will I get back with that jerk!"

"Good. I was afraid that you have had a lapse of sanity for a moment and decided to go back to the States for him." Susi paused. "So, what is it then?"

Andi took a small sip of her hot coffee and put her mug down on the table. "You'll just have to wait. I'm afraid you can't handle it in your fragile condition at the moment."

"I am not fragile," Susi protested. "I can handle it. Trust me." She paused. "Is it something bad?"

Andi shrugged and pretended to contemplate her answer. "It depends how you take it, I guess," she smiled at her then continued, "but you should really shower up before I tell you. You'll thank me later." Changing the course of the conversation, she added. "So, did you ever go back to talk to the photographer at the castle last night? He looked pretty lonely out there by himself in the hallway."

Susi's color changed to a slight red. "Well, I took a break to catch some fresh air and I went over to talk to him for a little while."

"And?"

"He took a couple more pictures of me, just for fun," Susi said.

"Just for fun?"

"Don't be so nosy!"

"Come on," Andi probed. "You can tell me. Did he tell you his name?"

Susi played with a piece of scrambled egg on her plate, then looked at Andi and paused until a smile cracked her serious face. "He not only gave me his name, which is Ralf by the way, he also gave me his phone number. He wants to take me out some time this week."

Andi jumped out of her chair and shouted in excitement: "Yes, you're going on a date!"

Susi grabbed her obviously hurting head with both hands. "Aaaah, not so loud! And it's not a date," she emphasized. "We are just going to dinner to get to know each other some more."

"Sounds like a date to me," Andi replied with a satisfied smile. "Now go grab a shower and get dressed, so I can finally share my surprise." She grabbed the half-empty plate and carried it to the sink. "I'll clean up in here. Hurry!"

*A*fter Susi left the kitchen, Andi turned on the radio and let the hot water run into the sink. She only had a few dishes, so she didn't want to bother with the dishwasher. It was 10 a.m. and the hourly local news came on.

"...when a small earthquake rattled the Heidelberg area Saturday night at 10:13 and lasted a minute and 34 seconds," the voice on the radio said. Andi stopped what she was doing and listened. "The magnitude of the tremors measured a 3.1 on the Richter scale and the vibrations were felt 20 km from the epicenter, as far as Schwetzingen and Mannheim."

Wow, she thought, that would explain a lot. Was this the reason why she felt so queasy?

"There were no injuries or major damage reported," the voice continued, and then changed the subject to other news.

A few minutes later, Susi walked into the kitchen.

"Wow, what a difference a shower makes," Andi teased her. "You're looking much better!"

"Thanks," Susi replied as she sat back down at the table. "I still feel off, though."

Andi joined her at the table. "You won't believe what happened last night."

"You fell in love?"

Andi rolled her eyes. "Are you kidding me? I just got here." She leaned forward and continued, "There was a small earthquake while we were at the party last night."

Susi looked at her surprised. "Oh, that would probably explain why the lights were flickering and the chandeliers where rattling. I couldn't tell if it was because of the heavy bass of the song that was playing, or I was getting dizzy from dancing."

"You mean, from drinking?" Andi grinned at her and then stood up.

"Wait here," she said, "I have something to show you. I'll be right back."

"Goody," Susi looked at her in anticipation. "I've waited all morning for you to reveal this apparent secret of yours."

"You'll see in a minute," she called from the hallway. Andi ran up the stairs and retrieved the ring from her nightstand. She tripped as she hurried back, and nearly went sailing down the first set of steps. She barely caught herself by clinging on to the rail. "I'm good," she yelled down. She felt her heart race as she straightened herself. That was close.

To her horror, she saw Volker on the bottom of the staircase looking worried at her. "Are you okay," he whispered.

Andi was mortified and felt the heat rising to her head. This guy must think she's a clumsy idiot. She wanted to run back upstairs and hide in her room to get away from him. That would have been a great idea, if he was a solid human being and could not walk through doors. Instead, she tried to smile at him, hoping that he didn't notice her red face and continued down the stairs. "Yeah, I'm fine, I think." She wouldn't dare mention that she had felt like a dork almost every time she met him so far. She picked up the ring that she dropped in favor of saving her skull.

"I will see you again in a moment," he said with a low voice as he vanished with a smile.

"What's that," Susi called from the kitchen.

Andi tucked the ring in her pocket and slowly walked down the last few steps to avoid a repeat of her humiliating fall. "Nothing, Suse."

As she entered the kitchen, again, Susi poured herself another cup of coffee. "What happened and who were you talking to?"

Andi grinned. "I was just trying to test the sturdiness of your rails. Now sit down, I want to show you something," she commanded.

"Yes, ma'am!" Susi sat on her chair as instructed. "So what is so important that you are risking breaking your neck over?"

"I'm about to tell you." Andi sat down on her chair and then began her story. "Yesterday at the party, I went outside for some fresh air. I was standing by the scaffolding when the earthquake hit, and this ring fell down from somewhere and landed by my foot." She dug the ring out of her jeans, picked off the pocket fuzz and handed it to Susi.

"This looks very real, and very old, and beautiful, aside from the dirt or whatever that is," Susi said as she stared at it in awe.

"Nice choice of words," Andi patted her on her shoulder. "But wait, it gets better." She took a glance over Susi's shoulder and saw Volker leaning in the doorway. Their eyes met, and they looked at each other for what only seemed a moment.

Andi's heart began to skip a beat as he held her gaze.

"Hello!" Susi patted her hand to get her attention. "Earth to Andi... what gets better?"

"Huh? What?" It took her a second to remember what she was talking about. "Oh yes, sorry! When I picked up the ring from off the ground in the courtyard, I saw a man dressed in medieval clothing standing by the fountain. I glanced back at the ring and back up toward the fountain, but the guy was gone."

Susi smiled. "And I thought that I had too much to drink!"

Andrea sighed in exasperation, "Just listen, will you," then continued. "When I came back inside, I showed Belinda the ring and she saw the same guy. After she quickly looked away to get my attention, he had disappeared again."

"So, what are you trying to say? You both saw a ghost at the castle? I know you're into writing about that sort of stuff, maybe you should change your genre over to small-town romance novels for a while."

Andi hem-hawed around a bit. "Uh, well, yeah. About the ghost, I mean. I saw him again last night in my room."

Susi nearly spit out the sip of coffee she just took.

"You're kidding! Are you sure that nothing hit your head during that earthquake? Maybe you have a fever - are you sure that's not the measles – that rash on your face?"

"Nope. Now that you've touched the ring, I want you to slowly turn around, look at the kitchen door, and tell me what you see. Ready?"

"Sure, I'll play along." Susi turned around not expecting to see anything out of the ordinary. Instead, she saw Volker standing in the doorway with his 17th century garb and a smile planted on his face, waving at her. "Nice, you finally found a decent looking guy. Did he drive here, because I don't remember him riding with us in the taxi?"

"Uhm, no. He doesn't need rides. He's a ghost, sort of."

"Yeah, whatever. Have a seat." She turned to him. "Can I offer you some coffee?"

"Nein, danke," he declined. "I can't have that."

"Ah, caffeine, I understand," Susie replied.

Andi rolled her eyes. "No, Suse, he literally can't have any coffee." She turned to Volker. "Can you show her the cup thing, maybe that'll convince her?"

Volker smiled. "Sure."

"Watch this, Auntie!" Andi said as Volker proceeded to grab Susi's cup of coffee and his hand went right through it.

Susi paled, and her eyes went large. She looked like she just saw a ghost. Well, technically she did.

"Did... did... did you just see that," she stuttered.

Andi smiled. "That's what I've been trying to tell you. Susi, meet Volker, from the year 1605. Volker, meet my aunt Susanne, but I think she prefers Susi."

He gave Susi one of those breathtaking smiles, and then bowed. "It is very nice to meet you, Frau Susanne," he said with his old Heidelberg dialect. "I'd kiss your hand but forgive me if I can't."

Susi was flabbergasted. "Okay," was all she could manage at the moment.

Volker and Andi caught Susi up with the legend and the dilemma he faced. The entire time, Susi had that deer in headlights look, as she gawked at Volker.

Finally, Andi couldn't take it anymore. "You know, that's kind of rude to stare at people like that," she chided.

"Uh huh," was all she got for a reply.

Volker laughed. "Don't worry. I don't mind."

"But I do," Andrea countered. "Get hold of yourself. You're practically drooling all over yourself."

Susi blinked a few times. "Sorry. I just can't believe that, uh, the way, uh, well."

"I know," he said. "I think you are handling the news very well."

Andi rose from her chair. "Okay, you guys talk some more, while I call Pete and Belinda to see when they want us to come over. They invited us for coffee and cake, and to examine the ring - you know those two are history buffs. Are you two up to it?"

"Sure." Susi nodded and turned to Volker. "So, what brings you here?"

*I*n the afternoon, Andi and Susi arrived at Pete and Belinda's apartment in the old section of town. When Pete opened the door, he took a good look at Susi. "Wow, rough night, huh?"

"I guess you could say that." Susi rewarded him with a smirk.

As Andi walked through the door, Pete broke out in loud laughter. "Honey, you have to come see this!"

Belinda walked out of the kitchen with a cake server in one hand the other held in front of her mouth, when she saw Andi's face. "I'm so sorry! I'm really not trying to make fun of you. Really!"

Pete cleared his throat. "So, what happened to your pretty face?"

At least he tried to be a little bit politer. "Stage make-up accident," Andi replied a little miffed. "You don't happen to have an antihistamine, do you?"

Belinda hurried over to the dining room table and set the cake server down. "Hang on, Andi. I think I do have some in the medicine cabinet. Why don't you guys take off your coats and have a seat? I'll be right back to join you."

Pete motioned them to get comfortable at the table, while he hung up their coats. When he returned, he took the seat next to Andi. "By the way, Andi, are you still looking for a job?"

She turned to him. "Yes, I haven't had much luck yet, because I did all my schooling and job training in the States and employers here don't know what to make of it and how to fit me in. Why?"

"A colleague told me that the University is looking for an English-speaking administrative clerk in the International Department. I spoke to the Personnel Department to get some more information about the position and they said that they were looking for someone like you." He got up, retrieved a piece of notepaper from his desk, and handed it to her. "Here is their contact information, if you're interested."

Andi's eyes lit up. She did not enjoy living on her savings and Susi's insisting of covering groceries and dining out. For her own peace of mind, a job was number one on her priority list. "What do you mean, am I interested?" she replied as if he had made the understatement of the century. "At this point, I would take any job to make a living, even if I have to clean houses."

"Well," Pete said, "I'm having trouble visualizing you as a Putzfrau, but if you give the University a call, they might actually give you a position."

Andi hugged him. "You really didn't have to job-hunt for me, but I appreciate what you're doing. I'll give them a call first thing in the morning."

Belinda reappeared from the bathroom with a pack of antihistamines and a tall glass of carbonated water.

Andi smiled in appreciation as Belinda sat the pills and water in front of her. "Thanks, you're an angel!"

"Not quite," Belinda looked at her husband and gave him a wink.

"Seriously," she added, "you've been so nice to me already. I don't know how to repay you."

Belinda waved her off. "Ach, forget about it. We wouldn't do it if we didn't like you. Anyway, I'll be right back with coffee and cake," she added on her way to the kitchen.

After everyone had their first piece of cake and exchanged a few pleasantries, Belinda couldn't wait any longer. "So, let's see it!"

"You mean, IT in regard to the ring or HIM?"

"What are you talking about, Andi? I'm confused," Belinda looked at her as if she was sprouting horns.

Pete shifted forward on his chair. "Oh, this ought to be good."

Andi and Susi looked at each other, pretending to contemplate whether they should let them in on their secret or not. After a short moment of silence, Andi finally gave in and explained. "Of course, you remember the ring that I found last night." The pair nodded in anticipation. "The guy, Belinda, who you swore was checking me out at the bar and disappeared - I'd seen him before, when I picked up the ring from the ground."

"Oh," Belinda interjected. "So, you found him again and got his phone number? - Or better yet, took him home?"

Andi snickered. "Well, you could say that."

"No way!" Belinda and Pete said in unison.

After glancing over the couple's shoulders, she smiled once more as she saw Volker's amused face, before she continued. "This guy you saw, his name is Volker and he's something like a ghost."

"Shut up!" Now it was Belinda's turn to laugh.

"I'm sure he is," Pete added. "Nice Halloween gag."

Andi grinned again. "I'm serious! Susi and I realized this morning that everybody, who touches the ring, could see him for some strange reason, as if there's some sort of connection. Actually, he's here right now."

Belinda looked around. "Okay, I'll play along. I touched the ring. Why can't I see him?"

"Because he's standing right behind you, silly!"

Belinda turned all the way around and if Pete hadn't caught her in time, she would have fallen off her chair. Volker just stood there in his usual outfit, a big grin pasted on his face, and waved hello.

"What? I can't see anything," Pete complained.

"That's because you haven't held the ring yet." Andi slipped it off her finger and handed it to Pete. He marveled at it for a few seconds, and then looked behind his wife, where indeed some guy stood grinning his butt off. "What in the world...?"

"Hallo, nice to meet you all," the ghost said.

While the newly initiated couple collected themselves, Volker conjured up a chair and a cup of ghostly coffee between Andi and Susi and joined them at the table.

It took a minute to catch everyone up on the story, before the subject changed to the ring. "So," said Pete, "now that we know what the ring does, let's take a closer look at it, shall we?" He went to another room and returned with a small box of tools. "I can't get all the muck off it, unless I use a special solvent, but I'll do my best to clean it as much as I can. In the meantime, Volker, why don't you tell us how you became a ghost, for the lack of a better term, and what we can do to help you find this jewelry box?"

Volker nodded and took a sip of his imaginary coffee. "After I was arrested and thrown into the prison tower, you already know that I became very ill. Since I did not know anything about the whereabouts of the ring, the princess summoned a woman from the outskirts of town, who was rumored to be a witch. Since she was miserable without her precious ring, I, as the apparent culprit of her loss, had to suffer as well. The princess forced the witch to cast a spell on me to live in unrest until the ring gets reunited with its box."

"Little did the princess know that I knew the witch," he continued. "Her name was Amelie. We had actually grown up together in Eppelheim. As we became old enough to work, I had followed in my father's footsteps as a mason and Amelie spent most of her time studying to become a healer, and soon, some of her other special abilities emerged." He smiled. "Andi really could use one of Amelie's healing spells right now to help her with her current malady." The round giggled as Andi grimaced at the jest.

"Amelie was forced to put the spell on me, or the princess would have punished her and her family for being disobedient. But to make my demise less severe, she left out a few inconvenient conditions, which the princess demanded, such as confining my soul to the tower after my death. Thanks to her, I at least had the privilege of roaming around the castle grounds and watch people as they changed, learned a little English and Japanese in the meantime and got to watch some TV hanging out with the security staff, so at least, I'm a little caught up with the times."

"So apparently the ring fell somewhere in a crack and it must've gotten knocked loose during the earthquake, I guess," Belinda speculated.

"This section of the castle was being worked on at the time when I was arrested. It is quite possible that it fell into some mortar between the bricks as the baron sicced those troops on me. That's a mystery we will probably never solve completely," Volker added with a sigh.

Susi took a bite of her second piece of cheesecake. "Well, we could go to the castle and look at the exact spot where Andi stood when she found the ring. Maybe there's some visible damage in the walls?"

Pete nodded. "Good idea, I'm almost finished with the rough cleaning of the ring anyway," and held it against the light to admire it.

"So what happened to the princess's jewelry box?" Andi asked.

"Of course, the baron still blamed the missing ring on me," Volker continued his story. "Being superstitious, as he was, the baron believed in ghosts. He found out that a witch put a spell on me and that I might come back to haunt him to take revenge for what he did to me. So the only thing that he could think of doing was to take it from the princess again and hide it in a place where nobody would ever find it. When the princess was away, he snuck into her room, and then announced to his cousin that he was going down to the market to visit a friend on the other side of the river. Since I could only trail him within the castle grounds, I do not know where he actually hid the box."

"Well, that narrows it down." Belinda commented not so confident. "It's either close to the market place or with his friend across the river, if he told the truth. So where should we start searching?"

Pete looked up from his work. "I have access to a wide variety of books and literature in the University Library and know many historians in the area. I can work that part."

Susi looked at Volker a bit more comfortable than she felt that morning. "I have to be back at work tomorrow, but I will try to do my best to assist with the search. I just don't know how much of a help I will be," she continued apologetically.

"Worry not. Housing your niece and taking her to the ball was more than enough. Without Andi being at the castle that night, who knows whose hands the ring would have fallen into. I am forever grateful for that," Volker's appreciative gaze turned to Andi.

"Maybe Andi and I can do some field work while she's still waiting on news about her job situation," Belinda suggested. "Just tell us where to go and we can check it out."

Volker smiled. "I can't believe that you are all willing to do this for me. You didn't even know I existed until today."

Andi pointed her finger at him. "Not true! I knew that you did exist, well, at some point in time. Actually, I found out about you the day I took the tour at the castle."

"And because of you, I lost a bet with my best friend," Volker added. When everyone looked at him confused, he told them about the crooked painting and that he had bet that a tour guide would notice it first.

"You did that?" Andi couldn't believe it. "You're such a prankster!"

"I try to do my best," he boasted, then winked at her, "especially if it gets a pretty girl's attention."

She was about to punch him in the arm and stopped millimeters short. Andi felt a small jolt of electricity as they almost touched and jumped in surprise. "Sorry about that," she said. "I forget that I cannot do that to you."

Volker only grinned in return.

A few minutes later, the humming of the miniature brush stopped. "Alright, this is about as clean as it gets without the solution to remove the remaining mortar," Pete announced.

Everybody rose from the table and walked over to the desk where Pete held the ring into the light. "Isn't she a beauty?" he asked. The polished silver ring was studded with several diamonds arranged around a large sapphire. In each corner of the diamond shaped ring, was a small ruby that coordinated perfectly with the colors of the jewelry.

The ladies and Volker sighed in awe. "This is breath-taking," Andi whispered.

"Beyond breathtaking," added Susi.

"I'm speechless," said Belinda. "I want one!"

"Anything for you, my darling," Pete cooed at his wife then became serious. "Maybe we should be careful about who knows about this ring. Sure, it's great for Volker to interact with living people again, but if the ring falls into the wrong hands, all chances of us reuniting it with its box will diminish. Also, if someone from the government finds out about it, they might confiscate the ring and display it in a museum. That would make our mission far more difficult than it has to be."

Everybody nodded in agreement. "I think that we

should not mention it to anyone else at this point and focus on the search, instead," Andi added.

"I have a safe that we could keep it in for the time being," Susi offered. "Can we still see you then?"

"I am not quite sure. Maybe we should try to lock the ring up when we get back to Susi's home and see if Pete and Belinda can still see me," Volker suggested.

*A*fter they finished their coffee, Belinda cleared the table, and put up the cake, and the group made their way to the castle. It was only a short distance to the funicular, so they decided that it would be easier just to walk instead of taking the car and finding a place to park. They had to buy combo-tickets anyway, even though all they were interested in was the courtyard. If they had waited another two hours, they could've gotten in for free, but with daylight fading, they probably wouldn't be able to see where the ring came from, so they just paid for the tickets and rode the funicular up to the castle. Since it already was late in the day, they got a section of the cabin for themselves and Volker joined them on the ride up.

The girls took a quick bathroom break at the stop before they walked to the castle. Andi looked in the small mirror as she washed her hands. She smiled as she noticed that her spots were fading. To her delight, Belinda's antihistamines seemed to work some of their magic.

They took their short walk to the castle entrance, when Andi felt her legs and eyelids getting heavy. "Gosh, I hate taking drugs. I'm about to fall asleep." She yawned for good measure. "That's okay, though. I'll tough it out."

"I could carry you for a bit," Volker suggested with a smug grin on his face.

Andi faked a quick laugh. "I'd like to see you try." As

soon as the words came out of her mouth, she remembered the slight tingling she felt when he about touched her hand. "Never mind," she added to cover up her embarrassment.

His ghostly face flushed. Apparently, Volker remembered the same incident from last night as they tried to shake hands during their introductions.

As they neared the entrance, most tourists were already on their way out of the castle. Andi noticed that some of them would look at her funny and kept their distance, which made her feel extremely uncomfortable. "Gosh, I wish people would stop staring at me," Andi commented as they walked past the leaving crowds. "They look at me as if I have an infectious disease like the measles or chicken pox."

"I think they are just jealous of your beauty." Pete winked at her.

"I second that." Volker flashed his big smile at her.

"Oh, stop it you two, and focus on why we're here," she said, hoping to avert their attention to something other than her.

As they entered the courtyard, they immediately walked to the scaffolding.

"So where were you standing when you found the ring?" Susi asked, looking around for any obvious signs of earthquake damage.

Andi walked a few steps closer to the walls and turned around to see where she was standing in approximation of the fountain across the yard. She looked back at the wall with the scaffolding and then down to the ground. "I think it was right about here." She glanced at the fountain again and moved a few steps over to the left. "No, I'm fairly certain that it was right here."

"I think so, too." Volker agreed.

Now that the spot was established, the group focused on the search for cracks or missing bricks in the wall.

"This may be nothing, but I see something over there," Susi pointed at a few rocks closer to the scaffolding from where they stood.

Pete looked up to search for the source of the rubble. "I see some pebbles on the edge of the first level of the scaffolding," he announced, then looked farther up. "I bet this chipped area on the second level is where our ring came from. It probably fell on the scaffolding, bounced off and landed where you stood."

"It's quite possible," Volker added.

Belinda wrinkled her forehead. "So why is it that it fell from so high up? Shouldn't it have been somewhere at ground level?"

"Actually, my men were working at that portion of the building when I was arrested." Then his expression turned into recognition. "When the guards came to fetch me, the baron followed them so that he could bellow orders at them and accuse me of my apparent crime. Not being accustomed to walking on uneven bricks, I remember him losing his balance and he almost fell off the wall, which would've been just fine with me, but who knows, someone might have blamed that on me as well."

"Can you get up there, Volker, and get a closer peek at the hole?" Pete asked. "I'm afraid that I can't climb up on the scaffolding without being discovered and banned from the castle."

Volker looked at him amused. "Well, sure. Though, it would've been a fine sight to see you being manhandled by some police officers yourself."

Pete looked at Andi. "It looks like your ghost has a sense of humor."

"I'm just kidding. Please forgive me," Volker apologized. "I want you to know that I am very grateful for everything you do."

"No offense taken," Pete replied with a grin on his face. "I'll just get you back one of these days."

Volker smiled in return and then looked up at the scaffolding, disappeared, and popped up on the boards of the second level. He scanned the wall for missing rocks and irregularities and found the suspicious damaged bricks, where some chunks fell off during the earthquake. The damaged area had a thin, yet long crack to the top and bottom of it. "I think I found the area where the ring could've been embedded," he shouted down.

"I wish we could give you a camera to take pictures," Pete shouted up, then kept his voice down as people were staring at him as he was talking to the scaffolding.

Volker smiled. "No problem, watch this!" He disappeared and popped up next to the group again. They huddled around Volker.

"So, what," Andi asked, "got another one of your ghostly tricks?"

"Yes, I do. As requested, here's a photo for you. The only caveat is that you can't put it in an album." He held up his hand and conjured up a Polaroid picture of what the crack and damaged sandstone bricks looked like from up-close.

"Amazing," Susi marveled. "I'd like to see a slide-show of what things used to look like in your time. Can you do that?"

Volker grinned. "Certainly. Maybe one evening I can make that happen."

"I'll hold you to it. A medieval slide-show presentation it is," Susi confirmed.

Directing his attention back to the picture, he pointed

to the crack. "I bet the ring was imbedded in the mortar between these two bricks."

Pete bent forward and put on his reading glasses. "I certainly agree with you. If your people worked on this section and the mortar was still soft, the ring could have fallen into the crack and in all the commotion, could have gotten stepped on and submerged. What a coincidence that our girl from America happened to stand right here to find it."

"I think it's destiny," Belinda added.

Pete looked at his watch. "Folks, I hate to break this up, but it's getting dark. Shall we head to the apartment for some refreshments before you leave?"

Susi nodded. "A cup of hot tea to warm up would be wonderful."

The four, plus one see-through, headed back to the apartment contemplating on what they were going to do next to solve the mystery of the missing jewelry box.

*T*he girls said their goodbyes and got into Susi's car to drive home. Volker also disappeared for a while to give them some space. Just before they drove off, Belinda came running out of the house with a small baggie in her hand. "Wait!"

Andi rolled her window down. "Yes?"

"I'm glad I still caught you! I meant to give you these antihistamines. You need them more than I do right now," she said out of breath.

"Thank you so much, Belinda. You're awesome." Andi replied. "If it wasn't for you, these spots would still be bright red."

"No problem. I'm just glad I could help. See you tomorrow!"

Susi then put her car into gear and they waved until they rounded the corner down the street.

Andi folded down her visor and turned the little light on, so she could look at her face in the small mirror. She was glad to see that her spots had faded even more since she checked her face in Belinda's bathroom mirror, after they came back from their outing. With any luck, they might almost be gone by tomorrow and she wouldn't have to endure people's stares in public any longer.

Once they arrived at home, Susi slumped into her favorite armchair. "I'm so kaputt!"

"That's because you drank like a fish last night and are still recovering from your hangover."

"Guilty as charged," Susi replied with a yawn.

Andi walked into her aunt's kitchen, poured some water in a glass, and plopped on the couch in Susi's living room. She swallowed another antihistamine and relaxed for a minute.

"Have you heard from your photographer?"

"No, not yet, his grandmother has her 80th birthday today, so he is spending the day with family. Besides, he's not MY photographer. Like I said, Ralf and I are just going to dinner sometime to hang out, nothing serious."

Andi smiled. "Whatever you say."

Susi shook her head. "No, it's not a date!" She then pulled her blanket from the back of the armchair and covered herself to warm up. A grin crossed her face. "Don't you think your ghost is hot?"

Andi about choked on her water. "Psssst, what if he hears us? I can't believe you just asked me that!"

"So, do you?"

"Will you stop?" Andi leaned forward and whispered loudly. "That is none of your business anyway."

"I'm just asking. You were so interested in my love life,

so I thought that it would be polite to share my interest in yours." Susi put on her best 'I won' face.

"Touché," Andi admitted and changed the subject to a less embarrassing matter. "Anyway, I do wonder if the ring has some sort of limitations. I mean, will everyone see Volker, or can he decide himself who will see him?"

"I can answer that," and Volker materialized next to Andi on the couch, except the cushion did not move.

Andi wanted to find a pillow and hide her face behind it. "How long have you been eavesdropping on us?"

"I don't eavesdrop. But I did walk in when you admitted that I was hot." Volker and Susi laughed hardily.

Andi felt her face burn. She grabbed an old newspaper from the end table and threw it at him. "I never said such a thing!" When she realized that the paper flew right through him and had no effect on him, she got up from her seat and stomped on the floor. "Okay, we need rules if we're going to work together."

"What do you have in mind?" He still wore this mischievous grin on his face.

"Rule #1: If you're in the room with us, you have to show yourself. Rule #2: The bathroom is off limits. I need my privacy. Rule #3: You announce yourself when you want to come into my room or any room, for that matter, instead of scaring me half to death every time you sneak up." She looked at Susi. "Since this is your house, do you have anything to add?"

"No, I think you covered it all."

"So what do you say? I think those are reasonable rules. Can you work with these?"

"Do I have a choice?" He put on his most innocent look.

"Nope."

"Okay, so I will always show myself when in the room,

I'll knock, or rather click my tongue, before I enter a room, I will not enter your water closet, and I promise to behave myself, or at least I'll try."

"That's good enough for me," Susi said. "Andi?"

"Good. Now that that's settled, do you think you can try to appear at Pete's apartment," Andi asked Volker.

"Sure, I will make an attempt."

"Let me give them a call to let them know you're coming." Andi picked up the cordless phone from the side table and looked for the correct speed-dial.

"Hello?"

"Belinda? It's Andi. I have you on speakerphone with Susi and Volker listening in. We're home now and we were wondering if you guys wanted to see if Volker can come see you with the ring being in our house."

"Sure," she replied. "Tell him he's welcome here any time and we're ready for him to swing by."

Volker nodded in acknowledgement. "I'll be back shortly. I know I can get there, but I don't know if I can show myself." He winked at Andi then vanished.

"Belinda, he's on his way. Can you see him?"

Belinda was silent for a moment. "No, not yet."

"Maybe it takes him a minute to get there," Andi pondered aloud.

"Oh wait, I can see him. He's waiving at us," Belinda announced. "The only thing is, well, he's very translucent. We can barely see him." She paused. "What did you say Volker? He is really hard to hear." The line was silent for another short moment. "Oh, okay. He said he is coming back to you guys."

"Bye, Volker," Pete and Belinda said in unison.

It took only a few seconds for him to return. "Knock, knock, I'm back!"

Andi smiled. "Now see, that's what I'm talking about. No surprises."

"Belinda, Pete? Are you still there?"

"Yes, we are," Pete's voice crackled from the speaker.

"I wonder if the ring is like a radio antenna - the farther you get away, the weaker the signal gets," Andi contemplated.

"So what we have to do, is either bring the ring with us when doing research or leave it here and we just have to get used to not seeing you."

Andi yawned. Apparently, her medicine was kicking in again. "Let's figure out the finer details another time. Belinda, do you still want to do research tomorrow?"

"Yes, of course I do. Should I come pick you up?"

"Actually," Andi replied, "I still need to stop by at the University about the job Pete told me about. I can take the streetcar in and call you when I'm ready to meet you."

"Nonsense," Belinda said. "It'll take you forever to use public transportation. I'll pick you up and take you to the University. Afterwards, we can grab a quick snack before we hit the archives. I get up with Pete anyway, so it's no trouble for me."

"Well, if you insist."

"I insist. I'll be there around 8.30, or is that too early?"

Andi smiled. "No, that's fine. I'll be ready."

They hung up the phone and Andi tried to stifle yet another yawn. "If you all will excuse me, I'm ready to go to bed."

"Good night, kiddo," Susi said. "I think I'll do the same. I have to work tomorrow."

Volker turned and waved. "Gute Nacht, ladies," he said, and faded away.

· · ·

*a*ndi slept like a baby as soon as she hit the sack, that is, until she turned over just a few inches too close to the edge of the mattress. In half-sleep, she felt her body teeter close to the abyss, and once she realized she was about to face plant on the floor, she woke up with a start and flailed her arms to keep from going over the edge.

With her adrenalin slightly elevated and the wonderful properties of her antihistamine worked out of her system, she sat in her bed, wide-awake. Hmm, what now, she thought. Her throat was dry, so she decided to get up and get some water from her kitchen.

She sat down at the table and drummed her fingers on the surface. Her thoughts drifted to the happenings of the past 24 hours. Just last night she spoke for the first time to a ghost, a darn good-looking one at that. If someone had asked her before, she'd swear up and down that she did not believe in ghosts. Her view has drastically changed since then.

Thinking of ghosts, she was wondering what Volker was up to. He's probably floating around somewhere in the area. "Volker, are you here?" she ventured with a soft voice. "Volker?"

He must have heard her, because his shape slowly materialized in the doorway. "Is everything okay?" He looked worried. "Why are you not sleeping?"

"I woke up, and for the life of me, couldn't fall asleep again." She made sure not to mention how she almost dumped herself out of bed. "If it's true what people say, ghosts don't sleep, right?" Hopefully, she was correct, because she didn't want to look like an idiot in front of him again. She wasn't exactly an expert in supernatural phenomena, she just wrote about what she believed how things could work in the other world, if there was such a thing.

"No, we don't sleep. There is no need to," he explained. "We are made of energy and do not have to sustain a body, so sleep is pointless for us."

She tried to wrap her mind around that one. "So, what do you do with your time when everyone human is sleeping?"

Volker's corners of his mouth turned into an amused smile: "I chit-chat with pretty, sleepless, polka-dotted ladies at two o'clock in the morning, for one."

Andi frowned: "That's not what I meant."

"I know," Volker added. "Normally, I put up with my mates at the castle, whom I've known for several centuries. You just learn to tolerate the ones you don't like. Sometimes even bad company is better than no company at all, especially if you're confined to a castle."

"So, when I called you, were you away?" She asked.

Volker nodded. "I've realized, since we've been linked through the ring, that if I tune in, I can pick up your voice when I'm away."

"That's cool! Can you hear what I'm thinking?" She just thought of how gorgeous he looked when he smiled and felt herself blush. Great, Andi, she thought, just think of something like scrubbing an oven instead of how mesmerizing his slightly uneven teeth are.

"I wish I knew what goes on in your pretty little head, but I think I already know." He winked at her.

"Yes? Well I was thinking of how we're going to find the jewelry box." She hoped he didn't catch on to her real thought, the one about him, the one that she couldn't get out of her mind. For God's sake, he's a friggin' ghost!

He let her get away with her subject change. "Pete said that he would start checking literature and such things about the legend." Volker wrinkled his forehead. Apparently, the search had been on his mind as well. "We could follow the genealogy of the baron. Maybe he has family that is still alive, and maybe they heard stories about him."

Andi's face lit up with hope. "And City Hall would be the best place to start. Are you coming with us, or will you be working with Pete?"

An impish grin appeared on his face. "You have the ring, so I'll be hanging out with you, I presume?"

Duh, she didn't think about that. "Of course. Well, since we have a lot going on tomorrow, I probably should try to get a few more hours of sleep. I'll need to be able to focus if I'm going to delve into someone's family tree. That ought to be quite a task." She rose from her chair. "Good night, Volker. Thanks for keeping me company."

"It was my pleasure. Have a good night and I will see you in the morning," he replied and vanished.

CHAPTER 5

The next morning, Andi woke up with a slight medicine head, but was elated when she looked into the mirror. Her once red dots were now barely visible. She clapped her hands in excitement and then made a mental note to thank Belinda profusely when she arrived to pick her up. They had a busy day ahead of them. First, she needed to go to the 'Uni' to see about the job that Pete told her about yesterday. Next, they planned to get busy with their research. She quickly stepped into the shower, brushed her teeth, and made herself look presentable, before she went downstairs to join Susi for a quick breakfast.

Twenty minutes later, her aunt left for work and Andi called Belinda to confirm that she would pick her up.

"So, are you ready to crack this mystery," Andi asked in English when Belinda answered the phone.

"I'm ready when you are, sweetie," Belinda answered excitedly.

"Actually," Andi said, "Volker had a great idea last night to track down any living members of the baron family. Maybe someone remembers stories being carried down through the centuries, and we may be able to find the box with whatever information we can glean from them."

"That's a great idea, Andi. Let's start with the archive at City Hall and comb our way through the baron's family history, and then we'll take it from there."

"That's exactly what I had in mind," Andi replied.

"Awesome. If you're ready, I can be there in 30 minutes, if that's not too soon."

"No, that's fine with me." Andi was eager to get started on the project, and any minute that she sat in the house, was a minute less she had to save Volker. "See you in a few," she added and hung up the phone.

Andi walked into the kitchen and finished her cup of coffee, while gathering her green pen and a big legal pad for taking notes.

"Good morning," Volker greeted her.

"Good morning," she replied without looking up while stashing her supplies in her bag. "Belinda is picking me up in a few minutes. We'll stop at the University then start our research. Are you still coming along?"

"Yes, I am. I'm curious to find out if any of the baron's brood is still around."

Andi tossed two apples into the bag, just in case they needed a snack and then plopped it next to her purse, so she wouldn't forget it on her way out. "I'm sure we'll come up with a few names of people we can contact..."

She glanced up at Volker and did a double take. "Wow!" She couldn't help but stare. Apparently, ghosts can change clothes, too. Standing in front of her was the modern version of Volker. He wore a red V-neck sweater with a white t-shirt underneath, a pair of perfectly cut Levi jeans, and some hiking boots to match the season.

Volker grinned at her. "What? I have to look the part when I'm going into public with you two girls."

Andi still stood there with her mouth gaping wide open but managed to form some words. "But nobody can see you."

"You two can, and I think it's a mighty good occasion to dress up."

"Well, I'm flattered," she said. "You clean up quite nicely." Oh no, she felt another blush coming on. Why does she keep doing that? She quickly looked away, pretending to search for something in a kitchen drawer, hoping that he did not notice the color change in her face.

They heard a car pull up next to the house. Andi peeked out of the kitchen window. Yes, saved by the bell. "Belinda is here," she announced.

"Already, then, shall we go," he asked.

"I'm ready." Andi grabbed the ring and her bag, and they walked out the door. "Are you riding with us or are you going to meet us there?"

"I'll give you some privacy and meet you at City Hall," Volker said. "You women folk talk too crazy for me to listen to this early in the morning. I'll hang out with my buddy Markus at the castle for a while to catch up."

"Okay, we'll meet you at the market place in front of City Hall?"

He nodded. "I'll be waiting."

*A*ndi climbed into Belinda's car. "Hi, Belinda."

"Hi, Andi," she replied with her Irish dialect. "Wow, your spots are almost gone. I'm glad that the medicine worked. You look great!"

"Thanks, Belinda. I'm so glad that they are not noticeable anymore. I was nervous about having to go job-hunting with red dots all over my face. What a first impression that would have made."

Belinda giggled. "I must admit, you did look highly infectious yesterday," she said. Belinda put her car in gear and they made their way into Heidelberg. "So, he's not here, right?"

Andi looked around, just to make sure. "Volker? No, not that I know of. And he has sworn to make himself known if he's around."

"So, what do you think? Isn't he cute?"

"I can't believe you're going there, Belinda!" Andi sighed. "Yes. He's cute. But he is also a ghost, in case you've forgotten."

"I'm just saying, too bad that he is not real."

"I know," Andi agreed. "I haven't been very lucky with men lately. Maybe, it's just the way it's going to be with me. I'll end up like Susi living by myself. It sure saves me a lot of heartache."

"Come on! You can't talk like this. You just haven't met Mr. Right yet," Belinda tried to cheer her up.

"Well, I'm just going to take life as it happens, and in the meantime, I'm going to write my novels and hope that my publisher will not drop me for the lack of romance in my books."

"What are you talking about?" Belinda looked at her surprised. "Look at the story that's unfolding right in front of you? That's right up your alley, and your research is already taken care of. Just ask Volker about medieval stuff you have questions about. He's the expert."

"I've already started plotting out a story about the legend, but I'm stuck."

Belinda thought for a moment. "Maybe you should write about THIS story. It's great fiction, even though it's real."

"You've got a point, but what if we don't find the jewelry box? I have to have the manuscript ready by this summer."

Belinda shrugged her shoulders and then smiled. "Just make up a happy ending."

"I can't do that if I tell the true story."

"But it's fiction, remember?"

"I don't know," Andi sighed. "It wouldn't feel right. I'll have to think about it."

They arrived at the University, and after driving around the block a few times, to look for a parking spot she could squeeze her Audi in, Belinda finally gave up and drove into the parking garage. "At least this one is cheap, and we can have them validate the ticket at the personnel office for a discount."

The visit at the University went very well. She had turned in her résumé and the person in charge of hiring for the department assured her that they would get in touch with her within the next week or two, although Andi had her doubts of getting the job. Several organizations already had turned her down already. They were probably looking for someone with a German education, which she hadn't had since middle school. Well, at least she tried.

The weather was mild, so they walked the few blocks and landed on the large market square in front of City Hall. They looked around for Volker.

"You did bring the ring, right?" Belinda asked.

"Yes, it's in my purse. I didn't want to wear it and have people asking questions." Andi looked around some more on the busy square. "Volker?"

"Here I am." Volker materialized next to them. "Sorry, I forgot the changing into visibility mode part."

In the meantime, Belinda gaped at Volker. "Wow, if I wasn't married, I'd snatch you up right away!"

Volker blushed. "Thank you for the compliment. Shall we go in and see what we can find out about the baron's family?"

The three of them walked into the archives and asked the clerk for access to the records of the baron. She typed in some names on her computer and presented them with a few microfiche sets. "I'll be right here, if you need me to look for more information," the clerk said. "The readers are over in the left corner. I'll be glad to help you, if you run into any problems."

The ladies thanked her and walked over to the microfiche readers. They sat down next to each other and began browsing the films. Volker sat between them, so he could see both of the screens at the same time.

They searched for a good hour, before they finally saw some names they recognized. "There he is," Volker shouted. "Go back one document."

"Pssst," Andrea held a finger in front of his mouth. "Not so loud!"

"Nobody can hear me but you!" His eyes twinkled.

Belinda looked at him. "Hello, I can hear you loud and clear," she chided.

"Sorry. Let's go back to that death certificate," he continued, trying to keep his voice down.

Belinda moved back to the last document. "Here it is. Ludwig von Dossenheim. He was born in 1565 and died in December of 1606. Let's make a print of this one."

"What year did you die, Volker," Andi asked.

"In September 1605."

"So this means he died a year after you were dead," Belinda thought out loud.

Volker leaned back in his ghostly chair. "He died of the pox. It was an ugly death, I've been told."

"Yes, it says right here," Belinda confirmed. "Cause of death: Small pox."

"So, it wasn't a slip on the ice when he was drunk?"

"No, but he has been known to look too deep into his cups at many occasions."

"Well good, deserves him right," Andi said. She despised him from the second she saw his painting.

"Let's find the marriage certificate," Volker added. "He finally took some poor duchess from Bavaria as a wife, since the princess was even less interested in him now that he only found half of her missing treasure. The duchess was already carrying his child before the wedding. So, we should find something like a birth certificate of the baby."

They took a short lunch break and returned to continue their search for any living family members. City Hall was about to close when they located the birth certificate of his son, Anton.

*T*he group met throughout the week, but the big plan was to go to the Irish Pub on Saturday to consolidate their research over a couple of beers. They walked into the pub, armed with their overflowing binders. Shai greeted them with a raised brow and then smiled, amused. "Oh, oh, that ought to be good! What's this all about?" He pointed at one of the massive binders.

"We're working on a secret mission," Pete replied and hung his coat on the rack behind their usual table. "We may let you in on the secret, once your customers are gone. You're going to love this one, considering your background!"

"You must've discovered another odd story to get lost in," Shai ventured and shook his head with a chuckle.

"Because I don't ever see you this excited unless you've found a mystery to solve."

"Close, but we'll tell you later," Pete reiterated as he sat down at the table.

"I can't wait. Does everybody want their usual drinks?" Shai asked.

Everyone nodded, and Shai rushed away to pacify an impatient patron hollering for service.

Pete turned his attention back to the binder in front of him. "Okay, let's see what we came up with this week." He opened his folder to a section he had tabbed as 'Ludwig'. "I have learned that the baron was pretty upset about the lost ring and that the princess would not marry him, so he began drinking more in town than it did him good." He took a swig of his ale. "Then, over the winter, he contracted a disease and died miserably."

"Small pox," Belinda confirmed. "We have the death certificate right here somewhere," and rifled through her documents. "Found it! He passed away in December 1606, a little over a year after Volker."

Pete continued, "One reference mentioned that the baron buried the jewelry box away from the castle grounds in an unlikely place, separated by a divide."

"Hmm, a divide? What could that divide be?" Susi pondered, "a wall or the mountains, maybe?"

"What about the Neckar River? Water divides many things," Andi suggested.

"That could be a good possibility, although, we would have to dig up the entire Holy Mountain across the Neckar, if that's where it is buried. It's like finding a needle in a haystack. We need to find more specific data," Belinda added.

"What have we found so far in terms of the baron's family?" Pete asked.

Andi opened her own binder. "We tracked his blood-line until the 1800s. We need a little more time to find details of anyone still living in this area."

Susi, who felt a little out of place due to not being able to contribute to the search as much as she wanted to, suddenly had an idea. "What about the witch's family line? Maybe we can also track down her living family members. Spiritual people are well known for passing down family histories and legends."

"That's a great idea, Susi." Pete turned to Volker. "You said that you knew the name of the witch?"

"Yes, we grew up in Eppelheim together. Her name was Amelie Winter."

Belinda raised her pen, ready to take notes. "I assume she was born in Eppelheim around the same year as you?"

"I believe she was a year younger than me."

"Okay, that's a start," Belinda scribbled on her notepad.

"I'll continue with the research of the baron's family this coming week," Andi offered. "Belinda, can you start with the research on Amelie?"

"Of course! I can hardly wait to see what we can find out about her. We've come a long way already."

Pete closed his binder. "And I will continue with my research on the legend, the divide, and anything jewelry box related at the Uni and the museums."

Volker became serious. "I know I've told you before, but I don't know how to thank you all for sacrificing your valuable time for helping me. I don't know how to ever repay you." He hung his head in humility.

Susi looked at him, "Hey, you still owe us a medieval slide-show, remember?"

He lifted his head. "Well, the medieval age was actually before my time. I actually lived in the Early Modern period, but I will be honored to share my memories with you."

"What about next Sunday afternoon when we relax anyway? We can meet at our house." Susi suggested. "I have a big, white wall in my living room to display the, uh, slide-show. I just have to take down some family photos." She turned to Volker. "Will that work for you?"

Volker nodded. "That would be perfect! I'll think of some nice images from my time to show you."

Andi smiled. "I can't wait!"

*L*ater that evening, business slowed down, and finally, the last guests had moved on to other places. Shai locked the front door for their usual private wind-down of their Saturday evenings. He brought five shots of schnapps, including one for himself, and another round of beer to the table.

Volker, as usual, sipped on his ghostly beverages. He enjoyed the group of friends, especially Andi. A slight chuckle escaped him, as he imagined how different his afterlife would have been, had a city employee from the Sanitation Department found the ring, while sweeping up the cigarette butts and cold tissues that littered the court-yard early Sunday morning.

"So what's the big secret?" he asked as he passed out the drinks and pulled out the chair between Susi and Andi to sit down.

Volker hung in the air in a seating position, before he realized what just happened.

"NOOOO! Don't sit there," the friends shouted in horror.

Shai looked at their reaction, obviously confused. "Did I do something wrong?"

Everyone stared at Volker, except for Shai, who couldn't see him.

He laughed when he realized that Shai almost sat in, not on, his lap. Everyone still stared at him, so to break the tension, he said, "I'm okay. No worries," and laughed again. "Will someone fill him in already?"

Pete was the first to respond. "I will."

"What? Who are you talking to," Shai asked, still looking confused.

"Shai," he said and paused for a short moment, "I only tell you this, because you have been such a good friend of mine and Belinda's during our ordeal, and I trust that you won't pass this on to anyone."

"I swear on my dead dog's grave," Shai raised his right hand.

"Great, so here we go." Pete took a deep breath. "We have another intriguing story for you - somewhat similar to ours."

Now Andi and Susi looked confused but did not say anything.

Pete continued to recount a short version of Volker's story and handed Shai the ring.

"I'll be damned," Shai said. "That ring is a beauty." He then looked up and saw Volker sitting in the gap. He did a quick double take. "You need to stop surprising me with all this paranormal stuff," he laughed. "Hallo! Mein Name ist Shai." He held his hand up in greeting. "Don't worry; I won't shake your hand. I'm used to paranormal visitors around here."

Volker smiled and gave a short wave back. "Hallo," he said. This one has been the most interesting reveal of all. He liked this guy.

Andi and Susanne still looked at each other puzzled. "Wow, what have we missed," Susi asked in awe. "What paranormal visitors? Hey, you guys have been holding out on us! You owe us an explanation!"

"We will fill you in eventually. Why don't we let these two get acquainted first?" Belinda settled them down. "Our story may take a while..." She winked at her husband.

"We will tell you soon. I promise," Pete reassured them.

Shai raised his beer, first to Volker, and then to the rest of the group. "Prost, everybody!"

"Prost!" Volker repeated, and took a sip of his imaginary beer, along with the others.

They hung out for another hour and then decided to call a cab as the yawns at the table reached a frequency of ten every five minutes.

"Good night, everyone," Shai said, as he let them out the door. "Volker," he called out, "if you like to keep me company until the girls get home, I'd be happy to chat with you while I finish up around here."

"Sure, I'll just let Andi know. I have to warn you, though. I will fade as the ring travels away from where I'm at."

"That's okay, I just need to talk to you for a short moment," Shai answered.

As the taxi pulled away, Volker appeared at the bar, while Shai was washing glasses. "I've seen the way Andi looks at you," Shai tested the waters, "and the way you look at her. I know this look when I see it."

"I know, she's the most beautiful woman I've ever laid my eyes on," he replied.

"So, this begs the question about what's going to happen between the two of you. Of course, you can tell me to get out of your business, but obviously, the gal likes you, and you have a, well, let's call it a slight challenge to deal with. What are you going to do?"

Volker thought for a moment. "I honestly don't know, Shai. I just know that I want to spend every waking moment with her, if she lets me, because who knows when we will see each other for the last time? It's like a gift that has been given to me from above, and I don't want this feeling to ever end."

Shai wiped the counter tops with a damp rag. "So do you know what's going to happen when the ring is paired with the box?"

Volker played with a cardboard coaster he had conjured on the clean counter. He didn't even want to think of the day that this would happen. "All I know is that I will be freed. It could mean that I'll disappear forever into heaven, or that I'll materialize and fall into a pile of ashes. I don't know what it means, and it scares me to death thinking about the day, when I can no longer see Andi."

"Only time can tell, my friend. I hope all works out for you two, one way or another," Shai said. "Hey, Volly, you're fading."

"Oh," Volker looked down at his hands. "I guess the girls are almost home. Let me make sure all is in order. I'll try to come by and see you occasionally, if you don't mind. You may not be able to see me, very well, though."

"You do that. Have a good night, friend."

*A*ndrea slipped into her pajamas and made a quick cup of tea to help her settle down a little. She heard something that resembled a knocking sound. "Are you in the mood for some ghostly company?" Volker stood in the hall outside of the kitchen.

"Of course, I am," she said with a tired voice. "Thanks for not scaring me to death this go around. I appreciate it." Actually, she started looking forward to their late-night talks. Andi pulled out a chair for him, so he could sit at the table with her.

"So why is a beautiful woman like you still unmarried?"

Andi shifted uncomfortably. She hated talking about that jerk and wanted to close that chapter of her life, but figured that Volker deserved to know what had happened, since she knew so much about his life already, so she started her story: "Well, I was in a relationship with this guy, who had promised me the world. The only thing he didn't promise was to marry me and start a family. You know, after a while, a girl wants just that. I guess he had some commitment issues. We spent five years together and we were about to take off on a cruise, which we planned months ago. Suddenly, he came home from work one day, telling me that he did not want to be with me anymore. The trip was booked on his credit card, so he simply changed my name to his girl-friend's name on the reservation."

Volker's face turned dark. "If I ever see this jerk…"

"That's okay. At least I found out when I did. It turned out that this wasn't his first side-step."

"So that's when you decided to come back to Germany?"

Andi shook her head. "I was stuck in a lease in a place that I couldn't afford on my own. I took a part-time job, on top of my regular work, while I was also revising my latest novel. After I sent the finished manuscript to my editor, I finally had some time to think about my options. I hated the place I lived in, so it didn't take long to come to the conclusion that I had to move out. Since my writing is not tied to any location, the thought of coming back to Germany crossed my mind. What did I have to lose? After I spoke to Susi about coming to live with her for a while, it didn't take long to get rid of my furniture," she continued. "I considered that to be a good omen, so here I am."

"I'm very glad you came," Volker said. "Do you ever regret your decision?"

Again, Andi shook her head. "Not in a million years. Actually, you're my inspiration for my new novel. I had no idea what to write about in my next book, and my publisher already bugged me about story ideas. You know, when I heard about the legend of the ring, I knew that's what I wanted to write about and that there was a good story in it."

"Did you ever guess you would get involved in a paranormal mystery like this?" Volker asked.

"Never! I didn't even believe in ghosts, but they do make for a good story."

"But now you believe?" His lip turned up into a breathtaking smile.

She smiled. "I do now. So, now it's your turn," she prompted. "Tell me a little about your life."

"Well, there's not much to tell. You already know that I grew up in Eppelheim. Back then, as you can imagine, it was a small village. Many of us were masons, but we had a few families with other professions living in our community. Amelie's mother was a healer, which came in handy when someone became ill or injured."

"This is so fascinating! Keep going," she urged, trying to visualize every word he said.

"For you, always." He shifted in his seat. "Amelie and I used to go out into the woods and pretend that we were knights. She was a tomboy, you know, and we used sticks to practice our sword fighting skills. One time, I reacted too slowly, and she accidentally scratched my skin with the pointy end of her stick. The scratch was deep, and she apologized repeatedly. Since her mother was a healer, she had already learned a few skills from her. She collected a few herbs, bound them together, and tied them to my arm. That's when I also learned that she had some special skills."

Andi wanted to take another sip of her tea. "Dang, I'm out." She didn't bother to get a refill. "Please keep going."

"As she took care of my wound, she kept mumbling some strange words. I did not understand what she was saying, but suddenly, I felt a tingling sensation in my arm. After a few minutes, she removed the bandage, and the only thing that was left was a faint scar."

"Unbelievable! Did that not freak you out?" Andi tried to put herself into his position.

"Not really. I trusted her. That doesn't mean that I wasn't amazed by what she did."

"So, were you two in love? You don't have to answer that if you don't want to. I'm just curious," she added.

"We liked each other, but not as lovers. We are more like brother and sister, since we both have known each other so long. Eventually, she found herself a man and moved closer to town."

"Have you ever married?" She couldn't resist.

"No, unfortunately I haven't. The girl I liked only had eyes for a boy from the neighboring village. I was devastated, but I got over it by throwing myself into my work as a mason at the castle and moved up the ranks in my craft. Because the castle needed constant repair due to battles and fires, I did not have to fear losing my job, unless I upset the royal family. Fortunately, I was well known for my quality work and it would take something catastrophic to get me out of favor with the family."

"Such as a stolen ring?"

Volker nodded. "Like a stolen ring. The rest, as you know, is history."

Andi shuddered at the thought. "Not many people get to hear about life in the 1600s from an actual person from that time. I am really looking forward to hearing more about how you lived." She could no longer stifle a yawn. "I'm sorry. I think the tea did its job."

"Well, good night, my fair lady. I wish you a wonderful night."

"Good night, Volker."

$\mathcal{B}$y Wednesday, Andi and Belinda found information about a living family member of Baron Ludwig von Dossenheim. His name was Frederick Edeler von Dossenheim. They copied his birth certificate and then called Pete to see if he could look him up online to get a phone number.

"I hope this guy did not inherit his ancestor's lack of morals," Volker casually mentioned as they strolled across the market square.

"We'll find out soon enough," Belinda replied, wrapping her scarf tighter around her neck. "Brrr. It's cold! I wonder if it will snow soon."

"Probably not until the end of the year," Volker replied. "And if it snows, it won't stick until January."

"We barely had snow in Savannah, and when we did get some flurries, the entire city shut down." She smiled as memories of building a grass-spiked snowman with her friends flooded her mind. It took every snowflake in the front yard to build this waist-high masterpiece.

Volker and Belinda laughed. "Not here, girl, snow or

ice, you have to be at work. We don't get snow-days here. If the roads are bad, people just take the bus, since most vehicles don't have winter tires for those few days, we get nasty conditions. You'll see!"

They made their way to the apartment, where Pete was waiting for them. "I've already checked the internet and found a phone number based on the name you gave me earlier. Our man, Frederick, lives in Schwetzingen, so only about 30 minutes from here." Pete retrieved his cordless phone and punched in Frederick's number. "Let's see if we can meet with him."

The phone rang four times, until a sleepy voice answered the phone. "Hallo?"

"Hello, am I speaking with Frederick Edeler?"

"Yes, and no, I'm not interested in your insurance, so if you'd excuse me," the voice sounded irritated on the other end of the line.

"Actually, I'm not selling anything. My name is Peter Wagner and I work for the Historical Department of the state of Baden-Württemberg. I understand that you're related to the late Baron Ludwig von Dossenheim?"

"Yeah, I guess. Do we have to discuss this right now?" Frederick's voice grew impatient.

"No, not at all. I'm working on a project and I'm interested in meeting with you in the next few days, at your convenience. I just want to get some insight into your ancestor's life and am hoping to get a different perspective of him coming from a family member, than of what is common knowledge."

Frederick paused for a moment. "I don't know what you want to know, but sure, I can meet with you. Will tomorrow morning work? Let's say around 10 o'clock? I can meet you at my office - I own Edeler Realties in Schwetzingen."

"Very well. I thank you for the time, and I'll be at your office at 10 a.m. sharp," Pete confirmed and hung up the phone.

"So what was your impression," Belinda asked.

Pete rubbed his chin. "Well, he sounded like he didn't want to be bothered with anyone. It strikes me odd that he has a real-estate company and treats his potential clients like he should be the one calling them." Pete laughed. "I don't know if I would want to buy my house from that guy. He didn't seem to be interested in selling anything, to be honest."

Andi's handy buzzed. "Who is calling me," she wondered as she dug for her phone in her purse. "Found it. Hallo?"

"Good afternoon, Frau Meyer, from the Human Resources Office at the University calling. May I speak with Fräulein Morgan?"

"This is Fräulein Morgan," Andi replied with some apprehension.

Frau Meyer continued: "I have good news for you. We're offering you the administrative position in our International Department you have applied for. Would you still be interested?"

Would I still be interested? What kind of question is that? Of course, she was still interested. She could get her own vehicle. She wouldn't have to turn every Euro over twice before spending it, and she could afford to buy decorations for her apartment... She reined in her excitement and attempted to keep a professional tone. "Yes, Frau Meyer, I'm very interested in the position."

They went over the most important details and scheduled an appointment for the next day to fill out the necessary paperwork.

"Again, congratulations, and welcome to the University of Heidelberg," Frau Meyer said and ended the call.

Andi stood in Belinda's hallway in disbelief. She did it! "I've got the job, everybody!" She skipped into the living room. "I can start Monday!"

*P*unctually, at 10 o'clock, Volker and Pete walked into Frederick's real-estate office. A young man in his mid-20s wearing a suit appeared from the back office. "Can I help you?"

"Yes," Pete extended his hand. "Peter Wagner. I have an appointment with Herr Edeler."

The young man grudgingly shook his hand. "Fred Edeler. You can come into my office, but I'm very busy and can only talk for a few minutes."

Volker found it hard to believe that this guy was busy and rather wanted a good reason to get rid of Pete. He already disliked this pompous, sad excuse of a human being. Maybe he was biased, because he loathed his ancestor just as well. Apparently, the apple does not fall far from the tree, he supposed.

"Well, let's get straight to business then," Pete suggested.

Fred nodded and motioned him to sit in front of his desk.

"Thank you. As we discussed on the phone yesterday afternoon, I'm working for the Historic Department of the state of Baden-Württemberg and am doing research on the old legend of Princess Margarete's ring and jewelry box. I'm sure this story has been passed down to you?"

"Well, somewhat," Fred acknowledged. "I'm not much into legends and I believe that this Ludwig guy was framed by someone."

"Really? I'd like to hear more about that," Pete prompted. "This puts an entirely new spin on what is commonly known of this story."

"According to my grandmother, Ludwig was supposed to marry the princess and when the ring came up missing, she changed her mind, because she didn't want to get married without her mother's ring. That mason stole the ring, because he loved the princess himself, but he got caught by Ludwig."

Volker's eyes narrowed. He had no interest in marrying the princess. Secretly, he always wanted to be with Amelie, but did not have the courage to tell her until it was too late, and she gave her heart to someone else. For over 400 years, he had lived with that regret, until Andrea came into his life. Pete continued to speak, which brought him back to the present.

"Is that so? How interesting," he commented and glanced to his right, where unbeknownst to Fred, stood Volker.

Amazing how Pete kept his composure with all the accusations that spouted out of Edeler's mouth. If it were up to him, he already would have punched him in his face for telling all those lies.

Pete continued: "What happened to the mason?"

"He died in the prison tower, where a witch had cast a spell on him. I'm sure you know how the rest of the story goes."

Pete leaned back in his chair. "So, what do you know about this jewelry box? Did any stories ever get passed down through the generations about what happened to it?"

"Not really, but the rumor is that the ghost will return when the ring is placed into the jewelry box. I'm not superstitious or believe in ghost stuff, but with me being family with that guy, I sure wouldn't want the mason taking revenge on me if he comes alive, or whatever happens to him, just because I'm the only one left."

Volker could barely resist the urge to use his fists to make him believe but thought that restraint may be the wiser option at the time.

"Are you sure you don't have any other family members of Ludwig's lineage left," Pete asked.

"Yes, as far as I know," he replied. "My parents passed away several years ago. Now I'm stuck with the family business. Why the sudden interest? Did the government find the ring?"

"No, the government didn't find the ring yet," which was the truth, however, Pete squirmed a little in his seat.

Please, don't give us away, Volker prayed.

Fred raised his eyebrows. Apparently, he sensed that something was up.

Before things could get out of hand, Pete rose from his chair. "Well, those were all the questions I had for you."

"Is there something you want to tell me," Fred asked suspiciously.

"No, not at all. I've taken too much time from your busy day already." Pete stretched out his hand. "Thank you for meeting with me."

Fred returned the handshake. "Certainly, Herr... Wagner?"

"Yes, Peter Wagner. Let me leave you my business card. Please feel free to call me if you can remember any more details regarding the legend."

Fred accepted the card and placed it on his desk.

·   ·   ·

*A*s soon as City Hall opened the next day, Belinda and Andrea continued their search about the Winter family. Volker decided that he wanted to work with Pete that day, so the girls were on their own.

By now, Andi and Belinda were experts in researching family histories and found information about Amelie's descendants quick. Apparently, Amelie's parents died when she was in her late teens. She had two children from her marriage that had survived and married. Her husband was killed during a robbery, shortly after their second child was born. They worked their way down the family lineage and by afternoon, they finally arrived at the current generation. One of Amelie's descendants was born in the area, so they decided to follow that lead.

"Wait," Belinda sat back in her chair. "Why does this name sound familiar? Where do I know this name from?"

"I'm sure there are not too many Amanda Herzleins in the area." Andi wished she had a cute last name like that. It translates into a German term of endearment: Little heart. Instead, her mom had married her dad, which had a common surname. Not that she didn't like her father's name, per se.

"I know it now," Belinda burst out with excitement. "Oops, I forgot we're still in the archives. I bet she's the owner of the nature shop in town. What's the name again?" She paused for a moment. "Oh yes, 'Was das Herz Begehrt.' That's it! 'What the Heart Desires'."

"Let's see if the clerk has a phone book, so we can confirm the address. We have to walk that direction anyway to get back to the car. Maybe the store is still open," Belinda pondered.

It turned out it was the right person, so the pair made their way to her store. They had to walk down Main Street for a few blocks and turned into one of the small alleys that were still covered in cobblestone. Almost half way down the dark alleyway, they saw the old sign for the tiny herbal shop, nestled in between the tall, old houses. They walked a few more meters, until they arrived in front of the store's display window, which was decorated with dried flower bouquets, wreaths adorned with colorful ribbons, baskets of assorted teas in small plastic bags, and random painted mushrooms and animals crafted from wood.

"What a great location for this little gem," Andi remarked. "The atmosphere for it is just perfect."

They admired the old writing on the window. "It looks so mystical," Belinda commented. "I love all the fairy stuff, the flowers and the beautiful nature decor. It so reminds me of home."

"So why did you come to Heidelberg?" Andi asked.

"Well, Ireland isn't what it used to be, literally."

Andi could sympathize with her. Eppelheim has changed a lot since she lived there as a kid. "I've never been in Ireland myself, so I'm not the one to ask, but I see what you're saying."

Belinda smiled at her and then continued, "I had fallen in love with Pete and he needed to return to Germany for his work. So, I decided to tag along with him."

"Do you still have family in Ireland?"

Belinda turned solemn. "No, not in this life."

Andi cocked her head. What in the world was that supposed to mean – not in this life. "I give up. You guys confuse the heck out of me. You know that, right?"

Laughing, Belinda stepped up the stairs and opened the wooden shop door for them, which had flowers and fairies glass-painted on its window. "Oh, good, it's still open. Trust me, we'll tell you the story tomorrow at the pub when Susi can be along to hear it as well."

They entered the store and they were greeted with the scent of herbs and incense and a large calico cat that was curled up on a pillow in a chair by the register. The lighting was dim and dried bundles of lavender and other herbs and spices were hanging from the ceiling. Soft music with an Irish theme filled the store, and the Zen water fountain by the register made a calming splashing sound. The shelves were filled with jars of diverse dried plants, a variety of mortars and pestles, crystals, oils and ribbons. In the far corner stood a large shelf with books about nature, healing, and legends and folktales.

"I like this shop," Andi admitted as she continued to explore each section, savoring the soothing atmosphere. "This is a wonderful place to escape from today's hectic world."

"That's the effect I'm aiming for," said a woman in her mid-30s entering the store from a back room, obviously pleased that someone appreciated her efforts of making her customers feel as if they entered a different world.

The woman's warm smile and positive energy that surrounded her made Andi feel welcomed.

"Are you searching for anything in particular," the woman asked.

"Yes, actually, we're looking for Amanda Herzlein," Belinda answered.

"That would be me. Call me Amanda."

Belinda introduced them, as Andi still looked around in awe.

Amanda then asked, "How can I help you?"

Belinda explained to her why they came to the store. "We are doing some research on the legend of Princess Magarete's missing ring and jewelry box. As we traced the family lineage to modern time, we found out that you're a direct descendant of Amelie Winter."

Amanda's eyes remained warm. "Yes, that's correct. Would you like to join me for some herbal tea that I just brewed? I can see a long conversation coming."

"We don't want to intrude on a Friday evening and at such short notice. We can come back sometime next week during your regular hours," Belinda replied.

"Ach was, I don't have many customers this late in the day and I'd be delighted to talk to you. Please join me in my herbal kitchen in the back, where we can sit."

They moved into the back room, and sat down at the small, rustic, wooden table in the corner. Amanda poured the brew from her kettle into some old-fashioned tea glasses. "Honey or brown rock sugar?"

"Honey, please," they both replied in unison.

After they finished flavoring the tea to their liking, Belinda opened the conversation. "Frau Herzlein, we're here hoping to learn more about Amelie and the spell she had cast on the mason. Are there any writings or stories that were passed down to you?"

"Please, it's Amanda or Mandy. Anyway, I know that Amelie was a healer, who was said to have special powers. The witch trials were in full swing at her time, so she had to be very careful and selective about when she used these powers. Of course, people were still superstitious then, and being a healer often came with the reputation of dealing with the devil."

"I can imagine," Andi interjected.

"She lived secluded with her two daughters on the outskirts of Heidelberg. While her husband was on his way to the market one day, someone robbed and beat him to death, so from then on, Amelie had to raise her children on her own. She supported her family by making tea blends, potions, and medicines for the sick. After the ring vanished, and only the jewelry box surfaced, the furious princess, who somehow found out about her powers, sent for Amelie. She forced her to cast a spell on the mason. If she failed to comply, the princess was going to accuse her of being a witch, which in turn meant certain death. Afraid that her two young children would not make it through the winter if she was killed, she agreed to put a spell on the innocent mason, who was already weakening by the day in the 'seldom empty', you know, the prison tower."

"So, to give Volker..." Oh no, Andi thought and quickly covered her mouth with her hand. How stupid of her! She couldn't believe that she just had blurted out his name and prayed that Amanda didn't catch on.

Amanda's eyes went large. "Wait, what are your names again and who are you doing research for?"

They repeated their names and explained that Belinda's husband works for the State, researching old legends.

"You said the name Volker. How do you know this name? There is more to this story, isn't there?"

Andi sighed, regretting the slip. "I hope this is not getting us into trouble, Belinda." She then turned to Amanda, determined only to give her the basics. "This might sound weird," Andi tried to prepare Amanda for what was about to come, "but since we had the earthquake, I've been seeing a ghost. His name is Volker. He is..."

"...the mason Amelie cast the spell on," Amanda finished for her. "I'll be damned! Is he here?"

This was not quite the reaction Andi had expected. "No, he's not with us at the moment. Does this mean you believe us?"

"Yes, of course I do." Amanda leaned forward in anticipation. "Please, continue."

When Andi finished, Amanda looked at her. "My

grandma used to tell me the story of Volker and Amelie many times when I was a kid. You see, there's another part of the legend that nobody knows. It actually is a family secret, but I think that now the time has come to tell that story."

She poured them another cup of tea and continued the tale. "The spell Amelie had cast had not only eased Volker's pain, it also allowed for him to finish his prematurely ended life when the ring and jewelry box are reunited. I assume you found the ring?"

Andi's eyes opened wide. She then looked at Belinda for guidance if she should tell her about the ring.

Belinda nodded.

"Yes, I did, but what did you just say? Being set free means that he's coming back to life?"

"Yes, Andi, it does. The story then continued with the prophecy that when the time is right, only the true love for Volker will find the ring, see the mason's ghost, and will approach the healer for help in the quest of finding the jewelry box."

"That's you, Andi," Belinda exclaimed full of excitement. "How romantic!"

Andi blushed deeply. She still couldn't get the part out of her head that Volker would come to life again.

"And you, Mandy, must be the healer."

Amanda rose from her chair. "Please wait here for a moment. I have something to give to you." She returned carrying an old book. These are instructions from Amelie, not the original, but a copy rewritten several times, as the original had become worn out over time. In the front, it says that it had last been transcribed in 1855 by my great-grandmother. According to the story, the scholar can interpret the notes in this book. Do you know who that can be?"

"This must be my husband, Peter," Belinda suggested.

"But I must warn you," she continued, "the baron still fears for revenge."

Andi looked at her puzzled. "Does that mean that the baron is a ghost, too?"

"I'm afraid so, but the story didn't say if he was a ghost or not," Amanda replied. "I just know that Amelie put a curse on him. That's why he became deathly ill with the small pox."

Belinda couldn't believe what she had heard. "Get out! She took revenge on him? She rocks! Good for her!"

Amanda smiled.

Andi looked out of the small window in the room. It was already getting dark outside. "I guess, we have enough information to digest for now," Andi announced. "We need to get home and have Pete get to work on deciphering this book."

Amanda fetched them a fabric bag to carry the book in. "Please, come back anytime you have questions about my family. I'll gladly help in any way I can," she said as she walked them to the door.

They thanked her profusely for all the information she had provided. As they were about to walk out the door, Belinda turned around one last time. "Amanda, would you like to join us all tomorrow evening at the Irish Pub? You can bring your husband, if you like."

"Oh, I'm not married," she said trying to hide a blush. "I can't seem to keep a guy around long enough without scaring him off with my…well…strange family background." She smiled apologetically. "Back to your invitation, yes, I'd love to come, if nobody in your group minds."

"Nobody will mind, silly!" Belinda interjected. "You're the key to helping us bring Volker back to life. You'll even get to meet him tomorrow, if he doesn't mind. We'll be there around 8 p.m. So, are you coming?"

"I can't wait!" Amanda gave them both a hug and sent them off to study the old book.

*D*ang, I should've brought my gloves, Andi thought as she held her handy to her ear while walking to the pizzeria. "Hurry up, Susi, answer the phone already!"

"Hello, Andi?"

"You've got to come out to Pete's house right now. We have some news that will blow your socks off," she said, trying to keep her teeth from chattering.

"Oh, Andi, do I have to? I just got home and I'm tired. Why don't you tell me over the phone or when you get home?"

"Susi! It's Friday night, for God's sake!"

"I don't know. I'm really not up to going anywhere else tonight."

Andi needed to change tactics. "We're getting pizza…," she paused for added effect. "I know you haven't eaten yet. Come on," she pleaded. "What do you say?"

"Okay, okay. I'll be right over."

Andi hung up the phone and shoved her frozen hands into her coat pockets. "Now let's go inside the pizza joint and get our food, Belinda. I'm freezing to death out here."

About 30 minutes later, Belinda opened the apartment door. Pete and Volker were already home from their research.

"You won't believe what we found out today!" Belinda set the fabric bag with the book on the kitchen counter.

Andi stopped in her tracks and almost dropped the

pizza boxes when she stepped into the living room and saw Volker smiling at her.

"Hi, Andi."

Amanda's words popped into her head: 'only the true love for Volker will find the ring.' She is his true love! '… finish his prematurely ended life when the ring and jewelry box are reunited.' He will come alive! Suddenly, the events seemed to catch up with her and she felt the room starting to spin around her.

Pete glanced at the three boxes Andi was holding, then back at Belinda, oblivious to Andi's wobble. "You found pizza?" Pete took a stab in the dark.

"That, too," Belinda replied. "You'll have to wait a few minutes, though. When Susi gets here, we'll let everyone know at the same time. Let's get the table set while we're waiting. I'll make some coffee in the meantime, unless anybody is up for something a bit stronger."

"Maybe after dinner," Pete announced and then turned to Andi. "Uhm, Andi? Alles okay? You look a little pale, there. Here, let me take these from you and have a seat." He walked her over to the sofa and made her prop her feet up on the Ottoman.

Volker looked worried. "Did you receive bad news?"

Still staring at Volker, she shook her head. "Actually, we received very good news. I just got a little dizzy, that's all. Maybe, I just need to eat something."

The doorbell rang. "That must be Susi," Belinda announced and opened the front door.

Susi took off her scarf, coat, and wooly hat and hung them on the coat rack before she entered the living room to join the rest of the group. When she saw Andi looking a little green on the sofa, she hurried toward her. "Oh mein Gott, Andi, are you okay?"

"Yes, Susi, I'm fine. Just felt a little off for a moment."

Pete clapped his hands. "Okay then, we're all here now. Let's eat! Andi, let me bring you a slice. Hawaiian, margherita, or salami?"

"Two pieces of the Hawaiian pizza, please," she replied. "I'm starving!"

Volker plopped on the couch next to her. "You know, I missed you all day."

"You did?" She tried to act surprised, so she wouldn't give away her true feelings for him. Changing the subject would probably be a safer route to take at this point. "Did you and Pete find anything exciting today?"

"No, nothing really earth-shattering. But I bet you've made some progress, judging by the urgency of this assembly."

"Oh, you wouldn't know the least of it," she said as Pete handed her a plate with her pizza. She sat up straight and took a big bite. A really big bite. Wow, she must've been hungrier than she thought, or was it just a distraction from the gorgeous ghost that was sitting next to her? Was he even still sitting there? She dared a quick glance in his direction. Big mistake. He sat slightly turned toward her, watching her enjoy her food.

Suddenly, the big chunk of pizza she had bitten off had a mind of its own and went down her windpipe. She felt panic setting in, as she fought to get some air. She tried to cough it up, but it didn't work. The pizza was stuck tight in her throat.

"Oh my God, Andi!" Pete rushed to her. "Are you choking?"

Tears welled up in her eyes and she began to feel faint. She managed a nod.

Pete pulled her off the couch, stepped behind her, then pressed his fists in and up into her belly. Nothing.

Susi and Belinda helplessly watched Pete's attempts to save Andi's life. "I'll call an ambulance," Belinda said.

"No," Pete said out of breath from holding Andi up. "Not yet, they're too slow anyway." He gave her another push. Still no success. "Hang on, Andi," he urged her then gave her one more forceful thrust, which finally did the trick.

With a gagging sound, the red, cheesy glob of pizza shot out of her mouth and on the hardwood floor. Andi took a few sharp breaths and gained her composure.

Pete guided her back to the sofa. "That was close. You have to stop scaring us like that."

"Sorry, Pete." She then looked on the floor and saw what used to be a piece of her dinner. Embarrassment washed over her. "I am so sorry! I'll clean up the mess."

"You are not doing anything other than sitting on the couch," Belinda demanded. "I'll take care of it. Do you want me to bring you some water?"

"Yes, please," Andi croaked. Her throat hurt, and so did her belly. "Thank you, Pete! I can't imagine where I would be if it wasn't for your help."

"You'd be with me," Volker said gently.

Once Andi was taken care of and normalcy had returned in the living room, Pete cut to the chase. "So, are you ladies going to keep us waiting all night? What did you find out today that was so exciting?"

"Actually, we found a living descendant of Amelia Winters," Belinda began. "Her name is Amanda Herzlein and she owns a small shop downtown, close to where we parked the car. Since it was on the way, we stopped by and visited her."

"Why didn't you call me," Pete asked, disappointment written all over his face.

"I would have," Belinda responded, "but since it is

such a small store, we didn't think that it was still open this late on a Friday afternoon. Don't worry, though, you can ask Amanda all the questions you like at the pub tomorrow."

"Unbelievable," Pete shouted. "You've invited a stranger to the pub? Belinda, have you lost your mind? What if she finds out about the ring?"

Andi did not expect that kind of reaction from Pete and felt it would be better to let Belinda calm him down.

"We've invited her, since she is such a huge part of the mystery."

"What do you mean, she is such a huge part," Volker asked. "Am I missing something here?"

Andi smiled at him. "Just wait a second. You didn't hear the whole story yet."

"There is more?" Pete looked at her in surprise.

"Actually, there's a lot more," Belinda continued. "Andi, why don't you tell them the rest of the story?"

Andi gave her the evil eye. Of course, she had to set her up with telling Volker the news. Hadn't she already been through enough tonight?

The friends looked at her in anticipation.

Belinda grinned. "So let's hear it, buttercup."

She started the story at the point when Amelie changed the spell. "Uhm, you know the part when the ring is reunited with the jewelry box and you will be set free?"

Volker nodded.

"According to Amanda, setting free means that you will come back to life to finish up your time on earth," she added. "How this works is beyond me, but that's what her ancestors passed down to her."

His mouth dropped.

"Tell him about the other part," Belinda prodded. "That one is even better."

Andi blushed. How humiliating. Andi stared at Belinda and mouthed: 'I hate you!' before she continued with the story. "Well, the one person who finds the ring and who can find the box is also," she shifted in her chair, not knowing how to say this, "is also…"

"Come on, Andi, spit it out," Belinda urged with a Cheshire cat grin.

Andi rolled her eyes. "Okay, the one who found the ring," she repeated, "is also your, uh, well, true love." Where's a pillow to hide her face in when she needed one? Instead, she held her hands in front of her face to hide from the stares.

The room went silent, except for Belinda's soft giggling in the corner of the room. "See, that wasn't so bad."

When Andi dared to look up again, she saw everyone gaping at her, including Volker, whose facial expression changed from shock, to disbelief, and settled on joy.

"You're the one? Really? What if I don't like you," he turned to her with a teasing smile.

She dropped her hands on her side. "Easy, I'll let you find your jewelry box yourself. Let's see how far you get that way!"

"You wouldn't?"

"I would. I came here to write a book, not to play Indiana Jones."

Volker frowned. "So, I'll be doomed forever, because my true love wouldn't bring me back to life."

She punched him in the arm, only to get zapped again. "Ooops, sorry, I forget you're nothing but a walking blob of energy."

"A handsome walking blob of energy, you meant?"

Pete then interrupted. "Okay, enough of the happy

banter. Now that we know that we can possibly bring you back into our world, how do we find the box?"

"Well, there's more," Belinda chimed in. "Amanda gave us a copy of a book that was originally written by Amelie." She handed the heavy book to Pete. "It has instructions in it on how to find the jewelry box, but the scholar has to decipher it. We think the scholar is you, Pete."

He examined the leather-bound book. "These pages are very fragile, and the handwriting is very difficult to read. Did Amanda say what language this is? I don't recognize it."

"It's coded," Belinda explained. "That's why it takes a scholar to interpret it."

"I think I've found my next project for the coming weeks," Pete beamed.

"On a more serious note, Amanda also warned us of the baron," Andi continued. "She didn't know any details but said that the baron will still try to prevent anyone from finding the jewelry box."

"Interesting." Pete rubbed his chin. "We need to be very careful then."

Susi clapped her hands on her lap as she stood up from her chair. "Well, I've had a long day and Pete probably can't wait to get rid of us, so he can start deciphering the book. Andrea, are you riding back with me?"

"Sure. I'm ready."

"I'm coming, too. Got room in the backseat?" Volker added. "I haven't been with my true love all day."

"I wouldn't want to get in the way of two lovers trying to get to know each other," Susi said after they arrived at home. "I'll take a long soak in the tub and then curl up in my warm bed with my favorite book."

"Good night, Susi," the pair called down from the stairs to Andi's apartment.

"Night, kids."

Andi took the ring out of her purse and set it on the nightstand. "Can you wait here while I change into my night-clothes? I just have to get into something more comfortable."

"Of course, my love," he said.

Andrea frowned at him. "That isn't even funny." She threw her hands in the air as she retreated into the bathroom. "No peeking!"

Volker looked at the bathroom door that she slammed shut between them. "I wasn't joking," he mumbled. As he waited for her, the thought of peeking in on her was definitely tempting, but he was raised with standards. He made a promise to her when they first met, and he was a man of his word.

When Andi returned in her pink t-shirt jammies, she motioned him to come to the kitchen with her. "You know I can't go to sleep without my cup of hot tea."

He couldn't take his eyes off her. She poured the hot water into a mug, containing a bag of vanilla-strawberry tea, and let it steep for a few minutes. When the tea was ready, they moved into the living room. She sat her cup on a coaster on the table, then plopped on the couch sideways and pulled her feet up into a lotus position. "Come sit?"

He followed her to the couch and sat on the other end. "Don't mind me if I don't pretzel my legs up like yours."

She laughed at him, which made his stomach do somersaults.

Their eyes met, but after a few moments, an awkward silence grew between them.

Andrea shifted in her seat and broke eye contact. "So, now what?"

Volker was a little rusty in the dating department, to say the least. How do you talk to your soul mate? Yes, he was good at making her laugh, pushing her buttons. The only thing he did not know how to do, was tell her how he really felt about her, without making himself look like a babbling idiot. To give his hands something to do, Volker reached for his ghostly cup of steaming Earl Gray. The uncomfortable silence between them unnerved him, so he said the first thing that came to his mind: "Uh, do you like flowers?"

She looked at him, and then burst into uncontrollable laughter.

He certainly did it this time. 'Do you like flowers?' Who says such a dumb thing to impress his 'true love'?

"I'm sorry," she said, followed by a little snort. "I don't think this is going too well. Should we watch a movie instead?"

Relieved, he agreed to sit through a light-hearted chick-flick with her. They laughed at funny scenes together, and for some unmanly reason, he had to admit that the movie wasn't all too bad, even though, he preferred action movies, like any other modern guy.

After the movie was over, Andi yawned, got up from the couch and shuffled slowly with her cup into the kitchen. "Can you get the TV?"

"Pardon?" He was about to drain some power from the TV to turn it off, when she walked back into the living room to turn off the lights.

"Never mind. I'll get it," and shuffled into the bedroom with another long yawn.

He looked at her amused. She still looked cute, messy hair and all.

"Will you come to my room and tell me stories from your home?"

"Any time, my love," he said and followed her.

She kicked off her slippers and crawled into bed. "You know," she mumbled, barely audible, "I enjoy spending time with you." She cuddled up in her fluffy down blanket. "Tell me how life was in your time, will you?"

"What would you like to know," he asked softly.

She smiled. "Tell me something that made you happy back then."

He thought for a moment. "Well, when I was a little boy and lived in what you now call Eppelheim, my mother was usually at home, cooking, cleaning, mending and whatever chores had to be done. My dad was a mason, too, so that's where I learned my craft. As a little boy, I always built small castles and other structures by piling rocks one on the other. I was so proud of myself. As I became older, my dad showed me the finer art of building and stone carving, and my miniature castles became more elaborate as I learned more about them. When I was twelve, I was old enough to accompany my father to work at the castle, where I did my apprenticeship. I took great pride in my work and soon became one of the preferred masons. Actually, next time we go to the castle, I can show you some of my work."

"I'd love that," she said with a soft, dreamy voice.

"Andi?"

"Hmmm?"

"When I come back to life, I'll build you the best castle my money can buy."

"Hmmm."

"Andi? Are you sleeping?" He leaned a little closer and the only answer he received was a faint snore. He smiled, sat back in his make-believe chair, and watched her sleep.

$\mathcal{A}$ ndi opened her eyes and saw that Volker was still sitting on the chair by her bed. "Good morning, sunshine," he said.

Andi rubbed the sleep out of her eyes and blinked, just to make sure she wasn't seeing things. "Did you sit here all night?"

"Yes, I didn't have anything better to do, so I figured I'd wait until you talked to me again."

"Wow," she said followed by a yawn. "That had to be as exciting as watching grass grow."

"Well, I've done that before, and I must say that I had more fun watching you, especially when you started to talk in your sleep."

Andi sat up straight, horrified and suddenly wide-awake. "What? What did I say?" Several scenarios ran through her mind.

"Ach, nothing special. You called my name and you said that you couldn't live without me. You did sound kind of desperate," he added for good measure.

"I did not say such a thing!" She wrapped her blanked

around herself to keep the morning chill from getting to her. "You're making that up!"

"Nope, not making it up. Well, maybe I exaggerated a bit," he admitted, "but you did make cute little snoring sounds.

"That's it!" She grabbed her pillow and threw it at him. Instead of hitting her intended target, the pillow went right through him and hit the wall.

He laughed. "Come on, mein Schatz, let's get ready for a new day."

Downstairs, Susi was already up and getting breakfast ready. "Good morning, care for some coffee?"

"Sure," Andi replied, still wearing her jammies and hair sticking out in all directions from her head. Volker already saw her being a mess this morning; he could endure another half an hour until she got some coffee in her system, she thought. "Thanks, Susi," she said and set the mug of the steaming brew on the table.

Volker did his magic and made his own cup appear. "Thanks, Susi, I'm good."

"So what's on the agenda today?" Susi spread some butter on her toast.

"Volker is taking me on a castle tour. I'm actually getting the real story with bonus insider information. Afterward we'll go into town to do some shopping and tonight, of course, we'll go to the pub," Andi said. "Somewhere in between, I'll have to find some time to work on my book. Do you want to come join us?"

Susi shook her head. "I'm actually spending the day with Ralf. He called last night to tell me that our pictures are ready and to see if I was free today. We're going to Mannheim to do lunch, and then we're going to the plane-tarium. I haven't been there in years. Afterwards, I'll meet you at the pub."

"That's great, you're going on a date," Andi cheered. "Call me if you can't make it to the pub tonight."

"Don't worry. I'll be back in time. I already told Ralf that I had plans in the evening. He was a little disappointed, but I told him that we can meet again another time."

"You're crushing his heart already, Susi?"

"I am not! Besides, I really do have plans."

They finished their breakfast and Andi went upstairs to shower, get dressed, and ready to go. The sun was out, and the fog had already lifted. Even though, it looked like it was going to warm up later, Andi wore a nice warm down jacket, a scarf and a hat to protect her from the cold afternoon chill. "Volker, I'm ready," she called out.

He materialized next to her and he looked stunning. He wore a black suede jacket with fuzzy lining, a pair of jeans, and his hiking shoes. She was tempted just to cuddle up to him, but some things just are not possible. She stuck the ring in her purse. "Okay, we're all set." She made sure she had her streetcar pass and her wallet on her. "Bye, Susi!"

"Bye, kids. See you sometime this afternoon," she replied.

As they left the house, Andi stuck her new Bluetooth device in her ear, so people wouldn't think she's crazy for talking to herself in public, even though, she always thought those things were annoying, and so were the people using them. In Atlanta, she always thought that total strangers were talking to her on the streets, but as it turned out, they were holding a conversation with their bosses or clients on the phone. Now she was one of them – an undercover ghost whisperer.

Volker took the seat across from her in the streetcar. "All those buildings you see over there did not exist in my time," he explained as she looked out of the window. "It was all forest and meadows, with a few settlements sprinkled in between."

"So how did you walk to work every day? That must have been a long way."

Volker shook his head. "Usually, I took my horse. That was one of the benefits of my good reputation at the castle, though I did not mind walking all too much, either. On a normal working day, I left my home at dawn and came home when it became dark again outside. Sometimes, I stayed in town with friends for a beer or two, but I wasn't one for drinking all that much and didn't like making a fool out of myself."

"I don't drink much either," Andi admitted. "I guess you could call me a social drinker, because I have to be in the right mood for it, if at all."

"The baron, on the other hand, was always there when we arrived. Maybe he went every night. The later the evening, the worse off he was. Sometimes, I'd see him talking his way out of catching a beating for cheating while gambling; other times he would sweet-talk women that belonged to someone else. It wasn't a pretty sight."

"Looks like our baron had a slight reputation for overindulging in the sins," Andi suggested.

Volker nodded.

The streetcar stopped, and more people got on. "I'm going to disappear for a while until we get off the streetcar. I don't relish the thought of being trampled on." Within seconds, all three seats in her section were occupied.

"Okay, Volker, I'll see you when it's less busy," Andi said.

"Wie bitte?" The old woman sitting across from her looked at her. "Did you say something?" she asked in German.

Andi realized that the woman wasn't familiar with the earpiece. "Nein, nein," she said. "Telefon," and she pointed at her ear.

"Ach so," the little old woman replied as she saw the device. "My granddaughter has one of those things. I thought you were talking to me."

Andi couldn't believe it. She had turned into one of THEM – the crazy people talking to themselves!

After a few more stops, she reached her destination and hopped on a bus taking her to the other end of the walking zone, close to the base of the mountain, where the 'Heaven's Ladder' led up to the castle. When they were alone again, Volker reappeared. Not many people were hiking up the stairs that morning, just the occasional tourist or jogger, so they had plenty of privacy.

"I used to walk these steps a lot," Volker reminisced. "Of course, they weren't as pretty as these new ones, but I was grateful all the same. Amelie used to walk up there with me when she needed to go to the castle apothecary for some special herbs. She was a very happy girl until her dad died, when she was a teenager."

"That had to be terrible for her, to lose a parent so young."

"She was a fighter, Andi, and I thank her for putting me out of my misery, even though, I was limited to the castle grounds after my death, it could have been worse. But I'll show you my favorite spot later on."

They finally reached the last one of the steps. Andi stopped to catch her breath. "I hate you! How can you not be out of breath?"

"Because I am a top athlete and you are just a girl," he said, winking at her.

She pretended to raise her arm, ready to strike him, when he jumped back to avoid her punch.

"You missed! Like I said, you punch like a girl."

Still out of breath, she shook her head and they continued to walk.

He caught up with her, and without thinking, she hooked her arm into his, except there was no arm to hook hers into. Instead, it fell through the air and another jolt rushed through her body. Both of their eyes got big.

"I'm sorry, I forgot..." she managed. "Can you feel that?"

He shook his head. "I wish I could. It scares me more seeing you jumping out of your skin every time we accidentally touch. Does it hurt?"

"Not really, it just surprises me. It's, well, very tingly. In a good way," she got goose bumps just thinking about it.

He smiled his most irresistible smile. "Maybe I should touch you more often?"

"Maybe we should get moving, because there are some people coming?" She pointed at the stairs behind them.

"Right," he answered.

They moved on toward the castle entrance. "You know, before my time, there were actually two castles here, an upper castle that stood about there," he pointed toward the hill, "and the one that you see right now, except it looked much different then. The towers had wooden roofs and were intact. Also, the gardens were not this spectacular. All of these niceties came centuries later."

She paid her entrance fee again. Maybe she should just get an annual pass instead, she thought, as much as they were coming here recently. However, she decided to go with the one-day ticket again, until she could afford it. She remembered, coming up here a lot when she was a kid. Her uncle, who had long passed away, owned a house a little farther up on the hill, so when the kids, during family reunions got bored to tears, they ran down to the castle for a little fun in the courtyard during twilight. They would look into the deep well, try to count the money in the fountain, or just roam around the grounds, pretending to be royals.

As Andi passed the witch's bite at the large gate, she couldn't help but ask. "Was that Amelie?"

He laughed. "No, I think it was just a flaw in the iron and it cracked over time."

"Hey, with what I've learned over the last few weeks, I can never be too sure," Andi giggled.

Entering the courtyard, Andi's gaze was automatically drawn to the scaffolding where she found the ring. "What a coincidence that I stood here just at the right time," Andi said softly, trying not to look at Volker, or draw attention to herself in the crowds. She had to admit that it was difficult to have him around in public.

"Mein Schatz," he replied, "I bet that this is no coincidence. I think that fate has a play in this. How else would a perfect woman like you come into my life?"

Andi straightened her jacket, just to distract herself from being embarrassed. "I'm far from perfect, and by now you should know that."

"Well, in my eyes, you are."

They walked over to the fountain. "Hey, I want to make a wish." She dug a Euro coin out of her purse. "I know it's a bit much, but I want to make sure it'll come true." She closed her eyes and tossed the coin into the water, where hundreds of others had done so already today.

"What did you wish for?" Volker looked at Andi with a raised eyebrow.

Andi gave him a look of exasperation. "If I told you, it won't come true, now would it?" She blushed, "Besides, I'm sure you already know what it is anyway, don't you?"

"I suppose so," he said, and then pulled out a bag full of coins out of his jacket pocket.

Andi smiled. "Do you always carry a bag of old magical gold coins around with you?"

"You never know when it comes in handy. I might need it to reinforce a wish one day. Our wish." He did as she did a few minutes ago and poured the contents of his bag into the well. Of course, the water did not splash with the impact of the ghostly coins.

Andi cocked her head to the side.

"Oh, sorry, forgot something," he said and conjured a little delayed splash in the fountain water.

They both laughed. "You're too funny. Well, with all the money and magic involved, our wish has no choice but to come true."

"Are you ready for more of the tour?" Volker asked.

"Of course!"

They walked around the courtyard. "The portion that was currently being restored was what we were working on before my death. You see, this castle was still being built, whereas the upper castle already stood. The main building of the residential area to the right was almost finished when I got arrested."

They moved on toward the terrace overlooking the city.

"Isn't it beautiful up here," she said looking down into the old town and watching the river weave through the valley.

"This has always been my favorite spot," he said.

"Has the old bridge been here in your time?"

"No," he shook his head. It came a little later, but there were other bridges before it that were either destroyed in battles or by large floating ice chunks in the winter. After my death, I used to come up here to this exact spot and watch it being built."

She turned around and looked across the terrace. "So, what's the true story about the footprint in the sandstone over there? The tour guide said that a fire had broken out in the upper floor of the building and everyone escaped, except for a knight, who wasn't familiar with the building. He then jumped out of the window, landed hard, and miraculously survived unharmed."

He shook his head. "That's an old wives' tale. There is another story of Friedrich IV, who liked his wine very much. One night, he fell out of a window in a drunken stupor and left that footprint."

She stuck her foot into the imprint. "Well, I definitely have small feet."

"Well, I think any feet bigger than the ones you have would look out of proportion to you." He stepped in the imprint himself and found it to be a perfect fit. "Should I let you in on a secret?"

"What's that? You jumped out of a window after a maiden you were in love with?" She couldn't help to feel a twinge of jealousy when she said that.

"Actually, you're pretty close with your guess." His eyes began to sparkle in amusement.

Great, he's laughing at me and I have to compete with the ghost of some medieval bimbo, she thought.

He continued. "The secret is that one summer day, my friends and I celebrated a little much and decided to come up to the castle to play a prank on the snobby royals." He lifted his nose and did his best impression of the sort that ignored all the lowly workers.

She giggled. "You're funny!"

"We found Friedrich sound asleep on the ground,

surrounded by the smell of cheap wine. We got some tools from my work shed, outlined my foot, and chiseled away on this soft sandstone tile, hoping that no one would see or hear us making all this noise. We then hid to wait for what was going to happen next. A few hours later, a duke went for a morning stroll and found the sleeping Friedrich lying on the ground next to the foot imprint. He kicked him to see if he was alive. The body stirred, and Friedrich covered up his embarrassing story by saying that he fell out of the window the night before."

Andi stared at the imprint. "This is not yours!" No way was she going to believe it.

He rolled his eyes. "Woman, how can I convince you that I am telling the truth?"

"Unless you have a witness," she gave him a smug grin, "I don't believe you."

Volker thought for a moment. "Of course, Markus was there with me. Let me go and get him, but I don't know if you can see him," he answered.

Andi looked at him perplexed. "I was joking. Then on the other hand, you never cease to amaze me."

"Wait right here," he said. "I'll go and find him."

She walked back to the railing and admired the scenery, shaking her head. "This is crazy."

Five minutes had passed, when Volker returned alone. "I brought Markus with me. Can you see him?" Volker looked to his right. "You idiot, why didn't you tell me you didn't make yourself visible yet. Okay, he said he's going to try to materialize."

Andi waited and looked to Volker's right. Sure enough, slowly a male figure started to appear. He was shorter than Volker and had blond hair. He wasn't as solid as Volker was, but visible enough. "I can see you," she said. "Hi, my name is Andi." She did not make the mistake again of trying to shake his hand.

"Markus." He nodded at her. "She can actually see me," Markus said turning to Volker. "She looks hot, too. Just like you described her."

She cleared her throat. "Uhm, hello? I can hear you!"

"Oh, my apologies. I just don't meet many live people who can see or hear me. My social skills have suffered over the years."

"So you two knew each other back then?"

"Yes, we were friends when we were still alive and are still to this day, with a two-year interruption, of course, while I was still enjoying life and he had already kicked the bucket," Markus explained.

"Excuse me for being nosy, but how did you die and why are you still hanging around?" Andi just couldn't help herself.

"Well, I met my end in early spring by repairing a bridge similar to this one down there. I fell in the icy water and I was caught in the current. Don't look so glum," he interjected. "I'm over it."

Andi was confused. "But what keeps you here? Shouldn't you move on to heaven or something like that?"

He shrugged. "I have some of my old friends here and I'm just not quite ready enough to give up all the fun."

"I still can't figure out what's so much fun about being dead, but never mind. So, is it true that this is Volker's foot imprint?"

Markus laughed. "Oh yes! And what a delightful night we had, especially, when the duke came upon the incapacitated Friedrich."

Andi still didn't believe a word she heard. "Volker, did you tell him what to say?"

He sighed. "Of course not. I don't know what else I can do to make you believe. You'll just have to trust me on this."

"And me," Markus added.

Andi gave up. "Okay. I'm done arguing with you two."

"Well then, I'll leave you two lovebirds alone. It was very nice to meet you, Andi. Feel free to summon me if Volker no longer loves you."

When hell freezes over, she thought.

"I heard that, and I'm crushed."

"What," Andi looked at him surprised, "you can read my thoughts?"

Markus chuckled. "Not really. I'm just pretty perceptive, that's all."

She shook her head. "Some friends you have, Volker!"

They said their good-byes and continued their walk to the castle gardens. It was a fairly quick walk, as Andi began to freeze. "We'll have to come back here in the spring."

"Who knows, maybe we could actually walk arm-in-arm by then," he said.

Andi looked up at him. "I would like that."

"*I* hope Amanda didn't change her mind about coming tonight," Andi told Susi as they settled in at their usual table in the pub. She moved the chair next to her out for Volker to sit on.

"Nah, I think she just didn't want to be here first, since she only knows you and Belinda," Volker suggested.

About 10 minutes later, the pub door opened. Andi first saw Pete, who carried a backpack containing his notes, no doubt, entering the large room. Belinda followed him, almost pushing him over as she tried to get past him.

"Brrrr, it's cold," she said with chattering teeth.

Andi watched Pete as he set down his bag. He looked like he had pulled an all-nighter. She could empathize. Every time she was working on a good scene in her books, she'd get lost in her work and time ceased to exist. "Wow, Pete, that's what I call a man on a mission," she remarked.

"Well, I only spent a few hours on the project."

"He's lying," Belinda corrected. "He didn't spend a minute away from Amelie's book, other than to go to the bathroom, eat a quick snack of whatever I put in front of him, and slept on the couch, if you could even call it sleep."

Susi patted on the table for them to hurry up and sit down. "I can't wait to see what you've found out so far."

"Shai, where's the beer? We're thirsty," Belinda shouted over to the bar.

Shai gave her a thumbs-up, filled a few mugs and brought them to the table. He passed out the brew to each of the friends, except for Volker, who brought his own.

"Susi had a date with Ralf today," Andi spurted out and grinned at Susi. She always enjoyed pushing her aunt's buttons.

Susi flushed. "It was not a date! We just had lunch and went to the planetarium. I would hardly call that a date."

"I would," Belinda agreed, and then frowned at her husband. "Hey, I can't remember the last time you took me out on a real date."

Pete, in turn, gave Susi a pretend evil glare. "See what you've started? My wife is getting ideas that I should wine and dine her, just because you went on a date with Ralf." His eyes twinkled. "I'm losing cool-points by association, here."

Susi shouted: "For the last time, IT WAS NOT A DATE!"

Several heads in the pub turned toward their table.

Pete began to laugh, and the rest of the group followed along. "It's all in good fun, Susi. We're just teasing you."

"Anyway, Ralf brought me the pictures from the ball if

anyone is interested." She dug them out of her bag and passed them around.

Belinda looked at the photos of Susi alone first. "They are gorgeous! Ralf really knows how to do his job well." Toward the bottom of the stack were the pictures with Andi. Belinda broke out into a hearty laugh. "I'm sorry, Andi, but every time I see these dots…"

"Let me see," Pete turned her hand, so he could look as well. "That's a classic!"

"I'm glad you find it funny," Andi responded a little uneasy as she remembered those itchy welts on her face.

The pub door opened again, and Amanda walked in, looking a little lost.

"Amanda," Belinda called out and waved, trying to get her attention.

Amanda looked relieved when she saw the group and walked toward their table.

"Everybody, this is Amanda. She owns an herbal store downtown. Amanda, these are our friends," she pointed at each of them as she introduced them by name.

Amanda smiled. "Hello, everybody. It's nice to meet you all."

"Please, have a seat," Pete offered. "Just not this one, Volker is already sitting in it."

"Really," she asked. "He's here?"

"Yes," Susi answered, "We'll introduce you guys as soon as things settle down a bit."

"Oh, goody, I can hardly wait!" Amanda sat on the other free chair at the table. "I never thought that I would be the one in my bloodline to see the legend of Volker unfold and having the honor to surrender the book to the scholar. Needless to say, I feel very privileged to be part of this quest."

"Volker says thank you," Andi interpreted, "but I'm sure that he can tell you that later in person."

"You're welcome, Volker," she replied.

Shai came to the table and greeted the newcomer. "Hello there. What can I bring you?"

"Do you have some Glühwein?" Amanda touched her cheek. "I can barely feel my face. It's so cold outside."

Shai smiled at her. "A cup of steaming hot, spiced redwine will definitely warm anyone up in a hurry." He winked. "It's coming right up."

Belinda leaned over toward Amanda and whispered in a not so soft voice. "So, what do you think?"

Amanda looked at her slightly embarrassed. "Uh, what do you mean?"

"Come on, I saw how you two looked at each other," she continued.

Andi came to Amanda's rescue. "Don't mind her. Just because she's married to stud-muffin over there, she thinks that everyone should be living in matrimonial bliss. She already tried hooking Volker and me up."

"But you two are destined for each other, so why not," Belinda defended herself.

She glanced over at Volker. "In case you have forgotten, we still have a slight metaphysical problem."

Belinda laughed. "But don't you see how romantic this entire story is?"

"Yes, I do. And you'll get to read about it, once there is a happy ending and the book is published."

"You have to admit, though, that this is very fairy-tale like," Amanda mused. "Your love has been talked about for hundreds of years. Who else can say that?"

Andi grinned. "Romeo and Juliet? But have any of you people considered how impossible our situation is at the moment?"

"Ladies, ladies," Pete jumped into the conversation. "Please be civil." He cracked a smile. "I'm just glad it's not me being the ghost, no offense, Volker."

"What are you all taking about?" Shai came back with Amanda's hot Glühwein.

"What we're talking about is how cruel these people are." Andi pouted then smiled.

Shai turned to Amanda and set the mug in front of her. "So, how did these folks drag you in here?"

Amanda stirred her hot drink with a spoon to cool it down faster. "I met Belinda and Andi at my store yesterday afternoon and they invited me to come tonight."

"You must have made a great impression on them," he said, "because they don't invite just anybody into their round."

"Let's just say that I had a little leverage to get me into the clique," she said with a smug grin.

Shai shook his head, and then walked to the bar to fetch another round of beers for the friends.

"So, what did you learn from the book that Amanda gave you," Susi asked. "Were you able to make any headway in deciphering the code?"

Pete reached for his bag and pulled out a spiral notebook. "I think I did make some progress. Amanda, your ancestor did not have the neatest handwriting. I must admit that I'm having some trouble making out letters, therefore, my progress is very slow." He opened the notebook and flipped through some pages.

"Ah, there it is," he said. He read the text that he had decoded so far aloud in German.

'For the man to come back to life, the princess's heirloom ring has to be reunited with the jewelry box it once was kept in. A spell from a witch will seal the deal.'

That's about as far as I got," Pete said. "It'll take me a

few more days to decipher the rest of the pages in the book."

"Well, we now know that we also need a spell from a witch," Andi remarked. "Great, I think we're fresh out of witches."

"Not necessarily," Amanda chimed in. "I'm sure you remember how Amelie had special powers. The women of her bloodline all share the same gift in various degrees."

"So this means that you can do cool tricks, such as turning Pete into an elephant," Belinda asked.

Everyone in the group giggled, except for Pete. "Honey, if I were you, I wouldn't joke around like that. Amanda might get some ideas and our apartment is not large enough for an elephant to live in."

Amanda laughed and shook her head. "No, I'm not turning anyone into anything. My special powers or magic, as some call it, relate to healing, like my mother and her mother's, and even further back than Amelie's mother."

"If Amelie's powers are also related to healing, how was she able to send Volker into the ghost world and the baron into death," Belinda asked.

"Healing can have many meanings," Amanda explained. "In Volker's case, healing means freeing him from his pain and allowing him to come back and continue his life after the wrong of the stolen ring has been righted."

Susi took a sip of her beer. "This makes sense, however, how did she bring sickness to the baron?"

"Let me explain it this way," she said. "There's good energy and there is bad energy. When you heal someone, the negative, say sick energy, is being removed from that individual. Healers have to channel that bad energy into something else or they themselves get sick. Most of the time, healers send the bad energy to some inanimate object, which neutralizes the bad energy. In the case of the baron, she saved up the enormous amount of bad energy she drew out of Volker and channeled it back into Ludwig von Dossenheim."

"That's amazing!" Andi liked Amelie more by the minute. She was just her kind of girl. "So you can do the same?"

"Well, yes," Amanda replied not so confident. "At least, I believe so. I've never channeled bad energy into anything alive before. I also need to know what the spell is to return Volker back to human form."

"I'll be working on that," Pete said. "Hopefully, I will get to that portion of the book some time this week. Your ancestors did an excellent job with coding the text."

Volker gave Pete a warning stare. "No pressure, but I do hope you take your time and get this right. I don't want to come back as an ant or a dainty little dandelion if you get any of the words wrong."

"Don't worry, good friend. Leave this up to the profession...uh...me. Actually, I almost have the code for all the letters I cracked. It just takes time to translate it all," Pete admitted. "But I do have an idea. I'll just type all the letters into my word processor, do a search for, let's say, all the letters 'a' and then replace them with the correct one. I'm such a genius. And thank you for my next free beer."

Shai overheard Pete's comment. "It's on the house, genius." Shai grinned and placed the fresh glass of foaming ale on Pete's coaster.

"Thank you, my man, for recognizing my talents. I knew that there was a reason why I return to this place every weekend without fail. Cheers!"

Shai turned to Amanda. "And you, my lovely lady? May I bring you a special welcome drink on the house?"

Amanda smiled. "Maybe a cup of peppermint tea

would be perfect." Their gazes lingered a few moments longer than necessary.

"It will be my pleasure," he said and reluctantly tore free from the gaze that hypnotized him.

Volker and Andi did not miss this exchange. They glanced at each other in return. Volker's eyes sparkled with delight.

Secretly, Andi wondered how it would feel like to kiss him. Just the memory of them touching made it almost impossible for her to imagine how a kiss would affect her. She forced herself to look away, or she would really find herself in trouble.

Shai returned with the tea and some honey and pulled up a chair next to Amanda. "How come I've never seen you around here?"

"I actually don't go out that often," Amanda said in a sad voice.

"I don't get around much, either. I spend a lot of time running this pub, even though I should let one of my trusty employees look after it occasionally and learn about the rest of the world."

Amanda smiled at him. "I feel the same about my store. For some reason, I can't stay away for long. I don't get many customers during the day, but the ones that find their way to me, usually leave happy, which makes my day."

"Okay, you two," Belinda interrupted. "It's not so crowded anymore. Should we take the risk now and get Amanda initiated? If you are ready, Amanda, that is."

"Initiation, that sounds so gang-like," Susi commented. "I think a better term would be enlightenment."

"Come with us," Belinda said and pulled Amanda up by her hand.

Andi searched for the ring in her purse and followed them.

In the bathroom, Susi made sure that they were alone before they proceeded.

Andi pulled the ring out of her jeans pocket and then handed it to Amanda. "Here, hold this for a moment."

Amanda stared at the ring. "Is…is this, THE ring?" Her eyes opened wide in wonder.

Belinda smiled. "Yes, this is the princess' long lost ring. Now that you have touched it, you will be able to see Volker when we get back to the table."

"Really," Amanda asked, but looked confused. "Isn't something supposed to happen? I don't feel any different." Amanda took a last look at the ring and handed it back to Andi.

"Nah, I didn't feel anything, either. Instead, I saw this beautiful medieval man standing a few meters away from me. Little did I know that he was a ghost. I didn't figure that out until he visited me in my bedroom later on that night." Andi smiled. "I guess I can be a little dense sometimes. Are you ready to meet Volker in person?"

Amanda gave Andi the most incredulously look. "What do you mean, if I'm ready? I've been hearing about this legend since I was a young child. How can I not be ready to see him?"

They walked out of the bathroom and Amanda headed straight for the table, followed by Andi.

"Try not to be so obvious when you see him," Andi whispered. "There are still guests in the pub."

"I won't." They kept walking past the divider wall with the coat rack then rounded the corner into the main room. Amanda turned around to Andi. "Is that him in the red shirt?"

"Yes," Andi answered. "Keep going," she urged.

As she came closer, Amanda stood still like a pillar.

Andi felt that something had just gone horribly wrong. "What's the matter? Are you okay?"

A few seconds passed, and Amanda fought to get her composure back. "I just heard a voice. Didn't you hear it?"

They shook their heads and then Susi replied, "I only heard the noise from the people in the pub and the music coming from the speakers. Why, what did you hear?"

"It was a female voice. She said something like, 'Child, be aware. He's still here to stop you. You must warn them!" Amanda shook her head. "That was weird. Who was it and who was she talking about?"

"Let's worry about that when we get to the table," Belinda said.

"Amanda, meet Volker. Volker, meet Amanda Herzlein, Amelie's granddaughter, skipping a few generations," Andi officially introduced them.

"Nice to finally meet you," Volker said. "But why are you suddenly so pale? You look like you've just seen a ghost."

"It's worse," Susi whispered.

*T*his evening, not many of Fred's friends were at his usual hangout, so he decided to leave the bar. Maybe he would get lucky and find a pretty girl to keep him company tonight.

It was ice-cold, and the fog began to freeze on car windows and street signs. He adjusted his ball cap and zipped his coat all the way up to keep warm. Fred didn't like winters, but at least Heidelberg was not the coldest spot in Germany.

He passed an alley with an Irish Pub sign half way down from it. Fred disliked pubs. That's where all the old people spend their Saturday nights – definitely not a place to meet women, in his opinion.

Fred walked on but felt this strange urge to go check it out regardless. He shook his head. No, he wasn't going to waste his time. There had to be a better place not far from where he was now – a place where young girls were looking for a man to be with tonight. If all else failed, he would go to one of the dance clubs on the outskirts of town, where he could usually find a date for the night.

Small fog clouds formed on every exhale as he pressed on. His expensive jacket, which was designed to look good, did not keep him warm at all. He began to shiver. Damn it! Go to the pub, a nagging voice repeatedly said in his head. He thought of his current condition and concluded that he could do well by getting out of the cold for a few minutes, before he'd continue his search for a more desirable bar. Fred stopped in mid-stride and did a complete 180 to head back toward the alley and the pub. Maybe, he'd see one of his buddies or clients to share a drink with.

Almost at the pub, he noticed that there were not too many people hanging around the front entrance to smoke. He checked his watch. It was almost 11. The younger crowds had probably moved on to the clubs by now, where he should be.

He stopped in front of the pub and peeked through one of the slightly warped glass panes in the window. The place looked almost empty. A man sat at a large table, engaged in an apparent light-hearted conversation with a waiter. He then saw four women walking from the back area of the pub heading toward the table in the far back, where the man sat. The girls must have done the 'powdering my nose' maneuver, which chicks always do when talking about a guy.

Shifting his attention back to the women, his gaze

stopped at the girl with waist-long black hair, which was held back by a clip. She had beautiful pale skin and he wouldn't mind dating someone like her.

Fred continued to watch the ladies making their way back to the large table, when suddenly, the first woman stopped and turned pale. He noticed how the other three women started fussing over her. A moment later, she continued to walk, and then looked at the empty chair. She said something to her friends, who nodded in response. The lady then stared at the empty chair and started talking to it.

He was confused yet intrigued. He wiped the now fogged up window with his fist to get a better view. He looked over at the table again. Nobody sat in that chair, yet everyone was looking at it smiling. Are they playing some kind of weird party game?

The black-haired beauty sat next to the guy and then kissed his cheek. Damnation. Maybe they are dating. He was looking for a wedding band, but he was too far away. It didn't matter anyway. It's not as if he never took another man's woman before. Actually, it takes two to tango. He smiled, satisfied with himself.

He looked at this man again. Where had he seen him before? Was he one of his clients? Maybe he was one of his friends' acquaintances. Suddenly, he remembered. That guy is the one who came to his office asking about his ancestor. When he met the guy the other day, he knew something shady was going on with him. Fred tried to remember the name on the business card he had left him. It was a common name. Thomas? Frank? Peter? Yes, Peter Wagner, or something like that.

He continued to observe Peter and his friends. Why were they talking to that empty chair? He watched a few minutes longer. Could it be a ghost? No way, he thought.

Ghosts don't exist, do they? The group became serious again. He truly was intrigued now.

"Hey, what's so interesting in there?" Some guy smoking a cigarette started talking to him.

He nearly jumped, as if he was caught doing something he wasn't supposed to. "Nothing. Just someone I know," he responded then returned to his view through the window, hoping the annoying jerk would go away if he ignored him.

"Ah," he said. "I broke up with a girl a while back, and she didn't waste any time hooking up with a new guy and go bar-hopping with him. Sorry, dude."

Fred just nodded. He didn't care what the guy thought. It was none of his business anyway.

The guy walked away again.

His curiosity was killing him, and to stay undetected, his best bet would be to hang around outside of the pub and wait for the group to leave. He would follow the girls and strike up a conversation to find out more about the empty chair.

However, the cold and his inability to control his curiosity landed him inside of the pub after all. He found a corner table by the window from where he had been watching. Fred took off his jacket and left his ball cap on to stay unrecognized and then sat with his back to the crowd. The waiter came to his table. "What will it be?"

"Ale for now," he replied.

"Very well," the waiter responded.

While Fred was sitting at his table, he looked around and saw a mirrored picture on the wall across from him. He noticed that he had a perfect view of the group's table and the empty chair. He heard them banter back and forth and could pick up some of the words they were saying. "...Amelia... lost ring... see ghost."

He perked up. Could this mean that the ghost of the mason had returned? The waiter brought his ale and walked away again, respecting his privacy, which was exactly what he wanted. He listened more closely. "... return to life... spell... ready..."

Suddenly, another group of people strolled into the door. They looked like they already had a few drinks and were in a good mood, judging by the noise level they brought in with them. So much for his ability to eavesdrop. Aggravated, he sat back and drank his ale, keeping a close watch on the group in the mirror.

*A*bout an hour later, the group was ready to call it a night. They paid their tab and put on their scarves and jackets. Shai helped Amanda put on her long wool coat.

"Before we go," Andi interjected, "do you guys want to come over to see Volker's slide-show tomorrow afternoon? The weather is supposed to be cold and drizzly anyway, so we could have a nice afternoon at our house with cake and coffee."

Pete and Belinda nodded. "We would love to," she said. "Amanda, Shai?"

Amanda nodded. "Sure, I have time tomorrow. Where do you live?"

"They live in Eppelheim, but we can pick you up on the way, if you like," Belinda suggested.

"That would be perfect." She turned to Shai, "Will you come, too?"

Shai struggled with an answer. He really wanted to see the slide show. More than that, he wanted to see Amanda again. However, he did not have anyone to cover him at the pub on such short notice, especially on a busy Sunday, when locals and tourists were out and about. "Unfortunately, I will have to work tomorrow," he finally admitted. This was the first time he regretted having to be at work, since he took over the Irish Pub five years ago.

He watched Amanda's facial expression change from hopeful to disappointed. Not knowing what to say next, he stuck his hand in the pocket of his black pants and rubbed his lucky coin, which helped him out of a pickle more than once.

Suddenly, Amanda dropped one of her gloves. "Oh!"

They both bent down to pick it up. On the way back up, their heads collided.

"Auaa," she said with a pained smile, rubbing her forehead.

"Oh, I'm so sorry, Mandy," he apologized and helped her back up. "Here's your glove."

She looked at him perplexed then they both laughed.

"Will you come back next Saturday?"

Amanda nodded, "If it's okay with your friends."

"I think they like you just fine," he replied. "I would really like to see you again, Mandy."

"I would love that, as well," Amanda managed. "Maybe I'll come by for a cup of tea one day. You know, my store is not too far from here."

Shai could not tear his gaze away from her. He thanked his lucky coin. "You can stop by anytime you like. I'll see you in the next few days then?"

Amanda nodded. "I'll see you soon."

*F*red was already waiting around the corner when the group went their separate ways. This guy, Peter, the beauty, and the woman who looked like she had seen a ghost, walked toward the hills. Since he already had Peter's business card, he did not worry so much about them. Instead, he decided to follow the other two girls, who walked toward the streetcars. Originally, he wanted to drive his brand new, decked out BMW to a club to impress the ladies, but tracking the two girls was much more exciting. He left his car in the parking garage, then waited until the girls were ahead of him, and followed them.

The wind had picked up and Fred felt the drizzle hit his face. Yuck, he thought, and tried to warm up by crossing his arms. After an agonizing 15-minute walk through the shopping area, they finally arrived at the streetcar stop. They didn't wait long and entered the #2 line to Eppelheim, which is half way to where he lived. Maybe they are going to Schwetzingen, too. Fred, purchased a ticket and sat nearby with his back to them, so he could listen to them talk. Apparently, the ghost was still with them; because they would speak and pause, then laugh out loud for no apparent reason. He had to admit that he was a little freaked out.

The doors of the streetcar closed, and it began to move.

His thoughts drifted back to the ghost. So how could they see or hear him? He had tried to concentrate but did not have any success picking up anything at all. Finally, he gave up and just focused on making sense of the one-sided conversation they held.

They soon arrived in Eppelheim. The older looking woman stood up first and pushed the stop indicator button. At the next stop, the streetcar came to a halt and the women got off, giggling about something. Fred exited through another door and leisurely followed them from a safe distance without drawing unnecessary attention to him. He thought it wiser not to approach the women this late at night, unless he wanted to find himself in jail.

Instead, his goal tonight was to see where they lived, not that he wanted to break into their house or anything. In the next few days, he could casually befriend one of the girls and find out more about this ghost.

He also concluded that he would have to take it upon himself to find out where the ring and the jewelry box were hidden. Never could he let these two items be reunited. Never in his lifetime! He did not want the mason to come after him and take revenge for all the bad things that befell him.

The girls walked into a driveway. Bingo. He made a note of the street, house number, and walked back to another stop to catch his bus connection to Schwetzingen.

"*A*re you ready," Volker asked when the friends had settled down in Susi's living room the following afternoon.

"We're ready," Susi confirmed. "Just give me a second to close the blinds, so we can see the pictures better."

Volker nodded. "Well, let's begin, then." He looked at the bare, white section of the wall, which had about ten nails sticking out from it, where normally Susi's family photos hung. He concentrated for a moment and made the first picture appear.

"This is what the castle used to look like when I was a mason there," he began. "Note the section that we were working on to the left. This must've been the place where the baron lost the ring and where my Andi found it."

Andi blushed. He said HIS Andi! Her friends must not have noticed, since they still gaped at the large colored castle on the wall.

"Amazing," Amanda marveled.

"It is beautiful," Andi remarked. "It's weird to see

something this old in actual color. I so expected black and white pictures, you know, like in old documentaries."

Pete agreed. "It is very fascinating to see a colored version of your world."

"I'll do my best to keep the colors as vivid as possible," Volker replied. "Unlike the ruins you see today, when the castle was still functional, most of the structures had wooden roofs, which have by now weathered away, of course."

"Look at all these people walking around the grounds in period clothing," Andi exclaimed. The ladies wore beautiful dresses with lots of lace around their cleavage and sleeves. The men wore knickerbockers with tall white socks and buckle-shoes. On top, they wore uniform-like jackets and just as much lace as the women. She imagined how it would be like to live during that time, but when her gaze drifted to the women's tiny waists, she thanked her lucky stars. How awful it must be to squeeze into a corset every day and not being able to breathe – all in the name of fashion. Then she remembered her assortment of skin-tight jeans she had squeezed herself into and using a can of hair spray a day, when she was a teen in the 80s. I guess, women were not so different back then, after all.

He moved on to the next slide. "This is the small village of Eppelheim around 1600. About 150 people lived here before I died. My house is the one right here in the middle." He pointed at the cozy white building with the wooden structure beams and a dark roof. "My father built it before I was born, and I lived in it all of my life, until that one fateful day."

Andi marveled at the pretty rosebushes that grew in front of the house and the blooming cherry tree that stood to its left. "Do you have a picture of it from the inside, too?"

"Of course." He changed to an interior photo of his house. "We used to live very simple back then. However, my father was very skilled at his craft, so he kept adding rooms over time."

Andi admired the rustic kitchen, which housed a wood-stove, a decent sized table and chairs, a rocking chair and quite a few storage shelves. She could live like that. Who actually needs food processors, blenders, microwaves and the like, when all one needs is a few simple tools like knives, butcher blocks, and potato mashers?

"Here is my room. Again, it's very simple with a bed, table, chair and a small closet. We didn't have much, and to be honest, didn't need a lot." His gaze shifted to Andi again and when their eyes met, he smiled.

Andi fanned herself with a napkin. This is torture. Does he even realize what he's doing to her? she wondered. She gave him a quick smile back and then forced herself to look at the photo. His room reminded Andi of an old version of her dorm room when she was a freshman in college. It was quite an adjustment to live with only the bare minimums, but she learned to manage.

"Amanda, here is a picture of Amelie in her teens," he continued.

Belinda's eyes grew large. "Look at the resemblance! I can definitely tell that you're a Winters' girl. You have the same wavy brown hair and pretty almond–shaped eyes."

Amanda smiled. "I have never seen a picture of her. She was beautiful."

Volker lingered a moment on Amelie's portrait until he moved to the next one. "I hate to ruin your evening; however, considering the circumstances, I believe a short mention of Baron Ludwig von Dossenheim is in order." A pompous man with whitish-gray hair, wearing a period floppy hat, was staring back at them.

"I hate that guy!" Andi saw the greed and evil in his eyes. She felt her stomach churn in distaste.

"If I were the Princess Margarete, I wouldn't want to marry him, either," Belinda stated. "Not even for all the money in the world."

"Alright then, let's move on. I have a final picture of my best friend in old and current times. This is Markus, whom I became best friends with while working at the castle as a mason. He was a carpenter in his day. We used to spend most of our spare time together. Markus used to get me into more trouble over foolish things than I cared for."

Andi couldn't resist. "After meeting him in person the other day, I can see how he rubbed off on you!"

Volker smiled. "Yes, I used to be a perfect son to my parents. However, with all the mischief swimming around Markus's head, I soon defied the rules myself and became a prankster, just like him." He winked at Andi.

"And the rest is history," Pete finished for him. "That was quite a wonderful and insightful presentation. Thank you, Volker, for showing us a glimpse of your life in another time."

Susi finished her cup of coffee. "So, do you miss it – your old life, I mean?"

Volker thought for a moment. "In a way, I do miss my family and friends, but if I could go back in time right now, I don't think that it would feel like home anymore."

Andi knew exactly what he felt like. Germany had changed so much from what she remembered as a child, but she never regretted coming back – especially now that she met Volker.

"So who is ready for seconds on cake and coffee," Susi asked. "Besides, we need some sustenance before Pete and

Belinda tell us their secret story that I've been waiting to hear for weeks now."

"Is that so," Pete flashed her questioning smile.

"It is so," Andi backed her up. "You guys have been holding out on us, and you owe us an explanation!"

Pete and Belinda looked at each other with love.

"Honey," she said. "I think it's time."

Pete nodded. "Well, I could get bribed into telling it, if I can have another piece of Susi's Black Forest cherry cake," and patted his belly.

"*S*o, let's hear your story," Susi nudged Pete after she took her last bite of her cake.

He checked his watch. "Well, it's already getting late, and Andi has to get ready for her new job in the morning…"

Susi scowled at him. "Don't you dare wriggle out of this one, buddy!"

Pete smiled, because he succeeded again in getting her riled up. "Ouch," he yelled. "What was that for?" He rubbed his arm where Belinda just had punched him.

"Enough with the teasing already, darling," she said.

Belinda's attempt to look stern failed miserably as the corners of her mouth twitched and her sparkling eyes betrayed her. He kissed her on the forehead, and began: "A few years ago, I was working on my PhD in Cultural Anthropology in Ireland. My research focused on Irish folklore and legends, as you can imagine. One day, I was out in the country following a story about fairy sightings. One of the local witnesses gave me directions to where he once had seen a fairy appear. I asked him, if he wanted to accompany me and show me the exact spot, but he unwaveringly refused."

"I probably would have done the same," Susi commented, "because you're such a meanie."

"Well, when I came to the location that the man had described to me," he continued, "I got out of my car and walked to this large tree. A few meters next to the tree, I saw a fairy ring, which is nothing but many mushrooms growing in a large circle. I took a few pictures, and was about to leave, when suddenly, this beautiful maiden in distress appeared out of nowhere within the circle."

Andi raised one of her eyebrows. "That wouldn't be our lovely, Belinda, would it?"

"That would be me," Belinda confirmed, batting her eyelashes at her husband. "I was supposed to marry this fairy prince from another kingdom, who was only out for more money and power," she explained.

Pete felt anger well up inside of him, when she mentioned the fairy prince, but then his facial expressions softened when she continued the story.

"My brave husband sent this guy to the hills to never return and the rest is history."

Volker cocked his head sideways at Belinda. "So you're a fairy? I thought that fairies have pointy ears and wings?"

She smiled. "Now, where have you heard that rumor? Do I look like I have pointy ears? Actually, our race is misunderstood. Yes, we do live in a different world, but we look like humans. We may dress a little different and can use magic, but deep down inside, we laugh, we weep, and we dance, just like you, Volker, or Amanda. Okay, bad examples. In other words, we are just like any other human you would meet on the street."

Amanda, who hadn't said much during the story, finally asked the question that was probably on everybody's mind. "So can you do magic?"

The room went silent, as the friends were waiting in anticipation for her answer.

Pete's face saddened.

Belinda's eyes widened and then she stood up and beat her fist on the table. "Ní bheidh mé a dhéanamh draíochta arís!"

When everyone looked at her perplexed, she repeated the words, this time in German. "Never will I do magic again!"

CHAPTER 8

*A*ll week, Amanda had been thinking about Shai. He was very handsome, and best of all, he didn't seem put off by supernatural stuff. *That's a first,* she thought. Finally, she had met a guy, who wouldn't think that she was cuckoo in the head, once he found out about her unusual store and special abilities.

A few days into the week, Amanda eventually picked up the courage to walk over to the pub for a quick cup of tea. Actually, she didn't care so much about the tea than seeing Shai again. She entered the pub, and a pretty waitress in her mid-twenties greeted her as she wiped down a table with a damp rag. "Have a seat anywhere you like," the waitress called over her shoulder with a strong Irish accent. "I'll be right with you."

Amanda picked a table close to the bar, so Shai could see her right away.

The waitress approached her table and brushed a stray strawberry blonde curl out of her face. "What can I bring you?"

"A cup of hot peppermint tea would be perfect," she

replied as she draped her coat over the back of her chair. She sat down and rubbed her cold hands together to get the feeling in her icy fingers back.

The waitress nodded with a smile and disappeared toward the bar.

While waiting for her tea, Amanda looked around. There was still no sign of Shai. Maybe he was busy working in the back, she wondered.

A moment later, the waitress returned with her tea. "Here you go," she said with a smile. "Be careful, the water is very hot."

The waitress was about to leave, when Amanda took all her courage, "Excuse me, please!"

She turned around. "Yes, honey?"

She froze. This time, she was really out of her comfort zone. What if this is his wife? He didn't have a wedding band on last time she saw him, but that doesn't mean anything these days. It's all or nothing now. "Is Shai here by chance," she asked as casual as she could muster. "He asked me to stop by sometime this week, when I was not too busy."

The waitress shook her head. "No, sorry, he's working the evening shift today. He won't be in for another two hours." The waitress looked at her as if she remembered something. "Wait, is your name Amanda, by chance?"

She nodded. "Yes, it is, why?" How did she know her name?

The waitress held her hands in front of her mouth in excitement until she spoke again, gushing words like a waterfall, "Oh my God, he's been talking about you every day. I should shut up, though, or he'll kill me. But I can't help it! I'm Kyla, by the way, Shai's sister." She stretched her hand out.

Amanda cautiously returned the handshake, not sure

what to make of the woman's outburst. "Nice to meet you," Amanda replied. *At least she's not his girlfriend, or worse yet, his wife,* and felt a wave of relief wash over her.

"May I sit down," Kyla asked. "I don't want to intrude, if you prefer to sit alone."

Amanda motioned to the seat across from her. "Please, I actually could use some company."

Kyla propped her head on her hand, looked at her and smiled. "You know, Shai is all gaga about you. I've never seen him so excited before, except when he got his first car as a teenager."

"Really?" Amanda felt the heat rising to her cheeks. *He likes her...*

Kyla continued. "When we worked on Sunday, he told me that he had met the prettiest woman he's ever seen, other than myself - I guess, he just threw that in to keep the peace around here - and that he can't wait to meet you again. But don't tell him that I told you."

"Don't worry, Kyla. Your secrets are safe with me." *What a fun girl,* Amanda thought. She wished that she had a kid sister like her.

"So, Shai said you own a shop here in Heidelberg?"

Amanda stirred some sugar into her tea. "I do. It's called 'Was das Herz Begehrt', but you probably don't know it."

"Are you serious," Kyla asked. "That's just a block away from here! I walk by there almost every day on my way to work. Unfortunately, I haven't made it inside yet, because I can never seem to be on time for anything. I love how you decorated the window, though. It's so inviting."

"Thanks," Amanda said. "Feel free to stop by any time. I can make some fresh herbal tea, for you."

Kyla smiled. "I'd love that. I have a feeling that we'll

see quite a lot of each other in the near future. You are just what my brother needs."

The bells of the front door chimed "Hi, Kyla, how was..." he stopped in his tracks "Mandy!" He hurried over to her table. "I'm so glad you came to visit."

Amanda smiled. "Yes, I actually do enjoy the atmosphere in here quite a lot."

"Scoot over, Kyla," he said, not breaking eye contact with Amanda.

"Actually, I'll just leave you two alone and finish up the tables, if you don't mind." Kyla winked at Amanda. She grabbed her rag that she had left on the table behind her and got back to work.

"So you've met my annoying little sister, haven't you?"

"Well, I actually like her quite a bit," she said. "She's very bubbly, isn't she?"

"That she is. She used to drive me nuts, but I got used to it." A smile crossed his face as if he remembered some challenging times with his sister, then continued, "Mandy, I'm so glad you stopped by. I know I'm repeating myself. My God, I must sound desperate. Please don't let me scare you away. I'm not really that great when it comes to talking to women. There is just something about you that gets me all nervous and tongue tied."

Amanda blushed. "Why? It's just me. I'm sure you have met much prettier women than me in the pub. I'm surprised you are not married."

Shai's face turned sad. "I used to be married, until I lost my wife and daughter in a car accident five years ago. My grief was so overwhelming that I couldn't function in my normal life anymore. My only hope was to start over in a new place and drown myself in work. So here I am."

"Oh, no! I'm so terribly sorry to hear that," she said

with genuine concern. "Dealing with a loss like that must be very difficult to handle."

He continued, "Well, I put all my time and money into this pub and actually make a decent living now. I just haven't been very interested in women, since the accident. The few I did go out on dates with, quickly lost interest, since I didn't have time to party on the weekends. I'm not sure if I would want to spend the rest of my life with a woman like that anyway. How about you? Someone should have snatched you up a long time ago."

Amanda shrugged. "Apparently, I have the ability to scare people away with my gift. Obviously, you know that ghosts are real, but I have some unconventional healing powers that make men run to the hills." Oh no, she did it again! She might as well finish her tea and put on her coat, before things got worse. To cover her mistake, she tried to justify herself, "I'm not some voodoo priestess or evil witch. If I can help someone with my gift, I will. I'm just a healer." She stirred her tea again and took a sip. "Just a girl trying to help."

Shai looked at her in amazement. "Wow, Amanda. Those guys are idiots!"

"What do you mean?"

"You're helping people; you make them feel better. If I was the lucky one dating you and I came down with the flu, I sure as hell would want you to take care of me, and nobody else!"

A smile escaped her sad face. "You're too kind." Is this guy for real? Not knowing how to handle the situation, she nervously looked at her watch. "I'm sorry, but I have to get back to the store." Did she just detect a twinge of disappointment on his face?

Shai helped her into her coat. "I apologize for not

being here when you arrived. Can I walk you to your store to make up for it?"

She nodded. "Sure, that would be nice."

"Kyla," Shai called over to the bar. "I'll take Amanda back to her shop. I should be back in a bit."

Kyla walked around the bar and gave Amanda a big hug. "Please come back soon. We serve small lunches during the day. So if you're starving, think of us. Besides, I'd love to chat more with you some day."

"I know what you're doing, Kyla! I'm warning you!"

She flashed him an innocent smile. "Hey, I'm not doing anything. I just want to hang out with my new girl-friend!" She squeezed Amanda's shoulder one more time for good measure. "Bye, guys!"

They left the pub and walked down a block on Main Street before they turned into her alley. When they arrived, she looked at him. "Do you have time to come inside for a few minutes?"

Shai nodded. "For you, my dear, always."

She unlocked the door to her shop and let him in.

His jaw dropped. "This place is awesome! It's almost like stepping back in time." He walked through the aisles and picked up a thing or two. "I had no idea that all these treasures were hidden in your shop. A lot of these decorations, like this engraved horseshoe, would work great with the Irish theme in the pub. I'll have to bring Kyla along one day and do some shopping. This stuff is truly amazing!" He looked at some Celtic crosses and moss-covered decor logs. "A lot of your vases and nature knickknacks would make nice center pieces for our tables."

Amanda smiled, "I'm glad you like what I have to offer."

A sheepish grin appeared on his face. "Oh, you don't know the least of it."

Oh my! How is she going to make it through the day with him teasing her like that? When he's gone, she'd have to brew herself a big pot of calming chamomile tea.

*A*ndi returned from her work each afternoon looking forward to seeing Volker. They realized that it was a bad idea to hang around her office during the day; so instead, he spent that time with Pete or Belinda in a semi-translucent state. Volker usually gave her some space to unwind on her way back home in the streetcar. They had abandoned the earpiece idea, because people still stared at her in a strange way when she was talking to herself, even with the device in her ear. Eventually, they figured that it would be less troublesome just to wait to talk until they were alone.

"Honey, I'm home," she announced, which was their code of saying that it's okay for him to appear and hang out for a little while, until she went to work on her novel again.

"Hi, Schatz," he said with a smile standing in her bedroom doorframe, looking stunning, as always.

"I'm so beat!" She stretched out on her bed and shoved her pillow under her head to get comfy. Her job wasn't physically demanding, but she was still trying to get the hang of the German business terms and different writing formats that she had to use for memos, which drained her mentally. "How did your day with Pete go? Did you find something cool?" She rolled over to her side and looked at him as he sat on a ghostly chair next to her bed. Gosh, she never could get enough of looking at him. She wondered what it would be like if he was real. Would he have kissed her already? Probably. Heck, there is no telling of how things would have been if he would only be solid. A little sigh escaped her.

Volker gave her a sad look. "I know. Me, too." He reached his hand out to her face, until he nearly touched her lips with his fingers.

She felt a tingle, not like the usual electric shock when she tried to slug him in the arm. Instead, a slow tingle intensified the closer he came to touch her. She looked at him in surprise.

He pulled his hand back, disappeared for a moment and reappeared next to her on the bed. They looked at each other, while lying on the pillows. "I wish I could hold you," he whispered. Their faces were only inches apart. "This is torture, yet, torture of the best kind."

He came closer. She closed her eyes and felt the tingle on her lips again.

"Oh my God," she whispered. "How am I supposed to survive this? Why can't you be alive?"

"I will be, my love. Soon, I will be," he said, barely audible.

The tingling intensified even more, and she almost thought that she couldn't handle it anymore.

Then suddenly the phone rang.

"No way!" Andi rolled to her back. "Whoever is calling, I hate that person, just so you know!"

Volker grinned. "You might as well answer it."

With a sigh, she dug her handy out of her pocket. "Hallo?" She listened to the voice on the other end. "Oh, hi, Pete." She rolled her eyes then let her head fall back on her pillow. "You know you have bad timing, right?"

"You are having dinner? Or what could I possibly interrupt?"

"Ach, nothing. So, what's up?" Andi turned on the speaker on her phone, so Volker could listen as well.

"I just wanted to call you to let you know that I found some more clues in the book," he said with excitement in his voice. "Apparently, Amelie had followed Ludwig when he snuck out of the castle one night and crossed the river. Since she had to wait to take the next ferry, she could only track him by his footprints, which lead up the Heiligenberg Mountain through the forest."

"Wow, Pete, good thing that the Heiligenberg is so big," Andi giggled. "We won't have any problems finding the box there."

"Very funny, Andi," he said. "Amelie followed him all the way to the top to the old monastery and hid behind one of the buildings to avoid being discovered." Pete paused. "Well, this is how far I've gotten. I still have several pages left to decode, but I'll have to take a break for now, or my eyes will permanently cross."

"I'd like to see that," Andi giggled then became serious. "Thanks, Pete, for doing all this work for us. You don't know how much this means to Volker and me."

Pete harrumphed. "Are you forgetting that my job is to research legends? This will not only benefit you two, it will also benefit me professionally, which is a nice by-product of just following my passion."

"You have a good heart," she said. "Please tell Belinda that I said hello and I can't wait to see you guys again on Saturday."

"Will do."

They hung up the phone and Andi turned to Volker. "Isn't this wonderful news? We just need a more pinpointed, location and we can dig up the box and put the ring in it."

"And have Amanda do the spell," he added, "which hopefully will be revealed in the book."

"Oh, Volker, we're so close to setting you free!"

He couldn't contain his joy. "Soon I will be able to kiss you senselessly, and there is nothing that you can do about it!"

"Who said that I want to do something about it?" She grinned at him.

"Well, in order for me to hug you soon, you will have to eat dinner first, because I can hear your stomach growling as loud as a wolf."

"You mean, a bear," she corrected him. "Are you cooking?" She laughed in delight and heaved her tired body off the bed. "Okay, never mind. I'll make it myself, but be prepared, you will learn how to make me breakfast in bed when you are solid again," and disappeared into the kitchen.

F red stood in front of Andi's house. This had become his after-work obsession. All he had to do is get a hold of this ring that they were talking about and he would be safe from the ghost.

He knew that the girl, Andi, worked at the 'Uni' but had not heard anything about the ghost from her. Apparently, she lived upstairs in the house, so he couldn't see her through the window, unless she walked right by it at night. She did appear to be talking to someone most times. He was certain that it must be the ghost, because nobody else, other than her aunt, would enter the house, and she usually spent most of her time downstairs.

He had also been to Peter's house. The pretty lady with him at the pub seemed to be his wife. Dang it all to hell, he thought. Why is she spending time with a loser like this professor, when she could be with him? He forced himself to focus on his task. He had not found the pale lady yet, but maybe they would meet again. Next Saturday, he had plans to go to the pub. He would make a short appearance, and maybe approach the group to find out what the hoopla was all about. He'd have to come up with a plan to lure some information out of them. Maybe he should play young and dumb and try to persuade them to spill what they know.

As the lights went off in Andi's room, he got into his BMW that he had parked down the street. He was determined to make his move the evening after tomorrow.

$\mathcal{I}$ t was Friday afternoon and Amanda had spent most of the day rearranging inventory on her shelves to keep Shai out of her head. Come on, Mandy, you're acting like a teenager, she thought, and tried to make herself focus at the task at hand. However, not even a minute later, she was back at square one. Will she see him tomorrow night at the pub? So far, she hadn't heard anything from her new friends. Did they not want her to come after she got Belinda upset last weekend? She couldn't blame them.

The bells above her front door chimed. Good, customers. She needed some distraction then was surprised that she saw Andi and Volker standing in her shop. Einstein, her cat, greeted Andi, who stooped down to pet him. Suddenly, the cat looked in Volker's direction and hissed.

"It's okay, Einstein, he's a friend," Amanda tried to calm him and picked him up. "I think he's not quite used to seeing ghosts yet," she explained, slightly embarrassed.

"Hi, Amanda," Andi said, while Volker waved at her with a smile. "I hadn't seen you all week. How are you?" she asked.

Amanda beamed. "Actually, I'm doing pretty well. I

went to the pub the other day for a cup of tea and Shai actually took the time to walk me back to the store."

"I think he likes you," Andi said.

"Really? That's what his sister told me, too," but Amanda didn't sound so confident.

"Come on," Volker encouraged her. "Give him some credit."

"You may be right," Amanda admitted. "Just so many men had left me, because I freak them out."

Andi grabbed her hand. "Shai is a good man, and I don't think you have anything to worry about with him."

"But we're here for a reason," Volker changed the subject. "We wanted to invite you to join us at the pub again tomorrow evening, if you don't have any other plans. Pete has made some progress with your family's book that he wants to share with us."

Amanda's face lit up. "He did? I can't wait to hear what he found out. Thank you for inviting me."

Suddenly, the phone rang. "Excuse me for a moment."

Amanda answered the phone. "Oh, hello, Shai!" She pointed with her free hand at the receiver and mouthed, "Oh my, God, it's Shai!"

Andi grinned and waved good-bye as they left the store. "See you tomorrow evening. We'll be there around seven," she shouted, before she closed the door behind her.

Amanda waved back and returned her attention to Shai. "Sorry, Volker and Andi just left. They invited me over to the pub tomorrow."

"So, are you coming?" The voice at the other end of the phone asked.

Amanda tried to contain her excitement. "Sure. I can't think of any better place to be."

"Well, that really makes my day, Mandy. I have to

work, though, but I'll sneak as much time away as I can to be with you."

Amanda couldn't help to feel flattered. "I can't wait."

"Me either. That's why I wanted to ask you if you were doing something tomorrow afternoon."

"I was going to check out the herbal plant exhibition at the Expo Center. Why?" Amanda was excited as a little schoolgirl. Was he going to ask her out?

"That sounds, uh, interesting. How about I take you to lunch first, and if you'd like some company, I can come with you to look at flowers. I don't have to be at the pub until six in the evening."

Amanda chuckled. "You would go to the plant exhibition with me?"

"Sure, you could teach me a thing or two about home remedies," he added.

"I just didn't think you would be into plants," she said.

"I may have a black thumb, but that doesn't mean that I do not appreciate nature."

Amanda giggled softly. "I'll be ready at 11." She gave him her address and they hung up the phone.

The next morning, Amanda paced in her apartment, ready to go on her date with Shai. She had dressed for the occasion. She wore a dark green knit dress with black tights and black suede boots that came up to her calves. Her brown, wavy hair was pulled back into a French braid and she wore just a touch of makeup. She waited.

At 11.30, he was still not there, and doubt crept up inside of her, muddling with her thoughts. No, maybe he was stuck running an errand, she tried to justify his tardiness. Hopeful that he would come, she waited another half an hour. Every five minutes, she kept peeking out of her window, but there was no sign of him. At 12.30, there was still no Shai. She called the pub to see if he was there, but nobody answered. That's strange, she thought. Maybe he didn't want to talk to her. He must have changed his mind. That horrible and all too familiar feeling of being dumped spread through her body like a wildfire. And there was nothing she could do about it.

Disappointed, she decided to go to the exhibition alone and called Andi to let her know that something came up and she wouldn't be able to come to the Irish Pub tonight.

*A*ndi, Susi and Volker arrived at the pub a little earlier than usual. "Hi, Kyla," Andi called over to the bar in English, surprised to see Shai's sister working the shift. "What have you done to Shai? Did you give him the night off?"

"Nah, he's nursing his mangled arm," she replied while pouring beer in a glass from the tap.

"How in the world did he manage to do that?" Andi walked over to the bar, expecting to hear bad news.

Kyla grinned. "Well, Goofball missed a step when he carried some empty crates into the basement this morning, landed on his arm and bumped his head a few times on the way down. He sure looks a mess. We spent most of the day in the hospital to get him all wrapped up, so I called in some reinforcements to help me run this place for a while," she nodded her head at the two young waitresses taking orders.

"That's terrible! Tell him that we hope he gets better soon, will you?"

"Why don't you tell him yourself? He refused to go home."

"Are you girls talking about me?" Shai stood in the doorway behind the bar.

Andi winced when she saw him. "Ouch, that had to

hurt!" With a decent sized bandage taped to his forehead and his casted arm in a sling, he truly looked like he's been through the wringer.

Shai attempted a grin. "It's not as bad as it seems. More importantly, did Mandy get here yet?"

"Uhm, I'm sorry to tell you this," Andi started, "but she's not coming. She called me this afternoon, saying that something came up and she couldn't make it."

Anger filled his voice. "I'm such an idiot! If I had turned on the basement lights, I wouldn't have fallen, and I wouldn't have stood Mandy up on our date. I'm such an idiot! Now, she thinks I changed my mind about being with her. I tried to call her, but all I had with me was her store number."

"That makes sense now, why she sounded so upset earlier." Andi dug in her purse for her cell phone, looked up Amanda's number and handed it to Shai. "Here, talk to her and tell her to bring her butt over, ASAP!" If anyone could persuade her, Shai could.

"Hi, Mandy," he said when she answered. "It's me, Shai. Listen, I'm sorry…"

Andi gave him some privacy and joined Susi and Volker at their table.

"So, Volker," Susi ventured again, "what did Pete find out?"

Volker sighed. "He's been very secretive and immersed in his work, so I've been hanging out with Belinda most of the time. He must be on to something though, because before I left to meet Andi after work, he had this big grin pasted on his face and told me that I'd have to wait until tonight, like everyone else."

"Whatever it is, it must be big," Andi concluded, feeling sick to her stomach for fear of how their lives would change, once they solved this mystery.

"Speaking of the devil," Susi announced as Pete and Belinda entered the pub.

Pete carried his usual backpack over his heavy coat. "Hi you guys," he yelled.

Andi had to laugh, as Pete stopped in his tracks when he saw Shai.

"My man, what have you done to yourself?"

"Running a pub is a dangerous business. I'll tell you in a minute." He handed Andi her phone back. "Thanks for letting me use this. Mandy has forgiven me and is on her way, as we speak."

Andi felt relieved. If only things between her and Volker were that easy. He must have noticed her watching him. They both knew that their relationship soon would drastically change.

As they were settling in, Amanda rushed in the door.

"That girl is almost as fast as I am in my ghostly state," Volker joked.

She ran straight to Shai. "Oh my God, are you okay?"

He hugged her with his good arm. "Now that you're here, I couldn't be any better!"

"Look at those two lovebirds," Susi cooed audible enough for them to hear.

Amanda gave her a disapproving stare, while Shai tried to hold in a laugh for Amanda's sake. It didn't work.

"What's so funny," she asked.

"You, my dear. You are cute when you get upset," he replied with a sparkle in his eyes.

"Yep, hopelessly in love...," Andi added. "How about something to quench our thirst?"

Kyla nodded. "Coming right up!"

Susi walked over to Amanda's side and pulled her lightly by her arm. "I'm sorry, I just couldn't resist. I didn't mean to make you upset. Come on and join us at the table, will you? I hear Pete has finished decoding the book. Shai, since you're worthless at work today, why don't you come and sit, too?"

Amanda grabbed her purse and her cup of tea and followed Susi. "Actually, I'm quite curious what Pete has discovered." Before she sat down, she stopped to talk to Belinda. "I am so sorry if I upset you last week. If I had known…"

Belinda stood up and gave her a big hug. "You are still worried about that? I should be the one apologizing for freaking out like that. You didn't know."

"So we're good?"

"Yes," Belinda assured, "if you can forgive me for my outburst."

Pete and Susi quickly pushed another table and some chairs against theirs, so they had plenty of room for everyone to sit. Once the friends had settled and gotten all their drinks, Pete unpacked his binder, which by now was overflowing with paper.

"I think you need to upgrade," Andi commented.

Next, he pulled out another stack of packets. "These are the transcripts of Amelie's book," he said with a big smile on his face. "I hope you're not too busy tomorrow."

Everyone's eyes were glued on Pete.

"What are you saying," Volker asked.

"I have finally deciphered the part of the book that tells the location of the jewelry box. It's buried at the Heidenloch at the Heiligenberg across the river. I have also decoded the spell for you, Amanda. It's all written in these packets." He handed them out to the group. "If all goes well, Volker could be one of us by tomorrow."

Andi looked at Volker, seeing the joy in his eyes.

"We can finally be together," he said, smiling at her.

Susi grinned. "Does that mean you're moving in?"

Volker's hearty laugh rang through the round. "If you let me, I would be forever thankful."

"You are practically living with us already, so I don't see why not. You would have to stay upstairs with Andi, though, because I want my privacy, got that?" Susi smiled sheepishly at Andi. "Sorry, honey. He's yours, not mine."

Andi grinned. "I think I can endure his presence for a little while longer."

The friends laughed. "I propose a toast to Amelie to help us bring back Volker."

Andi set her beer down. "What if it doesn't work?"

*F*red waited outside the Irish Pub contemplating his plan to get information about the ghost from the group inside. All week he had been waiting for the perfect moment to confront one of the girls, but for some reason, the right moment never came. Tonight, he would get to the bottom of this ghost business. He had the right to know. It was his family that is involved.

He looked through the pub window again and saw the friends sitting at a longer table today. How should he approach them? Get straight to business or play it safe? If he's to forward, they won't tell him anything. Maybe, he'd just play dumb.

Fred gathered up all his courage. It's now or never. He opened the door and went inside.

"Ah, Mr. Edeler, uh Fred," Peter said, though he did not appear particularly pleased with his visit.

The group looked at him as if he had sprouted horns. "The other descendant," he heard the chick with the braided hair mumble and watched her shift uncomfortably on her chair.

"Hello. Peter, wasn't it?"

"Yes," Peter said casually. "What brings you here? I haven't seen you in this pub before."

Fred shrugged. "I just wanted to try out a new place, do a little change of scenery from my usual haunts. May I join you for a little while? I see you still have a free chair," he said and hung his coat over it. He knew that their ghost would sit there. As he pulled the chair out from the table, the group stared at him in shock. He had that effect on people sometimes, especially when he was playing musical chairs with a ghost.

Fred signaled for a beer and sat down. "So, Peter, have you made any progress with my ancestor's legend yet?"

Pete took a sip of his beer. "Not much. With stories this old, it is sometimes difficult to find reliable information. I have to research the archives some more. Do you by chance remember anything that was passed down by your family that you didn't tell me yet?"

What a liar. He's covering something up. "Nah, not really. I just remember that the ghost of the mason is floating around waiting to take revenge or something like that."

The group listened intently to the exchange of words. "Yes, that's what I read, too. Can you tell me more about it?" Peter asked.

"Well, just that he gets freed, if the princess' ring gets reunited with the jewelry box. I wasn't much into these fairy-tales as a kid, so I didn't pay much attention," Fred admitted. "So, what about that mason ghost? Have you found out anything about him yet?"

Peter looked at his friends and then back at him as if waiting for the group to approve what he was about to say. "Just that he's supposed to spook around the castle grounds." He laughed uncomfortably, and his friends joined him. "I think this ghost is safely doing his pranks at the castle by shifting pictures and shutting doors on people. I don't believe that he will be set free anytime soon, at least until someone finds clues about the ring and the box's whereabouts," Peter concluded.

"I hope so, because I don't want that pissed off ghost to come after me, even though Ludwig has been gone many centuries now," Fred said.

"Now what gives you that idea," Peter asked. "Don't you think he's smarter than that and figured out that you are not the one to blame?"

Fred shrugged. "I'd rather err on the safe side than getting done in by a spook. I don't want him to come back. Don't even want to test the waters." Fred rose from his chair. "Well, I better get going to meet some friends of mine. It was nice talking to you. Enjoy your evening." Fred paid for his beer and left.

Except, he did not leave entirely. He watched through the window as the group focused on the empty chair again. Suddenly, the woman, Andi, sneezed and looked for a tissue in her purse. As her hand fished around in the depth of her bag, something shiny fell to the wooden floor beside her chair. It must be heavy, because the sound of it falling made the entire group look for it. Quickly, Andi picked up the object again, before someone would see it, and then dropped it back into her purse.

I'll be damned, he thought. They've got the ring.

CHAPTER 9

red did not want to miss his chance to intercept
the girls, so he drove to Andi's house and
waited in his car. He had parked down the street again, so
they would not get suspicious.

Thoughts of the ring raced through his mind. He had
to find a way to take it away from Andi and hide it in a
vault. Somewhere, only he had access to it, somewhere to
keep it safe from the friends. He would not risk the mason
taking revenge on him. No way!

The hours dragged on and nothing happened. Occasionally, a car drove by, but not the taxi he was looking for.
What were they doing? They were definitely not the club-
bing type, so they should've been home a long time ago.
Maybe they got too drunk and spent the night in town?
No, that wouldn't make sense; they live too close. He
checked his Rolex for the hundredth time. The hands on
his watch barely moved. It was getting late and he grew
more impatient by the minute.

Fred was about to give up, when a cab pulled up in

front of their driveway. He quickly got out of his car and carefully closed the door to keep the noise to a minimum.

The older woman stumbled out of the taxi first. She managed to open the gate and somehow unlocked the front door, while the other woman stayed behind and settled the cab fare.

This made things a lot easier on him. He raised his scarf and lowered his ball cap, so only his eyes were visible. Protected by the nighttime shadows, he moved toward the taxi.

Andi got out of the passenger seat. "Good night," she said to the cabby and closed the door. She looked around. "What is it, Volker," he heard her say. "Alright, I'll hurry."

The taxi drove off. Now would be his chance.

Within seconds, he jumped the gate that she had closed behind her and took a few long strides toward her.

She turned around and froze when she saw him.

This is too easy! Please don't scream, he prayed. He yanked her purse off her shoulder, hopped the gate, and ran off toward his car. He heard something fall out of the bag, but as long as it didn't sound like metal, he didn't care what it was. Fred's car was waiting for him at the corner, keys in the ignition. He scrambled into his BMW and sped off the other way.

Only after he drove out of the city limits, the possible impact of his actions caught up with him. Oh no, what had he done?

"Oh my God, Volker. He's got the ring," Andrea said, panic in her voice.

"Andi, remember, I love you. Go find the box and then come to find me."

"How can I worry about the box if you are gone?" Small tears formed in her eyes.

"He can't hurt me, remember?" Volker tried to console her.

"Oh no, you are fading!"

"It's Fred. Call the others," he said in a hurry. "You'll have to get the box today, before he sees the transcript of the book and puts two and two together. Don't call the police. They'll only question where you found the ring and it may only complicate things."

"I won't! I won't!" Andi watched in horror as he faded away into nothing. The last thing she heard from him was, "I love you, mein Schatz."

"I love you, too," she whispered into the darkness.

Quickly, she ran into the house to tell Susi, however, her aunt was groaning on her couch, and therefore not very helpful. She dialed Pete's number from their home phone.

"Pete, Fred stole my purse! Volker is gone!" A loud sob escaped her throat, before she continued, "We have to find the box right now! The ring is gone!"

Pete tried to calm her. "Slow down, Andi, what happened?" He listened as she told him the short version of the story. "Let me call Shai and Amanda to pick you up. They didn't drink anything tonight. Susi is probably not up to any of this right now. I'll grab some flashlights and tools and Belinda can drive me. She was feeling a bit off and didn't drink anything, either," he said. "We'll meet up at the Heidenloch at the Heiligenberg as soon as you can make it."

They hung up and a few minutes later, Amanda called. "Shai and I are on our way to pick you up. Don't wait outside alone. I'll call you when we get to your house."

Andi grabbed some small gardening tools from the

shed and shoved them into a bag. Next, she rummaged in the kitchen for a flashlight and some other things they may need. She was about out of ideas, when the phone in the kitchen rang.

"Andi, are you ready?" Amanda's voice sounded through the phone. "We're in front of your gate."

"I'll be right there!" Andi hung up the phone and ran toward the car. She kicked something in the darkness and looked down by her foot. It was her wallet. Thank God! She picked it up and looked inside. All her IDs and credit cards were still there, and with a sigh of relief, she stuffed it in the bag with her equipment. "I brought some more flashlights, and garden tools - sorry, that's all I could come up with in such short notice."

"At this point, I'm sure anything will help," Shai said.

They drove to Heidelberg, crossed the Neckar River into Neuenheim, and then rode up the Heiligenberg, until they reached the parking lot close to the Heidenloch. Pete's car was already there. They took their gear and joined Pete and Belinda in the search for the box.

Pete kneeled a few feet away from a hut that was built around the hole and he attempted to dig into the ground with a small shovel. "Hey, welcome to the Heidenloch. I'd love to tell you the story of it, but right now, I'm more worried about getting this jewelry box out of the ground. Can I have some more light, please?"

Andi shone her flashlight opposite from Belinda's.

"Thanks, Andi." Pete had to use a sledgehammer to force his shovel into the frozen ground, once he had gotten past the soft layer of pine needles and leaves. "Damn it! This is going to be harder than I thought."

Shai looked for another shovel. "Where can I dig? I only have one working arm, but it's better than nothing."

"Just start a little to the left of me. With any luck, one

of us will find the box soon. I had to guess when I was pacing out the distance, because they built this hut around the hole. But I'm certain that it has to be around here somewhere."

While holding the flashlight, Andi began to lose hope. Shai looked pathetic struggling with his small shovel. At this pace, they wouldn't get anywhere anytime soon. She had to do something to expedite the search. "Shai," she said, "do me a favor and hold this flashlight for me. I think that I'll take over digging for a while, if you don't mind."

*F*red finally arrived at home. He couldn't believe that he just stole the lady's purse. Man, I really screwed up this time, he thought. Hopefully, he'd have some time to get the ring into his safe deposit box before the cops would find him. He'd rather spend a little time in jail than having this mason take revenge on him. He grabbed Andi's purse from the passenger seat and ran into his house. Impatiently, he felt for the light switch in the kitchen and flipped it on. Next, he dumped the contents of her purse on the cluttered kitchen table. He found a folded document, lipstick, tissues, change. Where is the ring? Don't tell me she took it out of her purse? That would be just his luck. He stuck his hand into the bag to make sure he got everything out. The main compartment was empty, so he looked for hidden zippers. Why do these purses have to be so complicated? he thought.

Ah, he found a zipper in the inside of the bag. He opened it and pulled out band-aids, safety pins and... bingo! He removed the ring from the pocket and marveled at it. It was beautiful. A little old-fashioned for his taste, but that was to be expected from a treasure this old. All he had left to do was to drive to his bank in

Mannheim and store it in his safe deposit box. Maybe he'd even put that stuff back in Andi's purse and drop it off somewhere that she would find it. That's the least he could do for her. It also would greatly ease his feeling of guilt.

When he glanced up, he saw a tall man in medieval clothing standing in front of him. Surprised, he dropped the ring, fell backwards over a chair and lay sprawled on the kitchen floor. He scrambled back to his feet and stepped back toward the refrigerator. "Are... are you the mason?"

"Yes, I am. Return the ring," the mason demanded. "It is not yours to keep."

"Bu... bu... but I can't," he stammered. "If I return it, you'll become real and take revenge on me."

The ghost seemed amused. "I could take revenge on you right now, if I wanted to. Or I could haunt you until the end of your days. I wasn't going to do anything to you, but now after what you have done to Andi, I have changed my mind. How dare you rob an innocent woman?"

"No, please don't," Fred pleaded. "I just wanted to hide the ring, so you wouldn't be able to come back. I'm the only one who is left from that bloodline, and since my ancestor has been long dead, I thought you'd come after me."

The ghost tilted his head as if trying to understand what he was saying. "So, you steal Andi's purse? You commit a crime and tick me off in the process? What were you thinking? It is almost as if you wanted trouble."

"No, it's the opposite. I don't want any trouble from you. How did you even get here?"

The ghost grinned. "You brought me here by stealing the ring. When you touched it, you were able to see me. Now you are stuck with me, unless you return the ring to its rightful owner. Drive to Andi's house and return her belongings, including the ring," the mason demanded.

"No, I can't do that," Fred replied, looking to put some distance between him and the mason.

Suddenly, the mason swung his arm in rage. The lights flickered, and the ghost cleared a corner of his messy table with one sweep. Clutter flew through the air, barely missing Fred. "You will do as I say, or I will hurt you next! You do not want to experience what I am capable of."

Fred was terrified. He thought ghosts couldn't be violent. Maybe he was wrong. To escape the mason's wrath, he scrambled out of the room to get his jacket and car keys. "Okay, I'll return the stuff, but promise me to leave me alone." Reluctantly, he went back into the kitchen and tossed Andi's contents back into the purse.

They drove toward Andi's house. "Keep driving," the ghost told him, "I will check on Andi," then he disappeared and, within seconds, reappeared.

"She's already gone. Drive to the Heidenloch. What are you waiting for? Hurry," the mason urged him.

Fred stepped on the gas and took the Autobahn toward Heidelberg. At this point, he'd do anything to pass the ring and the ghost off to someone else.

"Keep driving," the ghost demanded and vanished again.

Fred glanced at the passenger seat just to make sure that the ghost was really gone. Relieved, he thought of what to do next. The ghost surely was unpleasant. He could probably do some real damage to him, once he regained strength after the box and ring were reunited. No, he couldn't let that happen. He was already in trouble. He had to make the ring disappear. Fred took the next exit, and with squealing tires made his way to his 24-hour safe deposit box.

Seconds later, the ghost sat in the passenger seat again. "Where are you going?"

"I'm taking the ring to a safe place, where nobody, other than me, can get to it."

The now furious mason yelled, "Turn this car around at once!"

No, he had to do this. Instead of turning around, he tried his best to ignore the annoying mason ghost in his passenger seat. His mind was buzzing. If he left the ring in his bank deposit box, he'd have a constant companion. However, he didn't believe that this ghost could do more harm than knocking some things off the table. If he could, he would have already done so. Eventually, he would give up and leave him alone. The only problem would be this group of ghost followers, but he could deal with them later. He didn't think that the Andi woman had recognized him, when he took her purse. Speaking of which, "Shouldn't you be with your girl-friend? I bet she needs you after what has happened to her." Maybe he'd leave again. Fred could only hope.

"I want to see where you're taking the ring first, so I can tell the others where to find it," the mason replied.

"I can save you the trouble. We're going to my bank in Mannheim, where I have a safe deposit box. Your precious ring will be secure there, even from your friends. You can leave now." He glanced at the passenger seat again. Dang, he thought. The ghost is still here. Oh well, he might as well get used to his new companion.

A few minutes later, they arrived at the bank. Fred swiped his card and entered the foyer, then swiped his card again and punched in a code on the keypad to enter the room with the deposit boxes. He stopped in front of box number 8934 and opened it with his card and another pin number.

He dug out the ring from his jeans pocket and stuck it in the drawer. Fred closed its lid, returned it into its cubby and let the door click shut. "So, mason. The ring is safe now and your friends can no longer get to it, not even over my dead body. Have a great life." Fred walked away.

"Not so fast. I'll be haunting you until the day you die," the ghost threatened.

Fred shrugged his shoulders. "Suit yourself."

He continued his drive back toward Schwetzingen. A few kilometers down the Autobahn, Fred noticed that the ghost began to fade. He smirked, as the mason now only was a waning wisp of fog. "Good riddance!"

With the annoying ghost gone, Fred decided to stop at his local bar for a few drinks to numb the nagging feeling of guilt and fear of what was yet to come. He knew that trouble had just begun and he was not looking forward to dealing with the aftermath. "Whisky, please!"

Three drinks later, he still did not feel the slightest buzz. That damn woman and her purse! Maybe it would ease his conscience if he just returned the damn thing. Pissed off about being such a soft egg, he paid his tab. He was actually in quite the mood for a little confrontation. Fred got in his car and sped off to the Heiligenberg.

*V*olker knew that Fred wouldn't go far for the rest of the night, when he parked his car in front of a bar. His first thought was of Andi. He was worried to death about her, after she had been robbed by that sorry excuse of a human being. Now that Fred was safely tucked away, he visualized Andi in his mind and found himself at the Heidenloch. He needed to tell her that Fred had the ring locked up in his bank.

She looked so sad, yet determined to dig the hole in the

hard, frozen ground. It broke his heart to see her suffering. If, or better yet, when things finally fell into place, he would make sure that he would never have to see her so desperate again.

"Andi, can you hear me?" She didn't even flinch. He cursed Fred's name for locking up the ring and keeping him from his love. "Andi," he tried again, much louder this time. Nothing.

Volker paced back and forth. How could he communicate with her, or any of his friends for that matter? He yelled again, this time from the top of his lungs then, in frustration, kicked some leaves on the ground, when they did not respond.

"What was that?" Amanda shone her flashlight to the spot where the leaves were kicked up. "That must have been a small wind gust."

Before she could look away, he kicked even more leaves into the air.

"Guys, do you think that Volker is doing this?" The friends stepped closer and looked at the small, clear spot on the forest ground.

"If this is you, Volker," Shai said, "can you try to write in the loose dirt here?" He moved a few more leaves to make more writing space.

Volker drew all the energy he could from the car lights, without draining the batteries completely.

His friends stared at the flickering headlights and then turned their attention at the bare spot.

He began to write: 'FRED RING BANK BOX MANNHEIM.' That's about all he could muster without draining their flashlight batteries as well.

Pete shook his head. "Son of a gun! I'd never thought he'd stoop that low, but then, I almost expected it. Let's get these cars started up to recharge the batteries, or we'll get stranded later."

He heard a small sob coming from Andi's direction. How badly did he want to hold her and comfort her, as small tears rolled down her sad face? She stared into the forest in front of her. "I love you, Volker," she whispered.

Not knowing how to respond, he kneeled down opposite of her and slowly kissed her on her lips.

She dropped her shovel, and with her gloved fingers, touched her mouth. Another sob escaped her and this time the tears began to flow freely.

Volker's heart broke. He did not want to make her feel worse. All he wanted to do was let her know that he was there with her.

Amanda rushed to Andi's side and hugged her. "It will be okay. We will save him."

Andi now sobbed uncontrollably in Amanda's arms.

Volker stood and watched, unable to console her. It tore him up inside seeing her like this. He felt her pain.

A few minutes later, Andi's sobs subsided. With new resolve, she grabbed the shovel again and began to dig even faster. "I have to find that box!"

Unwilling to stand around idle and watch Andi torture herself, he decided that he had to do something to help her. The only thing he could think of was to find Ludwig von Dossenheim - if he still hung around this ghostly realm.

Fred drove like a maniac into Heidelberg, crossed the Neckar River into Neuenheim, and wound his way up the Heiligenberg. He arrived at the covered hole in record time and parked his car next to the others. He saw the flickering of flashlights in the fog a few meters behind the hut and heard the group's voices echoing in the woods.

"Well, hello there," he shouted. All eyes were on him.

"Give me the ring back," Andrea yelled at him.

"Now, not so fast," he said. "Why would I do that? It already appears that I no longer have to worry about the ghost, unless I go to Mannheim. I guess, he's tied to the ring and as long as I keep my distance from it, he can't bother me." He felt pretty smug about himself. "By the way, here is your purse. I don't have a need for it anymore." He tossed it at the woman. "Everything is still in it, other than the ring." Fred felt better already. Nothing tops doing a good deed.

Pete walked toward Fred. "Are you really that dense? Do you really believe that Volker will take revenge on you?"

"The legend says so. Also, I'm the only one left to settle the score with, so guess what? The buck stops with me, and I'm not about to find out what he will do to me." He didn't care how hard they tried to persuade him into giving up the ring.

Peter carefully ventured. "You are aware that legends are stories of events passed down through generations. They are not all true, but of course, you are smart enough to know that." He paused to let the message sink in. "The mason, himself, told us that he does not want to harm you. He just wants his life back. He's not angry with you."

He didn't believe a thing Peter said. Fred recalled the altercations in his house and in his car earlier that evening. "Oh yes, he is!"

Suddenly, Fred's knees felt as if they were about to buckle. He saw a whitish glow in the in the shape of an older man appear in front of him. However, this was not the moody mason he had seen earlier. A few meters to his right, a little distanced from the crowd, appeared another ghost.

Andrea found her voice first. "Markus!"

Who the hell is Markus?

"I have Volker with me," Markus said. "He asked me to help him find the Baron Ludwig von Dossenheim."

The older ghost bowed before them. "That would be me, at your service."

Fred couldn't help but gape at his ancestor.

The man in the royal garb addressed Fred. "I understand that you are related to me?"

Fred nodded slowly, unsure what was going to happen next.

"I heard talk that the ring was found, and you stole it," the ghost continued.

Again, Fred nodded.

"You must bring it back immediately. I've been waiting here for over 400 years, protecting the jewelry box. I am tired, I will never get married to the princess, and I'm ready to move on, to whatever that means."

"But he'll kill me, if he comes back," Fred pleaded.

"Son, his anger is with me." The ghost turned his gaze next to Andi. "Mason Metz, for all the grief and pain I have caused you, I deeply regret what I have done. All these centuries ago, I made a mistake, because of my greed and my careless ways. I feared your revenge and the only way I knew to protect myself, was by hiding the box. Will you forgive me for the horrid deed I imposed on you?"

Markus discretely harrumphed, "Volker accepted the apology."

The ghost continued to speak to Fred. "All the mason wants is to continue living his life as a mortal with his true love," then he winked at Andi with a smile. "You, my son, have the responsibility to right the wrongs and return his life to him. He promised that he would not harm you. Now go and get the ring, so I can rest in peace!"

Fred nodded and scrambled to his car to fetch the ring from the safe deposit box. He still did not trust the mason.

*A*s Fred drove off to retrieve the princess' ring, Ludwig turned to them slightly amused. "Either you miscalculated, or you do take small steps," he said in a strong dialect, similar to Volker's.

Andi didn't find his joke very funny. She just wanted Volker to come alive and be with her. This was serious! She couldn't believe how anyone could joke about this task with Volker's life depending on the outcome.

Pete looked at Ludwig puzzled. "What are you saying? I took 13 paces to the north of the hole and then three to the west."

Ludwig laughed heartily. "I don't know who told you the number of paces, but it should be 18 to the north and three to the west." He demonstrated by walking into the hut to the edge of the hole and walked 18 paces out, through the wall of the hut, stopped, made a 90 degree turn to the left and walked three paces more. "This should be the place where the jewelry box is buried."

Andi's insides churned. If this is really the spot, and the jewelry box is still there, she could hold Volker in her arms tonight. Or not. The butterflies fluttering around inside of her stomach made her feel queasy.

Shai walked over to her. "Are you okay? You look a little nervous."

"I'm okay," she managed.

Pete fetched his big shovel and walked to the spot where Ludwig stood. "Please, allow me."

Ludwig stepped aside, and everyone watched anxiously

as Pete removed the loose layer of leaves and soil. As he dug deeper, the frozen dirt again was more compact.

With trembling hands, Andi shone her flashlight at the spot where Pete dug.

"Please, let me take over," Shai took the flashlight out of her hand.

Relieved, she released her iron grip and let it slide into Shai's waiting hand.

Pete continued to dig for another 15 minutes until he hit something metal with the tip of his shovel.

Andi sighed as Pete lifted the dirty, golden box out of the ground. It was studded with what appeared to be colorful gems. Carefully, he removed more dirt with Andi's little garden shovel. He handed the box to Belinda, who used her empty fabric bag to wipe off the majority of the mud, and then handed the box to Andi. "Since you are the true love, we leave it up to you to open it."

Andi carefully inspected the jewelry box then laughed. "Heck no! I've watched too many horror movies; next thing you know, I'll open the box and somebody's rotten finger bones are neatly arranged in it."

"Chicken," Shai teased, and Ludwig giggled.

Andi glanced at him. "Did you have something in there when you hid the box?"

"No, Ms. Andrea. It was empty," he confirmed.

Slowly, she tried to open up the metal box, but it wouldn't budge. She didn't want to break it. "What now?"

"Maybe we need to clean the hinges better," Pete suggested and took the box from her. "Let me see some of the bottled water you are holding, Belinda."

She handed him the bottle and he poured some water over the hinges to wash out the dirt and debris. He gave the hinges a final swipe with his gloved hand, and then handed it back to Andrea. "Here you go. Try now," he said.

Andi carefully wiggled the lid, and indeed, the hinges now seemed to work. With her heart almost beating out of her chest, she lifted the lid a few millimeters at a time. Suddenly, a roach-like beetle crawled out of the box and on her hand. Andi screamed and tossed the box a safe distance away from her and then shook the bug off her hand.

With the impact, the lid broke off the jewelry box and came to rest a few inches away from the box itself.

When she realized what she just had done, she held her hand in front of her mouth. "Oh my God, what have I done? What if the magic no longer works now?" Tears came rolling down her face again. She couldn't believe how a small bug like that could ruin everything. How could I be so skittish, she scolded herself? "Stupid, stupid, stupid," she yelled.

Everyone around her went silent. Even the ghost.

Discouraged, Andi hung her head low. "Let's try anyway…"

*A*s Fred drove to Mannheim to retrieve the ring, he kept thinking that he couldn't believe what he was about to do. What if Volker was just pretending that he wasn't going to harm him, until he came back to life, that is? He wasn't so sure what to expect. Then, there was the matter of his ancestor. Of course, Ludwig wouldn't mind giving up the ring. His princess was already dead, and he was sitting on that hill for centuries. Naturally, he was bored. He would want to get the hell away from this place, too, if he were trapped like Ludwig.

Fred yawned. It had been a while since he had pulled

an all-nighter like this, which was usually with a pretty girl. Come to think of it, he would've been better off just going to a club, instead of robbing the Andi chick. Then he might have been at home by now, having steamy sex with an exotic beauty. He shook his head in disbelief.

Almost in Mannheim, he looked at the passenger seat and saw Volker materialize. He rolled his eyes. Great, him again. He tried to think of something intelligent to say, but then decided to cut to the chase: "How do I know you're telling the truth about not taking revenge on me," he asked the ghost, eyes fixed on the road.

Volker looked back at him. "You would have to trust me, since I have no proof. However, I promise that I'm good for my word. Please know that I am very grateful that you are returning the ring to Andi."

Fred nodded and continued to concentrate on the road.

They drove into the city and soon arrived at the bank. Fred used his card to gain entry to the facility and then into the room with his lockbox. He punched in his code and opened his cubby to retrieve the ring. Fred glanced at the sparkling piece of jewelry once more, but disdain replaced the awe that he had felt the first time he saw it. He stuck it in his jeans pocket, closed the small cubby door and returned to his car.

"I've got it," he announced with a big yawn and headed back to Heidelberg. The silence in the car was awkward and uncomfortable. Fred was not in the mood for chatting. He fought to keep his eyes open but caught himself dozing off every few minutes.

"Are you okay, Fred? Maybe we should find something to talk about to keep you awake," Volker suggested. "Not that I mind an accident, since I'm already dead, but I rather have this ring delivered before sunrise."

Fred nodded again between yawns. "Okay, so, how do you know Ludwig?"

Volker sighed. "Great, you couldn't find a better topic, huh? But I guess I owe you the truth." Watching Fred drive, he continued: "It all started when I was working as a mason at the castle. One day the princess admired my work, I was pretty damn good, I must say, and she paid me some compliments. Baron Ludwig must have overheard the conversation and he became jealous. His plan had always been to marry the eligible princess to lift him up in station. However, for her to choose him as a bridegroom, he needed to impress her, and he couldn't accomplish that while she was admiring my work. To get the focus off of me, he set me up and tried to get in the princess's favor by returning the ring and its box, which you already know did not work out the way he had planned."

Volker had filled him in with the remainder of the story until they arrived in Heidelberg. Fred just wanted to get this over with and take a nap. They crossed the bridge to Neuenheim and headed for the mountain. He rubbed his burning eyes with his fingers as he listened with half an ear to what Volker was saying. His mind still drifted off every few minutes.

Suddenly, Fred sat up straight in his seat. "What was that? Did you say something?"

Volker looked at him concerned. "Are you sure you're okay to drive? You look like you are about to fall asleep."

He then yawned again. "I'm good. I can make it."

Suddenly, a family of wild boar came out of the wood line and crossed the winding mountain road in front of his car. He swerved to the left, barely missing the first one. Not that he cared much about the pigs, but he knew of the damage a full-grown boar can do to his new vehicle. When he failed to regain control of his vehicle, Fred cursed and gaped in horror as his car went off the road and down the hill into the forest. They came to an abrupt stop, when his five months old luxury BMW wrapped itself around a fir tree.

Fred woke up with his head resting on the steering wheel. He had a massive headache. What the hell happened? He thought. Was he bleeding? Pain shot through his left arm as he tried to feel his forehead. Instead, he lifted his right arm and adjusted his rearview mirror. Damn. He had a large gash where he must have hit the steering wheel. He looked over to his passenger seat, but only found a tree trunk where Volker had sat before the accident. The seat itself was now somewhere squished behind him. It dawned on him that his beloved car was a total loss and he hung his head in defeat.

"Fred," Volker called from outside of his driver-side window.

He blinked the dripping blood out of his eye, so he could see where the voice was coming from.

"I've told the others. They are on the way and they have called an ambulance."

Fred nodded and closed his eyes for a while.

What seemed like hours later, Shai and Amanda finally stood outside of his car.

"Your car sure makes a nice Christmas tree ornament," Shai joked. "Just needs a little more color, that's all. You should've bought a red Beamer instead."

Fred sighed. "What happened?"

"Volker came to get us. He said that you swerved for some boar. Since he couldn't help you himself, he came to get us. Pete already called an ambulance. It should be here soon. While we're waiting, can you hand us the ring, so we can continue with the ceremony?"

He heaved his arm up, shifted to reach into his right

pocket and pulled out the large ring. By now, he wanted nothing more than to get rid of it. "Here you go. This damn thing is nothing but bad luck!"

Shai took the ring from Fred and handed it to Amanda with a mischievous smile. "I don't suppose you could do some magic on him to fix him up, Mandy, could you?"

Amanda looked at Fred. "I'd like to help you, but I already hear the sirens down the hill. Let's let the professionals take care of you." She grinned back at Shai. "We'll wait with you until the medics are here, but I do believe you'll be taking a trip to the hospital."

"Great," Fred cussed. "I had plans for tomorrow."

"I'm sure they can wait a few days," Shai said. "Okay, medics are here." Shai gave Fred his business card. "Call me if you need anything."

Fred slipped in and out of consciousness and heard bits and pieces of Shai explaining to the emergency doc what had happened, while the medics worked on him.

"So what brings you folks up here this late at night, or early in the morning, rather," the doc asked.

"We were on a date." He winked at Amanda, who in turn snuggled up to him and smiled.

"Good thing you found this guy," he said. "Before you move on, please give the police officer your info and a short statement," he pointed at the Polizeiauto that just rolled up. "We'll take care of Mr. Edeler."

Fred heard a car drive off as the medics loaded him onto a stretcher and carried him up the hill to the ambulance. He looked one last time at his car then his world went black.

· · ·

*A*ndi stared at the approaching headlights.

"That's Amanda and Shai," Volker announced.

Another wave of anxiety welled up inside of her. She looked at Volker, whose face had dread written all over it.

"She has the ring," Shai announced, while Amanda waved it up in the air for everyone to see. "Fred is on his way to the hospital, that poor soul."

"I bet he's talking about all sorts of crazy stuff like ghosts, witches, and such in the ambulance," Belinda giggled. "They'll probably keep him in the psych ward for a while, before releasing him out into the public again."

"There is such a thing as karma, I do believe," Pete said, holding his belly from laughing so hard. He harrumphed as he tried to regain some seriousness. "Shall we commence with the ceremony before the first joggers arrive?"

The group grew somber as they gathered in a circle. Amanda handed the ring to Andrea. "I believe this is yours?"

Andi's hands shook, when she accepted the ring then looked at the jewelry box, which was now in two pieces. A thousand thoughts cursed through her mind. How could she be so squeamish and toss the box? Will it still work? What if it doesn't? Could she live with the guilt of being responsible for trapping Volker in his form forever?

Volker looked at her. "It'll be alright, no matter what happens."

"How can it be alright when I destroyed the box by being such an idiot?" Tears were streaming down her worried face. "Your life was in my hands and I tossed it."

He tried to soothe her. "Come on, Schatz. We don't even know if it is broken. Let's try it. I am so ready to finally hold you in my arms and kiss you like there is no tomorrow!"

Andi saw a glint of a smile on his face and tried to pull herself together. "And what if this doesn't work? What happens if you disappear forever?" The thought of losing him horrified her.

"I can only hope that I will return to life and be with you. However, should something go wrong, know that I will be in a better state than I am in now. And most important, remember that I love you. We have to live with what fate hands us. I only hope that if you were meant for me, that I would be allowed to return to you. God, I hope so."

Andi watched Volker rake his fingers through his hair. This could be the last time she would see him do that. She committed every single second of these last moments to her memory. "I love you, too," she finally managed.

A moment later, Pete broke the silence. "Well, let's do this." Belinda hooked her arm into his and cuddled up a little closer. "Andi," he handed her the box, which he tenta- tively repaired with some duct tape that he still had in the trunk of his car. "You know what to do."

Andrea looked at Volker one more time with tears in her eyes as she held the ring in one hand and the mangled box in the other. Will he return? Will he vanish? Will she see him ever again? She took a deep breath. "I'm so sorry if this doesn't work. I love you."

Volker braced himself for the worst. "I love you, too, no matter what happens."

Andrea inserted the ring into the metal jewelry box and closed the lid, bracing herself for some sort of magic, maybe some strange light emanating from it, or maybe a tingle of electricity. She waited and stared at the box, then at Volker.

Nothing happened.

Andi sobbed. "I broke the damn thing!"

"Not so fast," Pete interrupted. "We still need to do the spell. Amanda, are you ready?"

She nodded. "You didn't mis transcribe any of the words again, did you?"

"I certainly hope not," he assured. "Let's give it a try."

Amanda closed her eyes to concentrate. When she opened them again, her eyes were focused on the jewelry box with the ring inside. Loud and with determination, she spoke the words from the book:

Vereinigt für immer.
So der Schatz in der Truhe,
Wie der Geist mit seiner Versprochenen.
Unzertrennlich für immer,
Von nun an.

When she had finished, all eyes were on Volker, even Ludwig's. Slowly, Volker began to fade.

"Something is happening," Belinda exclaimed.

Andi mouthed a final, "I love you" at Volker just before he was gone. She looked around searching for any sign of the real Volker to appear. Nothing. Seriously, what did she expect? That he would appear out of thin air from behind a tree? That he would materialize in solid form right in front of her? Whom was she kidding? He was a ghost, after all. Confused and disappointed, she walked off and sat on the nearby bench.

The baron still stood next to Pete. He bowed deeply to the group. "Thank you for releasing me. It is time for me to move on now. I am free." With a somber smile, he vanished.

Belinda looked at Amanda. "What just happened? Did we release him instead of Volker? Was there anything weird in the spell?"

Amanda shook her head. "Unless Pete found something in the book that mentions Ludwig's ghost..."

Pete also looked perplexed. "The book just mentioned Ludwig's death, but not that he was cursed. Maybe he just meant that we released him from his bondage with the box?"

"Only time will tell," Amanda added. She joined Andi on the park bench and drew her into a hug to console her. She lifted Andi's chin. "He probably has to go through some sort of transformation. Give the spell time to work."

Andi was devastated. "What if I lost him?"

They waited a little longer to see if there was any sign of Volker, but when the first daylight broke, Pete walked up to Andi and kneeled in front of her. He looked up at her and propped his hands on her knees. "I think we should go home. If he were to come back, he would have already been here."

Andi lifted her hand and wiped a hot tear from her cheek. Besides freezing her butt off and almost falling asleep while sitting down on the bench, she really wanted to stay and wait for Volker to return. What if he comes back and she misses him? No, she couldn't leave without him. She had to wait.

Amanda tried her luck. "I know it's tough, but you really should go and get some rest. Maybe he is at home waiting for you?"

Andi stood up. "What if he is not waiting for me at all? Or what if I go and Volker is left here in the woods?"

Pete put a hand on her shoulder, "Let's get some rest and we will come back later to check the area again."

Andi just couldn't abandon Volker. The despair nearly tore her heart into pieces. "He will come back! Maybe it just takes a while. He may appear just as we leave. I can't do it!" She no longer could hold her tears and just let them go. Belinda drew her tight into her arms again and let her sob.

When she was all cried out, Amanda offered her another tissue, which she gladly accepted and blew her nose. Maybe the others were right. She needed to get home and get some sleep, warm up, and get some food into her tummy. "I'm ready," she admitted. "Let's go home."

CHAPTER 10

*a*ndi woke up a few hours later, when the afternoon sun hit her face. She turned around to keep the bright light out of her swollen eyes. "Volker?" She whispered his name, just in case he was in the room with her. "If you can hear me, can you give me a sign?" She waited a few moments, but nothing happened. Disappointed, she hugged her pillow a little tighter.

As she lay in bed, she recounted the last minutes she had with Volker last night. His face at the moment they said their final good-bye was burned into her memory. Her heart ached for him. Would she ever see him again or was the memory of him all she had left?

Her mind flashed to another scene - the fateful moment when she opened the jewelry box and the bug crawled on her hand. How could she be so stupid to toss the box away? She was such a wuss! And because she broke the box, Volker was now gone forever.

Suddenly, a pain so sharp as if someone stabbed her with a knife pierced her gut. It was all her fault! He could have been alive and lay next to her right now. She couldn't resist reaching out to feel for him, but as she expected, all she found was her pillow and her sheets, and no Volker. Disappointed and feeling guilty, she grabbed her blanket and curled up into a ball, trying to shut out the world.

Twenty minutes later, her stomach made unmistakable growling sounds. Annoyed, she tried to recollect when she had her last meal. Thinking back, she realized that she hadn't eaten since she and Susi stopped at a take-out window and ate a gyros, before they went to the pub last night. Even though that usually kept her satisfied for many hours, it didn't hold until mid-afternoon. All she really wanted was to stay in bed and wallow in her sorrow. However, her stomach had other plans, when another fierce growl announced the need for food.

Reluctantly, she rolled out of bed and shuffled toward the kitchen. Still sick from all the guilt and sadness, she didn't have an appetite. She opened the fridge, but nothing seemed fit to fill her void. Next, she looked through her cabinets and found half a box of oatmeal with chocolate chips in it. I guess, that should do, she thought. She grabbed a bowl from the other cabinet, dumped some oatmeal in it and topped it with cold milk. She always enjoyed eating her oatmeal cold. After she put some food in her belly, she hopped into the shower. Maybe she'd feel better afterward. She had to get on with her life. Somehow.

Just as she finished blow-drying her hair, the phone rang. "Hello?"

"Andi, it's Pete."

"Hi, Pete, what's up?"

Pete ventured slowly. "Belinda and I were thinking of checking the Heidenloch in a bit. Would you like to come along?"

Andi's hopes for seeing Volker were low, but what the

heck, she thought, maybe it would give her closure, if nothing else. "Yes, I would like to come with you."

*W*ith mixed feelings, Andi rang Pete and Belinda's doorbell. She had time to think about the odds of finding Volker while she was riding in the streetcar, and eventually concluded that it was very unlikely to find her love on the mountain. On the other hand, she had to try. She still had hope.

Belinda opened the door and enclosed her in a tight embrace. "I'm so sorry for what you are going through! I wish things would have worked out as planned." Belinda let go of her and led her into the dining room.

Pete sat at the table with a cleaning cloth in his hand. The jewelry box with the ring inside sat in front of him. "I know it isn't much of a consolation, but I repaired and cleaned the jewelry box for you as good as I could." He handed her the shiny golden box, topped with pretty gems in a similar fashion as the ring itself.

"Thank you, Pete. I love it," she said rather robotically, remembering how she broke it.

Pete motioned her to have a seat. "It's the least I could do for you, and your future will be secured, if you choose to sell these items. Just don't tell anyone that you 'found' them and the other circumstances, because, technically, those artifacts should go to the state."

"Don't worry. I think I would rather hang on to them anyway," Andi contemplated. "It's all I have to remind me of Volker."

"Listen," Belinda took a seat next to Andi. "I talked to Amanda while you were on your way up here. She said that she would like to try the spell again this afternoon, if you are okay with it."

Andi nodded. "I don't think it would hurt if we tried, do you?" She looked at Pete for direction.

Pete shook his head. "Maybe, now that the box is fixed, we could get the spell to work. What have we got to lose?"

"Right," Andi said with little hope in her voice. "I'm all for it."

"Great!" Belinda replied and got on the phone to return Amanda's call.

Amanda showed up twenty minutes later and they all squeezed into Pete's car to drive to the Heidenloch. Andi's first impulse was to look around for clues that Volker had been here or that he was alive. She found one of their small flashlights they had forgotten when they left this morning. She walked around some more, trying to find anything else that could prove that he was alive. "Volker," she called. "Are you there?" Silence.

A few steps farther, she found the hole that the box was buried in. She looked a little closer, just in case she missed something. Nothing. It was empty. Her stomach began to cramp up again. This was hopeless.

Pete called them all into a circle, holding the box and ring. "Shall we start with the ritual again?"

Pete handed the box with the ring inside to Andi. She accepted it with shaking hands. This time, she would do everything in her power to hold on to it.

"Maybe we should start all over again and remove the ring from the box first," Pete suggested.

Andi held on to it with an iron grip, and then opened the lid of the jewelry box with the other. I can do this, she thought. Next, she took the heavy ring out. Maybe taking it out of the box would make Volker appear again. She wasn't sure about the magic behind the two items, but they were connected somehow. Maybe taking out the ring is like activating a light-switch and Volker would appear?

Expecting to see him materialize any minute, she looked around. Nothing. This was becoming increasingly frustrating. It was because of her that Volker wasn't standing right beside her, or was he? She looked over her shoulders. Again, nothing.

"Let's begin with the ceremony," Pete announced, ripping her out of her thoughts.

"Andi, would you like to insert the ring into the box again?"

With trembling fingers, she did as he instructed.

Pete then looked at Amanda. "We're ready when you are."

Amanda walked up to Andi and placed her hands-on top of the jewelry box that Andi still held in her hands.

Last night, Amanda did not touch the box while performing the spell. Could that be the reason it didn't work?

Andi watched as her friend spoke the same words that she did just a few hours ago:

Vereinigt für immer.
So der Schatz in der Truhe,
Wie der Geist mit seiner Versprochenen.
Unzertrennlich für immer,
Von nun an.

When she was finished, the group paused for a moment. Again, nothing spectacular had happened. Did they miss something important? she wondered.

Disappointed, she placed the box into a fabric bag and

walked toward the car. Her heart was heavy with grief. Why did she always have this terrible luck with men anyway?

Pete looked at his transcribed copy of the book. "Maybe I missed something, or maybe I have a word wrong. I'll go over the spell again this week and see if we're missing a piece of the puzzle. Until then, shall we get out of this cold?"

*A*ndi sniffled and moaned as she tried to breathe. "Amanda, I need your help," she pleaded on the phone, followed by a rattling cough. "Can you come by and do some of your magic on me? I feel like I'm going to die with this flu."

"Sure, just let me gather up some items and I'm heading your way. I was going to close up early anyway, because of the snowstorm they're expecting for tonight."

"Thank you, Amanda, you're a lifesaver," Andi replied, unsuccessfully suppressing a cough.

After hanging up the phone, Andi crawled back into her warm bed. It had been almost four sad and lonely weeks since she last saw Volker that night on the Heiligenberg. She wasn't entirely over her loss of him, but she carried on with her day-to-day life as normal as she could. Her job at the University kept her occupied, and occasionally she went into town after work to enjoy a cup of coffee at the pub or hang out with Amanda at her store for a while. Something about her shop made her feel as if she was stepping into another world, where all her worries faded away.

The doorbell rang.

Andi crawled out of bed again, rubbing her eyes. She must have dozed off. Dang it! Where was her other slipper?

She didn't want Amanda to freeze to death outside, so she just wore the one she could find. Thank God for floor heating. Andi made her way to the door opener and buzzed her in. "Come on up," she said, coughing from straining her voice.

Amanda walked up the stairs with a basket full of herbs and cloths. "You don't look so good," she said when she got a good look at Andi's wild hair and red nose, then smiled as she looked at her feet.

"That's because I don't. Come on in and make yourself at home." She shuffled her way into the kitchen in slow motion. Her head throbbed without mercy and her nose was running a marathon.

Amanda made herself busy in the kitchen and brought a large pot of water to a boil. In the meantime, she mixed several herbs together in a bowl.

Andi watched as she took a small portion of the mix and filled a tea egg, the little egg-shaped metal filter on a chain, and hung it into a teapot. She poured hot water over it and let it steep for a few minutes. Next, she poured the rest of the hot water into a large bowl and added some chamomile. She set it in front of Andi and handed her a towel. "Here, Andi, hang your head over the bowl and cover your head with the towel. The steam will unclog your sinuses and you will feel much better afterward."

Andi did as she was told. She could feel the steam working on her stuffy nose and sore lungs. However, it didn't take long until she got bored. "How much longer do I have to do this?" Her back also began to hurt from bending over the bowl.

"Until the steam is gone, of course."

Andi heard her giggle.

"Have some patience."

"I hope I'm not keeping you from seeing Shai tonight,"

Andi continued. The pair had been inseparable for the last few weeks and spent every waking moment together.

"No, he's working tonight, and I'll go help out after I'm done here. He found out yesterday that they will remove his cast next week, just in time for Christmas."

Andrea grinned. "That's good news. That means, he won't need your help anymore?"

Amanda smacked her on the back with a clean towel.

Andi flinched. "Okay, so I deserved that!"

"I think the steam is getting to you," Amanda teased. "Actually, we're going to throw a little private Christmas celebration in the evening of Christmas Day and were wondering if you'd like to join us. We were going to do it at Shai's house, but we figured that we have more space at the pub. Of course, Susi and Ralf are invited, as well."

Andi nodded under her towel. "That would be awesome. I don't know if they have plans, but I would be... by myself... anyway..." She felt hot tears mingling with the steam on her face. She would be alone. Without Volker.

Amanda put her hand on her back and said with a soft voice, "I think that's enough breathing therapy for today. Here, I have a clean towel, so you can dry your face."

She uncovered her head. "Got some tissues," she asked. "Because you don't want to see what's been coming out of my head." Andi needed a moment to compose herself again.

Amanda grinned. "It's okay. It's all part of the treatment. Here you go." She handed her a fresh tissue and a cup of her special brew.

While Andi blew her nose and dried her face, Amanda went into the bedroom and straightened the bed for Andi.

"Eeew," Andi yelled into the bedroom. "What did you

put in there? This is the worst tea I've ever tasted! No offense."

"Nobody said that medicine has to taste good. It's the cure you are after. You are not drinking it for afternoon tea-time," she said with amusement in her voice. "When you're ready, can you come into the bedroom? I have one more thing for you."

"Oh, I like you, but not that way, sorry."

"I'm glad you got your humor back," Amanda said, "You must be feeling better."

Andi shuffled into her bedroom. "I can feel a difference, now that I can breathe. What do you want me to do?"

"Just lie down on your bed and relax."

Andi did as she was told and stretched out on the bed.

Amanda placed her hands slightly on top of Andi's forehead and moved her way down to her belly. "This is to unblock some negative energy in your body. Concentrate on your forehead and feel your sinuses drain and free the positive energy in that area..."

They continued with this session for quite a while, until Amanda sat back and announced, "Okay, we're finished. How do you feel?"

Andi opened her eyes. "You are amazing, Mandy!" She sat up on her bed. "I haven't felt this good in a long time. How did you do this?"

"Well, it's the total package of old remedies, Eastern medicine and a touch of my own magic." She winked at Andi.

"Wow, who needs a doctor when I have you?"

Amanda smiled. "I'm just glad you're feeling better. Now drink your tea!"

"That's not tea, that's witch's brew!"

. . .

*V*olker regained consciousness. He slowly opened one eye and then the other. As he moved his head to the left, he saw a window. It must be nighttime, he thought. He then moved it over to the other side, saw that the door to his room was open, and people in white uniforms walked by his door. Where was he? How did he get here?

Glancing toward his side of the bed, he noticed a machine with a bag hanging on a metal stand. From the machine, which had red numbers blinking on a display, he saw a thin hose leading to his left hand. A word popped into his head: Infusion. That must be it. Maybe he was in an infirmary, a hospital.

Slowly he tried to move his right arm. It felt heavy and his muscles were sore. He tried his left arm. Same thing. What happened to him?

Next, he tried to sit up, with little success, so he just leaned back again. He had not felt this weak in ages, since he had become sick with dysentery. On a positive note, he had to admit that he did feel a little better, his gut was still churning, but he felt rested for the first time in who knows how long.

A woman dressed in white walked by his door. "Hello? Can someone help me?" He felt embarrassed asking for help, but he needed to know what was going on and where he was.

"Well, hello, there. You're finally awake," the woman in white said. "My name is Angelika, your nurse for the night."

Volker blinked. Okay, a nurse, so a hospital it is, he hoped. "Where am I and how did I get here," he asked her.

"You are at the University Clinic in Heidelberg.

Someone found you two days ago half-frozen to death at the castle. You were pretty sick and in a coma. Luckily, someone found you in time or you wouldn't be with us right now." She squeezed his good hand. "Let me check your IV. It looks like we can give you a new bag in about 30 minutes. What is your name, by the way? You didn't have any identification or clothes on you, so we are still trying to figure out who you are."

He closed his eyes and thought for a moment. "I think my name is Volker. For some strange reason, I cannot seem to remember very much."

"Okay, Volker, it is then," she acknowledged and wrote it in his chart. "Can you remember your last name and where you are from?"

Again, Volker strained his mind trying to recall anything from his past. Why couldn't he remember simple things about his life? What an idiot I am, he thought. He must be very sick not to remember his own name. Then suddenly, the name Metz came to mind. "I do believe that my last name could be Metz, but I am not absolutely sure. And I think that I live in Eppelheim."

The nurse made a note of the additional information. "Good, this gives us something to go by. Do you want us to notify any family members?"

He shook his head. "I don't even know if I have family. I cannot remember."

"That's okay." The nurse tucked his chart back into the file compartment attached to the front of his hospital bed. "Why don't you rest, and we'll have someone come to talk to you in the morning that specializes in patients with amnesia."

Volker crinkled his forehead. "With what?"

The nurse smiled at him. "Sorry, amnesia is a condition where people have trouble remembering things after traumatic events or brain injuries. Hopefully, we can get you up to speed shortly." Nurse Angelika waved at him on her way out. "I'll check on you throughout the night. Just push this button next to you if you need anything."

He was alone again. What in the world happened to him? So, someone found him at the castle, naked and frozen. What was he doing there? He remembered being sick and he definitely was dressed. Maybe someone robbed him of his clothes as a joke? What about his family? Why couldn't he remember his family? Frustrated with his inability to think, he decided to close his eyes and let his thoughts wander wherever they may. Maybe something useful would show itself.

As he drifted off to sleep, a face appeared in his mind. It had to be the most beautiful woman he had ever seen. Her brunette hair was tied in a loose ponytail. Her eyes were blue as the sky and she had the cutest dimples on her cheeks when she smiled. Who is this woman? Does he know her? Is he married, or does he just wish that he were hers. With her face in mind, he drifted off into a peaceful sleep.

*T*he next day, Volker still felt pretty stiff and sore. He was just about to finish his breakfast, when a doctor came to visit him. "Hello, Herr Metz. My name is Dr. Schmidt and I am a psychologist. I would like to help you with regaining some or all of your memory, if that is alright with you."

Volker nodded as he swallowed his last piece of bread then asked Dr. Schmidt, "Do you think that I will remember everything? Who I am? My family?"

Dr. Schmidt pulled up a chair and sat next to Volker's bed. "Mr. Metz, I would hope that you can achieve a full recovery, however, with amnesia, you can never be quite sure how much memory a person regains. It depends on the extent of damage you have experienced and how your body can repair itself. It also takes time for your brain to recover. Some patients may never remember everything."

Volker frowned. "I can remember flickers of my past, but I cannot make sense of them."

Dr. Schmidt crossed his legs and rested his notepad on his knee. "Why don't we start with what you do remember? I hear you know your name, where you are from, but you do not have an address yet, correct?"

"Yes," Volker agreed.

"Mr. Metz, or may I call you Volker?" When Volker nodded, Dr. Schmidt continued. "We will have some police officers come by later on this morning, who will take your fingerprints. Sometimes, they help determine the identity of amnesia patients and we can track down your family members."

"What if that does not work," Volker began to worry that he would not have a roof over his head, once he was well enough to be released from the hospital.

"Let's not worry about that until the time comes," Dr. Schmidt intervened. "Your job right now is to try to remember as much as you can, so we can find your family, which will also be a big part of your recovery process."

*T*hree weeks after he woke up, Volker was moved to a transitional home. He was allowed to leave the grounds, but he still had to go to daily sessions with Dr. Schmidt.

Each day, he remembered more about his past, but strangely enough, most of his memories seemed to take place during another time. No family members had come forward so far, and he was beginning to wonder if something was seriously wrong.

After one of his morning sessions, Volker strolled through downtown Heidelberg. He walked by a store called 'Was das Herz Begehrt'. As he looked at the display window, a feeling of nostalgia washed over him. Why does that store seem so familiar? He wanted to go inside and see if he got more flashes of recognition, but the sign said it was closed for lunch.

Making a mental note, he decided to come back after a while. Volker was just about to leave, when he heard the sound of voices and the door lock clicked open.

"I'll see you at the pub tomorrow," a female voice said. "Thanks for the tea, Amanda."

Amanda? Why did that name ring a bell? Was that the woman whose pretty face he had been seeing ever day in his mind?

He heard the ringing of a dainty wind chime and the sound of the door shut. Someone was leaving the store. Maybe it was a friend of the owner. He walked closer to the entrance to see if the store was now open for business again. He was almost at the steps, when he suddenly heard the sound of a shoe catching on something, followed by a yelp. Alarmed, he stepped in front of the doorway just in time to see a woman come falling down toward him. Thanks to his freshly regained quick reflexes, he caught her just in time.

"Are you okay" he asked the woman who clung to his arms.

The woman slowly looked up at him, disbelief in her eyes. "Volker?"

How did she know his name? He looked closer. Could this be? In his arms, he held the woman of his dreams.

The best part was that she recognized him from somewhere.

She hugged him, as if she had not seen him in ages. Not sure about how he should react, he held her in return. She sobbed into his jacket. "Are you alright? Did you hurt yourself?" he asked in his normal old German way.

The woman looked up into his face. Her cheeks were red and wet from the tears she had cried. She looked very happy to see him. However, something she saw in his expression made her smile fade.

Not knowing what to say, he looked at her, "Do I know you?"

New tears welled up in her eyes and the expression of confusion turned into obvious pain. He felt like such a tool for hurting the woman in his arms.

She let go of him and backed up a step. She sniffed. "You don't remember me, do you?"

Oh no, what should he say. "I am sorry...," he stammered.

"I'm sorry. I must have mistaken you for someone else. I have to go now." She turned around and took a step back up toward the store entrance, probably to seek consolation from her friend.

Volker just stood in place, not sure what just happened. One minute, he looked at a store display, the next, he found this beautiful woman sobbing in his arms.

The wind chime rang again as she shut the door behind her. Like the idiot he was, he let her get away. He raked his fingers through his hair in frustration. She knew his name. She must know him; otherwise, she wouldn't have been so emotional. Who was she?

He could not let her slip away like this. Finally, his good senses returned, and he walked up the steps to the door and turned the handle. The wind chime sounded again, but this time it was also mixed with the sound of heart-wrenching sobs coming from the back room.

Should he wait for them to return or follow the sobs? He chose to walk toward the back.

"He didn't remember me, Mandy!" The woman cried, obviously hurt. "I know it was him!"

The other woman tried to console her. "Andi, a lot has happened. I'm sure he will remember you, just give him some time."

He thought for a moment. So this beautiful woman is called Andi? Why does the name sound so familiar? He dug in the deepest corners of his mind but did not come up with anything but white space. Risking that he would be thrown out, he slowly stepped into the back room, where he saw a woman with long, wavy hair console the woman of his dreams.

Volker softly knocked at the wall to announce himself and not to scare them. "Excuse me," he then said. "I don't want to intrude, but I think I might need your help."

*T*he woman looked at him and recognition showed on Mandy's face. "Volker! It is really you!" Mandy walked over to him and touched his arm. As if surprised what she saw, she turned back to Andi while still holding his arm. "Oh my God, Andi, he's real!" She looked back at him. "You have come back!"

Now he was thoroughly confused. What did she mean he was real? "Come back from where?"

Mandy looked at him in wonder. "You mean, from when? Are you trying to say that you don't remember anything that happened over the last few weeks?"

Volker shook his head. This was getting bizarre.

Mandy let go of his arm, walked over to the table and

pulled out a chair. "Here, have a seat. This might take a while. How about some fresh brewed hawthorn tea?"

Volker took a seat, not quite sure what to expect. For some reason, the mention of the tea triggered another memory. "Thanks, I think a friend of mine used to make hawthorn tea all the time. She was a healer."

The women looked at each other. "That friend would not happen to be Amelie?"

"Do you know her?" he asked.

"No, not directly," Mandy said. "We are related though, and it is definitely part of the story." She pulled out another chair from the table. "Here, Andi, you could use some tea, too."

Volker looked at Andi and could not take his eyes off her. What was wrong with him? He never felt like this about a woman before.

"So, Volker, meet Andrea, Andi meet Volker." They shook hands as if they had met for the first time.

"It's a pleasure to meet you," he said, feeling more at ease, now that Andi smiled again.

"I'm Amanda, but my friends call me Mandy," she continued the introductions.

Volker couldn't help but wonder out loud. "Am I in the latter category?"

Amanda nodded. "You most definitely are."

Volker already felt as if he was among friends but could not help being on guard. Did he really want to hear the story?

"I don't know what you remember," Andi started, "but do you remember being a mason, working at the castle?" Andi then told him the highlights of the legend up to the point where he was sick and in the prison tower.

As she told his story, bits and pieces came back to him and he nodded when something sounded familiar.

"Now stay with us on this one. This is where it gets tricky, so please hear Andi out."

"I will," Volker agreed as he sipped on his tea. "I am actually very interested in what happened next."

Andi took a deep breath. "Well, you have to promise not to run. We are not crazy."

He nodded. "I promise," he said with a smile on his face. "How bad can it get?"

"You have no idea," Mandy added.

"So," Andi tried again. "I went to this dance at the castle..."

Volker was not sure if he should believe what she had said. There are no ghosts. But what if there were? Andi said that she found the princess' ring and her friends found the box to complete the quest. Apparently, Amanda is a witch, and brought him back to life with a spell from the ancient book. He had thought he was crazy, but now he was not so sure about the two women sitting across from him. That's too bad. He really wanted to believe what Andi said, and that they were in love, but the story was made up. He stood. "Well, ladies, it was nice talking with you, but I have to go back to where I am staying."

"You don't believe me?" Andi looked as if she was close to tears again. "How can I convince you that I am telling the truth?"

Volker thought for a moment. "You are right. I have a difficult time believing you. It is quite a story you were telling, but it's a legend. And since I can't remember much, I may just believe what you are saying, just because it makes sense. But this nonsense about ghosts and witches, I think, went too far. I have to go."

"How can I make you believe?" Andi was about to get desperate. "You and Markus made the foot imprint on the terrace at the castle. It was a prank that you played on

Friedrich, who passed out after drinking too much. How am I supposed to know if you didn't trust me enough to tell me the story behind the legend?"

Volker sat still on his chair. "Who told you that? How do you know Markus?" He was torn between two worlds. It can't be, he thought.

Andi repeated. "You did, you big goofball! You told me! And we met Markus when you made me wait at the terrace the day you gave me a tour of the castle. Do you remember now?"

Volker shook his head. "No, I don't." What was it with this girl? "I will go now." He stood up and walked to the front door.

"Please come back, if you do remember anything. It will mean a lot to us and the others," Mandy said. "I am in the store during the week and Shai owns the Irish Pub down the road."

"Thanks, I will." Volker opened the door and with an empty feeling in his stomach left the two women behind.

On his way back to the main drag, he found himself in front of the Irish Pub. How in the world did he get here? He never came to this place before. He shrugged his shoulders. He might as well go in for a cup of hot tea, since he was not allowed to drink any alcohol per doctor's orders.

He entered the pub and looked around. It was fairly spacious. In the left corner stood a large table. Might as well sit down there, he thought.

The bartender, who had an arm in a sling, came from the back, carrying a rack of beer with his good hand. "I'll be right with you," he said, then suddenly dropped the case hard on the floor. "I'll be!" The bartender walked around the bar to the table. "Volker, is it really you?"

Volker looked at the bartender confused. "Yes, my name is Volker. How did you know? Are you, uh, Shai?"

Carefully, Shai poked him into the arm. "You're alive! The spell worked!"

"Don't tell me you believe in this hocus-pocus, too?" Volker shook his head. "Just like the two women in the store."

"You met Mandy and Andi already?" He shook his head again. "Unbelievable! It's about time you showed up! Andi was heartbroken when you disappeared. She thought that you had moved on to wherever ghosts go when they are finished with what they needed to do."

"Why does everyone keep saying that," Volker asked. "I can't remember a thing. Yes, Andi is the most beautiful woman I have ever met, but all this other stuff does not make any sense to me."

Shai slapped him on the back. "It's good to have you back. You might not remember us, but we sure remember you, friend. Please don't be a stranger. Andi needs you, and the rest of us truly enjoy your company."

"I will keep that in mind," Volker said. "I think I will go now and digest everything that happened today."

*V*olker lay in bed that evening. His mind spun. Everything seemed so very familiar to him, yet he could not remember these people. He must be friends with them, but for the life of him, he could not make sense of them saying that he was a ghost. How could this be? The other thing he could not wrap his mind around was these memories of an earlier time. Was he reincarnated and remembered his previous life? That has to be it. How else could he explain visions of Amelie, who lived 400 years ago in the New Modern period? Of course, he also knew what today's modern conveniences are. Thankfully, he did not forget any of those, or he would not have been able to transition into a temporary home this quickly.

His thoughts drifted to Andrea again. Who was she? Apparently, they must have been close, as Mandy explained when she took over that part of the story that seemed to be difficult for Andi to share with him. Poor girl, she must have felt so bad when he did not recognize her. Yet, there was that possibility that everyone was in on the story and the group would try to take advantage of him, take his money, which he did not have. Or was he rich? If only he knew.

Volker closed his eyes, and soon he was off in another world. At first, he was roaming around the castle grounds. The weird part of the dream was that he was able to float through closed doors like a ghost. He knew that it was only a dream, probably brought on by today's events, so he just let the story play out. Soon, he found himself watching the going-ons at a Halloween party and remembered his eyes being drawn to this one woman sitting with friends at a table close to the wall. Hey, it was Andi, he realized. He almost did not recognize her with all the dots on her face. This dream was very entertaining, he admitted.

Then the scene changed. He found himself in the courtyard of the castle in the middle of a mild earthquake. There was this woman again, holding a ring in her hands. She then looked up right at him, which surprised the heck out of him, because no one could see him before, other than his ghost friends at the castle. Wait a minute, ghost friends? This dream was getting stranger by the minute.

Another scene change. This time, he was in a room with Andi and her dots were no longer swollen, but they were still red. She actually touched his arm and withdrew it quickly, as if she was being electrocuted. She looked away as if she were ashamed to meet his gaze.

The scene changed again. He was in Shai's pub now, having a good time with the group he was sitting with. Andi and Mandy were there, so was Shai, and someone named Pete and a pretty woman they called Belinda. Next to Andi sat Susi, who looked too young to be her aunt. Her aunt? He felt as if he belonged.

Volker's dream flashed back to Andi's room. She was on her bed, looking at him with longing in her eyes. He was lying next to her and millimeters away from touching her lips with his. Then to his regret, her phone rang.

Finally, the scene changed to an area in the woods. He remembered that spot - the Heidenloch. They had dug out a box from somewhere nearby the hut that now stood over the large shaft. The last thing he remembered were Andi's last words, 'I love you!'

His alarm went off. "No way," he grumbled. "Stupid alarm clock!"

It took him a moment to drag himself out of bed. All he could think of is Andrea's sad face when she said good-bye. What a dream! His heart felt heavy. He then remembered her embarrassment and disappointment, when he saw her yesterday. Her heart had practically broken into pieces right in front of him. Could there be a possibility that the story the women and Shai told him was true? Volker began to doubt his sanity. Come on, Volker, ghosts and witches? If he told his therapist about this, he would lock him up in an institution for good.

Once he showered and ate a quick breakfast, he made his way to the hospital for his morning session. "So, Volker, how are you doing today?" Dr. Schmidt asked him. "Something seems different about you today."

"Yesterday, I ran into a woman, who knew me," he started, careful not to reveal any of this ghost story stuff.

"She seemed to like me a lot, but I think, I really hurt her feelings when I did not recognize her," he admitted.

"Did seeing her trigger any memories?" Dr. Schmidt scribbled something in his chart, and then looked at him as he waited for an answer.

Okay, stay focused, he thought. "Not until I fell asleep last night. I had a dream about her. We knew each other, and well, we were about to kiss, when the alarm clock went off this morning." Volker shifted in his chair and leaned back. "Maybe that's all it was, a dream."

"Do you have plans to see her again?"

Volker nodded. "She begged me to meet her at her friend's store again after work, where I saw her yesterday. I have so many questions to ask her. Maybe she can even verify some of the things I dreamed, if they were indeed memories."

Dr. Schmidt nodded. "That would be a start. I would suggest that you to carry a notebook and write things down that you learn about yourself or any memories you have. You could also write down names and addresses of people who recognize you. Remember, your housing arrange-ments are only temporary and hopefully, we could track some family of yours down."

"Hopefully," Volker agreed.

*A*ndi broke away from work as soon as she could. Maybe Volker would be at Amanda's shop waiting for her. She walked down to the alley where the shop was located and almost fell into a jog in anticipation of seeing him. She yanked the door open and immediately saw Mandy stocking some herbs in the shelves. "Did he come back?"

Mandy looked at her with regret in her eyes. "No, honey, there has been no sign of him yet."

Andi's face fell in disappointment. "I was hoping he would be here."

Mandy put down a jar of dried lavender then walked over to her. She wrapped an arm around her waist and led her into the back room. "I think it's tea time, don't you?"

Although, she didn't really feel like tea, what else was she going to do? After all, she was early. Maybe he would get there soon. "Do you think we scared him away by telling him too much?" Andi rested her head on the palm of her hand. "I mean, wouldn't you think that I was crazy if I told you that you once were a ghost when we met for the first time?"

"You have a point there, but don't underestimate him. Maybe it just takes time for him to get used to the idea," Mandy added.

"Or he'll avoid me like the plague every time he sees me on the street somewhere."

The door opened, and the wind chime rang. Both women looked toward the door. Andi jumped up first and peeked out from behind the curtain that separated the store from the back.

"Is that him?" Mandy got up herself and walked toward the curtain.

Andi just shook her head. "Customer," she said and walked back to the chair, where she waited until Amanda returned.

Ten minutes later, the customer walked out of the store with a book on herbal remedies and some teas to help her with her cold. Mandy returned to the back room and joined Andi with her black cherry tea.

Andi about dropped her cup when Volker was standing

by the curtain, smiling at her. "Let me guess, the lady that just left, when I came in, bought some herbs for her cold?"

The girls stared at him.

"Is this a bad time?" He looked for a clock. "I think I came a little early."

"No, no, no," Mandy said. "Please, take your coat off and have a seat."

Andi caught herself still staring at him and quickly shifted her gaze to Amanda, who retrieved another cup from the cabinet.

"Andi," Volker finally said. "I am so sorry for hurting you yesterday. I just wish I could remember..." he trailed off. "Can I ask you something, though?"

Andi's gaze lifted until their eyes met and she nodded. She wanted to reach out and touch him so bad, but she knew that she needed to give him space.

"You did not talk about this when we last saw each other, I just wanted to see if I remembered something, or if it was my imagination," he began. "You said that I was a ghost. What happened when you came too close to me?" He blushed a little.

Andi felt her face flush. "Well, when I accidentally touched you, it felt like I was getting shocked by an electric current." She blushed even more and contemplated not continuing, but if it helps him remember, if she can make him believe... "You tried to kiss me one night, and well, Pete, with his perfect timing called."

Volker's face went pale. "I remember. It is true, then?"

Andi nodded. "So you believe me, then?"

He smiled at her. "I think I do. It will take me a while to be myself again, but all I want is to spend more time with you." Volker held out his hand for her on the table.

She looked down and hesitated a moment in fear of getting shocked again, but then put her hand in his.

"Let's start fresh. Hi, my name is Volker. Have we met?"

She was close to tears. Not sadness, but tears of joy and relief. "I do believe we have," she choked.

Volker then stood and pulled her to her feet by the hand he still held as if he had no intention to let it ever go again. He moved around the table and almost crushed her with his embrace. "I will never leave you again! I swear!"

Andi could no longer hold back her tears. And when a particularly large one fell on his hand, he lifted her chin with his hand until their eyes met. He lowered his face and kissed her.

"Don't mind me. I'll be in the store putting herbs in the shelves, just minding my own business," Mandy said with a sing-sang voice disappearing from the room.

*V*olker felt a little nervous about meeting the rest of the friends. Andi had explained to him on the way to the parking garage that they usually met at the pub on Saturdays, but since everyone wanted to meet Volker right away, they decided to hang out at the pub an evening earlier than usual. Pete, Belinda and Susi had not had the chance to meet him yet in person, so this was the opportunity for everyone to become acquainted again.

"You'll like the rest of them. They are great people," Andi had promised him. He just had to trust her, he supposed.

They arrived at her parking spot and she clicked her remote to unlock her little metallic blue Honda Civic. "How do you like my new, well, used car? I just got it two weeks ago. It took me forever to find an automatic."

He had no idea what she was talking about, so he just nodded. "It looks very nice."

"I still have to get used to driving it in the city, but it gets me from Point A to Point B," she rambled on.

Volker smiled. She looked so cute when she became flustered. No wonder he fell in love with her.

Andi drove Volker to his temporary home, where he quickly changed into some evening clothes for the pub. His jeans and dark blue sweater were donated, but he hoped that Andi didn't mind all too much.

As he walked out of the bathroom, she gaped at him. "What's wrong? Should I put on the other clothes again?"

"No, no," she managed. "You look fine. Very fine."

A smile tucked on the corner of his mouth. For a minute, he thought that he was wearing his shirt backwards. When she still stared at him, he walked over to her and took her into a tight embrace. Minutes passed, and he did not want to let go of her. He was mesmerized by the fruity smell and the softness of her hair. Volker lifted her chin and kissed her on the forehead. "We better go, before my room-mate returns."

She nodded and slowly pulled herself out of his embrace.

He locked the door behind them, and then left a message at the reception area that he would return late and wrote down Andi's handy number, if someone needed to reach him. He then searched for her hand to hold as they walked to her car. Never will he let go of her again!

On the way to her house, she told him more stories of the times they had together, like the trip they took to the castle, the movie night, and the slide show he did for Susi.

Volker remembered bits and pieces of what she told him and laughed out loud when he remembered something funny.

When they stopped at the front gate of her house, he saw a couple getting out of a car in their driveway.

"Oh look," she exclaimed. "Susi made it home from work already. The guy with her is Ralf. They also met at the Halloween ball. Are you ready to meet them?"

Volker turned to her and brushed a finger over her cheek to move a strand of hair behind her ear. "She is not as pretty as you are, but if she has the same family traits, she probably is okay to hang around with." He smiled at her. "No, seriously, I don't mind."

"Hey, guys," Andi called. "Susi, I have someone who wants to meet you!"

Susi walked toward them, leaving Ralf standing in the driveway. "Oh my gosh, Volker! I know you might not remember me, but it's so good to see you! You should have seen Andi when she came home last night. She was crushed that you didn't recognize her, but now it looks like all is peachy, is it not?"

Andi gave her aunt an evil stare. "Thanks, Suse, I can always depend on you to spill confidential information."

Susi laughed. "Regardless, I'm glad you are back among the living. I'm sure Pete and Belinda will ask a million questions of you."

"That's quite alright. Andi has already filled me in on what to expect tonight. But I think I'm in good company, at least that's what Andi has told me," Volker admitted.

Andi turned to him. "Well, I have to get ready for tonight. Do you want to hang out with Susi and Ralf while I shower?"

Before Volker could respond, Susi dragged him and Ralf into the kitchen. "Come on, you two, I'll make us some tea while she is getting herself to look somewhat presentable." She turned around for a second and winked at Andi, before she disappeared with them in the kitchen.

Volker caught the tease: "I think she is already beautiful the way she is, but if she feels more comfortable..."

"I heard that," Andi hollered down the stairs.

Volker enjoyed being in this house. He found it entertaining how Andi and Susi were constantly teasing each other. There was definitely a strong bond between the two of them. He wondered if it had always been that way.

"So, I'm curious," she ventured, "you really don't remember anything since you passed away? Of course, you can tell me to shut up anytime that I get too nosy. It's just hard for me to comprehend what it must be like to be in a position like yours."

Volker's lip twitched. "Actually, I've been enjoying the stories everybody has told me so far. Some of them seem to trigger memories and dreams. This morning, I woke up from a vivid dream about Andi. At first, I thought I dreamt of something that the girls had told me yesterday, but when I spoke to Andi earlier today, she confirmed things that she could not have possibly known, unless she was there. That is when I finally realized that the girls were telling the truth."

Susi looked at him in awe. "I'm so glad that you two found each other again." With a twinkle in her eyes, she hooked her arm under Ralf's, who sat next to her, then turned back to Volker. "Hopefully, you'll remember more as time goes on. It's good to see Andi happy again."

Volker nodded. "I feel so bad for hurting her feelings yesterday. If I could only turn back time and start over."

"But you can," she said. "This is a fresh start and you're off to a mighty good one already."

They both looked at the stairs as Andi came running down the steps. She was finished in record time. She wore a pretty pink sweater and jeans. Her hair was falling over her shoulders in big waves.

Once he looked into her face, he was done for it. He barely noticed the subtle make-up she wore for him. The only thing that he could see was her pretty blue eyes and her glossy lips.

She smiled. "So, are we ready?"

*T*he Irish Pub was crowded, but Andi didn't care. She was with Volker and that was all that counted. She had her arm tucked under his as they followed Susi and Ralf to their table. Pete and Belinda were already there and waiting for the arrival of their mythical friend.

As soon as Belinda spotted them, she jumped up and down in excitement and waved them over. "Here they are, Pete!"

It took a few seconds until Pete spotted them in the crowd, and his expression was almost comical when he saw Volker by her side without her arm falling through thin air.

Andi waved back as they approached the table. Belinda squeezed past Pete's chair and the wall and gave Andi a big hug. "You look so happy!" Belinda then turned her attention to Volker. "Oh my!" She hesitated, not certain if she should hug him or not.

To Andi's surprise, Volker warmed right up to her and took her into a warm embrace.

"You are solid," she said as he let her go. "I am so glad that you are back!"

"What is all this commotion about?" Shai came up behind them with a big grin on his face. "You act like you have never seen this man before in your life!"

Pete, who joined the group, extended his hand to Volker. "Not in this fabulous condition, at least. Welcome back to the world of mortals," he joked.

"Well, let's get settled, here," Susi suggested. "I think

we can get a lot more catching up done with a nice glass of beer in front of us."

"That'll be tea for me, per doctor's orders," Volker interjected.

Belinda added, "I'll have tea, too. I'm driving tonight."

"Me, too," Andi added. "I don't want to make a bad impression on my first real date with Volker."

"Too late," he laughed out loud. "Remember the night we first met? You already looked quite a bit into your cups that evening."

Andi's face lit up. "You remember that night?" She wasn't sure, if she should be embarrassed, especially when she recalled the strange dots on her face, or if she should be happy that he remembered. Well, she hadn't been that drunk, and after she saw him in her bedroom that night, she was pretty much shocked into sobriety anyway.

"How could I forget?" He shrugged his shoulders and sat back in his chair. "I've been getting flickers of images in my head, which I assume is my memory trying to creep back into my head. I must say, you looked especially cute with the polka dots on your face."

Andi sighed and rolled her eyes at him. "Thanks for bringing that experience up again!"

Volker wrapped his arm over her shoulder and gently drew her toward him. Apparently, he was not used to his strength yet, and Andi felt herself being lifted from her chair.

"Eeek," was all she managed to get his attention.

He looked at her and must have realized that he was about to drag her off her seat. His facial expression changed from mischievous to 'uh-oh, I screwed up,' and caught her just in time, before she fell between their chairs.

As he held her tight, she felt an intense jolt surge through her, just like when he was a ghost, but this time it was different. He looked into her eyes and all she could see was a sea of green as she was being swept away into another world, a world where only she and Volker existed.

"Ah, Amanda, finally," Pete called out.

Leave it up to him to ruin another intimate moment, Andi thought.

Volker gave her another quick squeeze, smiled at her and gently let her down on her chair. "Soon, Schatz," he whispered in her ear.

Mandy waved at the group. "Sorry I'm late. I took a little nap, so I'll still be awake when Shai closes up tonight."

"Don't worry," Susi said. "You just missed the most fun parts of the evening." She shrugged and turned to her beer. "I'm kidding, Mandy. We're really just getting started."

"So, did anyone hear or see Fred recently," Andi asked casually.

"Who is this Fred again?"

Belinda explained: "He's the living family member of Ludwig, the one who stole the ring from Andi, because he was chicken that you would beat him up."

The friends laughed.

"He wrecked his precious car, when he had a good talking to from his grand-grand-whatever-grandfather and he brought the ring back to us, so we could perform the ceremony."

Volker did not laugh. "I remember now. I think the kid was just scared and for some strange reason, I feel sorry for him. Maybe I'll go talk to him one day."

Pete gave him a strange look. "Really? Why would you do that? He caused nothing but problems for us."

"I understand. However," he continued, "I want to make sure that he knows that I am not here to make his life miserable. That doesn't mean that I want to be best friends with the man."

Andi had mixed feelings about what he just said. "That's very honorable of you. I'm just not sure that I can forgive him for stealing my purse."

He touched her face. "Schatz, you don't have to if you don't want to. It's just something I need to do for myself. Just one meeting, that's all."

She nodded then sighed, "Okay."

They spent the rest of the evening joking and laughing. When most of the customers had left, Shai joined them as he usually did. Eventually, the time came, when Volker and Andrea had to go their separate ways for the night. Pete and Belinda took Volker back to his temporary facility and Susi, Ralf and Andi took a cab back to Eppelheim.

During the ride home, Andi was sad that Volker had to return to his place for the night. Of course, they would see each other again in the morning, but it didn't lessen the pain of being apart. On the upside, he promised to talk to his doctor about getting permission to move out first thing on Monday. Susi had given her blessing that he could live with them. 'Who else is going to keep my Andi company, while I'm staying with my Ralf on the weekends?' Susi had asked her. She smiled at that memory. Finally, her aunt had found a good guy to be with. If only things weren't so complicated between Volker and her.

*A*ndi honked her horn in front of Volker's place. It only took a moment for him to storm out of the door. "Finally, we have some time alone together," he said as he climbed into her car. He leaned over and gave her a quick peck on the cheek. Andi actually hoped for a more prolonged kiss, but she didn't want to rush him, especially since she parked in front of the facility where he was staying for the time being.

"So, where are we going," he asked.

"What do you have in mind?" Oh no, did she just say that? "I mean, where do you want to go?"

Volker's smile grew bigger with each attempt she tried to wriggle herself out of the awkward conversation she had started. "Why don't you just start driving and we'll go from there. I just want to get away from here."

"Why don't we walk through the Christmas market in town," Andi suggested. "I haven't been to the one in Heidelberg since I was a kid." She couldn't help but smile when she remembered the times when her parents took her to the Christmas market and bought her some roasted chestnuts and some Kinderpunsch, the non-alcoholic version of the famous Glühwein.

"Let's do that. I love seeing you happy like this." Volker looked at her a few more moments. "How can I resist giving you anything in the world that you want, when you reward me with your happiness?"

"Hmmm," Andi responded. "That's good to know. I have to remember that for the future, when we disagree on buying furniture."

Volker suddenly became serious. "You mean that you are actually considering keeping me around for a while?"

Andi couldn't believe what she heard. She looked at him and saw that he was indeed serious. Quickly, she glanced back to the road and nearly hit the car stopping at a red light in front of her. She stepped on her brakes hard, making him lurch forward.

"What are you saying?" Andi continued: "Do you really believe that I'm keeping you around like a stray dog, just because I felt sorry for you?"

"No, that's not what I meant. I'm just hoping that you

would actually love me, even though I have nothing to give in return right now," he said, apparently embarrassed to come to her empty handed.

The light turned green and she gently pushed on the gas pedal. "How shallow do you think I am?" She felt herself getting more upset with each word. "For your information, buddy, you have no idea how much I have fallen for you. You weren't even real when it happened." Her iron grip on the steering wheel relaxed. "I have enjoyed every moment we spent together, even though we couldn't touch." A single tear made its slow trail down her face. "Then, when you were gone, I missed you so much, I couldn't even function right. It felt like I'd lost a part of my soul."

Volker gently brushed her tear away with his thumb. "My God, Andi, I did not know..." he trailed off.

She then found a parking space on a side street close to downtown, which she not so expertly claimed. Once she put her car into park, she looked over to Volker, who sat stunned in the passenger seat. Their eyes locked and she could not break away. It seemed like time stood still until he leaned closer to her and kissed her with lips so tender that she thought she would melt into a pile of goo. Never had she experienced a kiss with so much love and gentleness. Just when she thought that she could not handle it any longer, Volker gave her one final quick kiss on her lips, before he pulled away from her.

"Wow," he finally managed.

She looked at him big-eyed, "Wow," she repeated, because her brain had turned into mush and was incapable of forming new words.

Volker was the first who got his speech back. "Didn't we want to go somewhere?"

Andi answered with a slow nod. "Let's get some fresh air, or we'll never make it out of the car."

"Wait a second," he said as he unbuckled his seatbelt and left the car. A moment later, he opened her door, helped her out of the vehicle, and closed the door again behind her. After she locked up, he took her chilled hand and they walked to the Christmas market.

Only a few more days and they would be together day and night.

*A*ndi spent her first day of her Christmas vacation waiting for the phone to ring. She kept herself busy by scrubbing her already clean bathroom, and then moved on to tackle the kitchen. Volker's session ended at 10 in the morning, and it was almost noon. Did something go wrong?

She jumped when the phone rang and answered it on the first ring.

"So are you coming to get me, or do I have to find another ride home," he asked.

Andi jumped up for joy and looked for her car keys. "So, he said yes?"

Volker's voice sounded just as excited as her own did. "Yes, he said yes, Andi!"

"I'll be right there." She slammed the phone on its cradle, grabbed her coat and drove to the facility.

Twenty minutes later, she rolled up at the main entrance. Volker already sat outside, with a few plastic bags with all of his belongings on each side of him.

"I am here to pick up a certain Herr Metz. Would that be you," she teased him.

He picked up his bags off the ground and carried them

to the car. "Ja, das bin ich," he replied and loaded his stuff into the trunk of her car.

It only took her seconds to unbuckle her seatbelt, get out of the car and run into his waiting embrace.

When she began to shiver from the cold, he gave her a quick kiss and guided her toward the driver's side door. "Let's get out of the cold. I'm ready to go home."

She nodded and reluctantly let go of him.

"I still have to come to my daily sessions," he said as they drove to Eppelheim. "And I will do my best to find work as soon as possible. Dr. Schmidt gave me a few contacts in the masonry business. Maybe someone is willing to give me a chance to show my skills."

"With your experience, people would be crazy not to hire you," she said. "But let's not worry about that today. The first thing we have to do is get you settled. Tomorrow, we can start with the other stuff."

They arrived at the house and carried his bags into her bedroom.

She could feel the uncomfortable tension in the air when they both looked at the bed in front of them.

He finally broke the silence: "Uh, I can sleep on the couch, if you want me to."

Andi didn't know what she wanted, but after hesitating for a few moments, she agreed with him. "Okay, I'll get you some sheets, a pillow and a blanket." She did not want to rush him. Heck, he had barely even known her a week as a human. Maybe he needed some space, which was all well with her. Perhaps they needed to spend some time with each other first, before changing their sleeping arrangements.

Volker took his shaving kit and arranged his items neatly on one side of the bathroom sink. "I hope this side is okay with you," he asked her.

She smiled at him. "Yes, take all the space you need." Her dreams had come true, but why was she still feeling so apprehensive? She should be the happiest person in the world. A lone tear rolled down her face.

Alarmed, Volker looked at her and pulled her into a hug. "What's the matter? Have I done something wrong?"

"No," she sighed, trying to keep from falling apart. "I don't know what came over me. I've been waiting for this day for weeks, and now that it's here, I'm a nervous wreck. This is all new to me." Deep in her mind, she still feared that he was eventually going to leave her, just the same as the other men in her life did. Alone the thought of losing Volker again, terrified her to no end.

He squeezed her tighter and stroked her hair. "It's all new to me, too, Schatz. Maybe we should take things slow," he suggested. "No pressure, as they say in the movies."

She nodded. "How about we go into town and get you some necessities? We should also stop at the grocery store. I didn't know what you like to eat, so I figured I'd wait until you got here."

Volker ruffled her hair and flashed her one of his knockout smiles. "Hmmm, I can't wait to try your cooking."

Andi grinned sheepishly at him. "I wouldn't be so excited, if I were you. I've been known to ruin quite a few dishes in my life."

"It can't be worse than what they served at the facility."

Good, if he uses cantina food as a point of reference, she'd come out on top. "A dinner date it is!"

· · ·

*V*olker enjoyed his time in town with Andi. Before they tackled the shopping, she introduced him to her favorite Döner place. He had trouble holding the massive flatbread without all the stuffing falling out of it when he took a bite. She laughed at him, when a big glob of shredded cabbage, engulfed by the spicy yoghurt sauce, fell on his shoe. He cursed then took his small napkin and cleaned his mess. "Why do they only give you one napkin if they know their food creates spills?"

She laughed at him some more. "There is a fine art to eating those, you know?"

He watched her carefully as she demonstrated the correct way to eat a Döner, but after two more mishaps, he did not care anymore and ate it any way he could.

After they filled their bellies, she found him some nice clothes to wear for the Christmas party being held at the pub the coming weekend. He felt a little strange trying on these modern clothes, but Andi repeatedly assured him that he looked very handsome.

Finally, they manage to buy a buggy full of food at the grocery store. He had no idea what half of the stuff was or what it tasted like, but he just had to trust Andi again.

Back home, he watched her throw some long sticks into a big pot of boiling water.

"We're having angel-hair pasta and tomato sauce for dinner, since it's already late," she announced.

The thought of eating hair did not sound so appetizing to him. He didn't care if it belonged to angels. But he would try it, just to make her happy.

"Alright, here you go," she said and sat a big bowl full of the hair, covered in tomato sauce, in front of him. "Do you want some Parmesan cheese on top?"

"Sure," he replied. He would try anything that would

make the hair slide down into his stomach without gagging.

She joined him at the table with her own plate. "Enjoy," she said and twisted the hair on her fork and put it in her mouth.

He almost gagged.

"What?"

"Nothing. I just never ate hair before." He didn't want to look like a weakling, so he tried to get some of these hairs onto his fork, which turned out to be a harder task than he expected. Finally, he managed to lift a hair on his fork to his mouth without losing it. He dreaded what he was about to taste.

She laughed at him again. "Silly, this is not hair. It's angel-hair pasta. Noodles. It's just named that way, because it looks like, well, hair. Trust me, you'll like it."

He opened his mouth and put the fork with the angel-hair in his mouth. It didn't all fit, so he sucked it in and splashed Andi with tomato sauce. "Oh, I'm so sorry."

Andi held her belly, she was laughing so hard.

After he moved it around in his mouth a few times, he realized that it just tasted like the noodles that they served at the facility, except her sauce tasted much better. Pleased with his dinner, he took a big fork full and shoved it in his mouth. "You have more?"

"What do you want to do next," Volker asked once they had cleaned up the kitchen. "Do you want to watch a movie?"

Andi smiled at him. "Sure, let me make us some tea first, though."

When she returned, he was sitting on the couch,

staring at the remote in his hand. "How do you make this work?"

"Hang on," she replied and put the two cups of tea on coasters. "I'll show you how."

It took Volker some persuading, but they settled on an action film. He sat back on the couch, ready to enjoy a good movie.

Andi grabbed the folded blanket and put her feet up on the couch. She spread the blanket over both of them, and then cuddled up to Volker.

He looked down on his chest and smiled. Cuddling with her could become one of his favorite evening rituals. He lowered his arm from the back of the couch, onto her shoulder and caressed her as the movie started.

Ten minutes into the movie, she looked up at him.

"Yes, mein Schatz?"

"I can't believe you are real now, and I can actually hear your heart beat." She lowered her head again and laid it on his chest, listening for the thump-thump of his heart.

"You don't know how lucky I feel to have you in my arms right now. The entire time I've known you, I wondered what it would be like to hold you, and to kiss you. It tore me up inside not being able to."

She raised her head again and looked him in the eyes, a big smile forming on her beautiful face. "It feels like this," she said as she stretched to kiss him.

"I am the luckiest man in the world," he responded as he met her half way. He never had anyone kiss him as tender as she did. Within seconds, he pulled her across his lap and held her tight. He didn't want to let her go. He couldn't. The way she kissed him made his head spin. "Woman, what are you doing to me?"

Andi backed up and faked a yawn. "Oh, darling, I'm sooo tired. I think I need to go to bed."

He could see the passion in her eyes, and when her dimples showed, as she tried not to smile, all he could do is pick her up and carry her to her bedroom and close the door behind them.

*O*n Christmas day, Andi stood in her bedroom, dressing for the celebration at the Irish Pub.

"Here, let me help you with that," Volker said as she tried to close the clasp of her necklace.

"Thanks," she replied and showed him how to do it.

"Susi and Ralf are almost ready to go. They asked me to check on you."

She turned around and kissed him on the cheek. "Just tell them that I'll be downstairs in a minute."

Volker smiled at her. "What if I don't want to leave right now?"

"Stop it with that cute smile! You know I can't resist when you do that," she scolded him.

"As you wish. I shall wait with the others downstairs." He paused. "And Andi?"

"Yes?"

"Hurry!"

She rolled her eyes in exasperation. "Alright already." She squirted a few sprays of perfume on her wrists and neck. "I'm ready. Let's go!"

He took her by the hand and walked her down the stairs. "She's ready," he announced.

They packed into Ralf's station wagon, where they had room for all the gifts. It was snowing, and the roads were slick, but Ralf expertly drove them to the pub and they arrived safely. The girls enlisted the guys as gift bearers, though the men did not agree with the terminology as they grumbled from the parking spot all the way to the pub.

"Their pack-mules is what we are," Ralf complained.

Shai held the door open for the last guests to arrive. "Merry Christmas and thank you all for coming," he greeted them. "Just unload the gifts over there." He pointed at the big table close to the bar.

Andi looked around and couldn't believe how beautifully it was decorated. "Amanda, did you have a hand in all this?"

She nodded. "Do you like it?"

"I love it!"

They joined their friends at the festive table.

"We set up a little buffet over in the corner," Shai explained. "Help yourself, if you get hungry. And for our American friend, I have some eggnog in that green pitcher. Sorry about the color, but it's an Irish pub after all."

Andi felt tickled that he thought of her. She wasn't much of an eggnog fan, but just for the effort, she would have a glass later on. "Thank you, Shai."

As the friends were about finished with their food, Pete tapped a spoon on his wine glass. "Can I get everyone's attention, please?"

The group silenced.

"I have an announcement to make." Pete cleared his throat and then seemed a little choked up. "As you may have already noticed, Belinda hasn't been feeling all too well the last few weeks."

Oh no! Andi didn't like the sound of this and then looked at Belinda, who sat next to her husband with a big grin on her face. Andi was confused.

"She has been to the doctor," he continued, "and I have to tell you that, well, we will be welcoming a baby into this world around August."

The friends broke out in cheers and gathered around, congratulating the parents to be.

Andi was relieved. At first, she had thought that something terrible was wrong with Belinda. She turned to Volker. He looked at her with so much love in his eyes. She couldn't be any happier. Maybe one day, he would make the same announcement.

They continued the festivities with the gifts. Susi and Ralf gave Shai and Amanda a picture frame containing a gift certificate for a photo shoot at Ralf's studio. Next, Belinda and Pete gave Andi and Volker an annual pass to the castle.

There was only one last gift left on the table. It was a small box with a pretty bow on it.

Andi watched as Volker retrieved it from the table.

"This is a present for my beautiful Andi," he said and got on his knee in front of her. He handed her the box.

Andi suddenly became nervous. Could he…? No way. Not yet. She fumbled with the bow and carefully detached the wrapping paper from the little box. With shaking hands, she slowly opened what appeared to be a jewelry box. Inside, propped in some cushions, she found the sparkling princess ring.

"Andi," Volker began, "since the moment I laid eyes on you, I knew that you were the one for me. Everything began with this ring. Without it, we would have never met. Every second I had to spend away from you was torture. I never want to go through that again. Therefore, will you, Andrea Morgan, marry a poor soul like me?"

Andi wiped her eyes with her free hand. Did he just propose to her? She couldn't believe it!

The room was silent, except for the silly Christmas song in the background.

Pete harrumphed.

Andi looked into Volker's green eyes and the answer was clear. She couldn't live without him – not again. They were destined for each other, or so the story goes, so what could go wrong? "Yes, Volker, I will marry you!"

The friends broke out in cheers again.

Volker took out the ring from its box and slipped it on Andi's right ring finger, as it was customary in Germany. "I love you so much! A life without you would be a life not worth living." He picked her up off her chair and twirled her around in a tight embrace. "You just made me the happiest man alive!" He then stopped spinning and kissed her like there was no tomorrow.

All Andi could do to keep her knees from buckling was to hold on to him for dear life.

When he finished kissing her, he whispered in her ear, "I have a less noticeable ring for daily wear at home."

EPILOGUE

*A*ndi stood in her bedroom looking into a large
mirror. She wore a beautiful 1600s-style white
lace-wedding gown and had fresh flowers, ribbons and
baby's breath braided into her hair. The room was buzzing
with excitement, which didn't help with her already
strained nerves.

Belinda touched her big belly. "Oh, I felt a kick!"

Andi walked toward her. "May I?"

Belinda nodded. "Of course."

She laid her hand on Belinda's belly and waited for the
baby to move again. "I'm telling you, that little girl will be
trouble when she is born!"

"I can't wait another six weeks. I'm ready for her to
come out of my body now! I can't eat, and I can barely
sleep. I'm so exhausted!"

Andi smiled. "But please wait until after the wedding."
Suddenly, she felt a tiny hand, or was it a foot, glide along
the inside of Belinda's belly. "I just felt her move! Hello,
little Molly," she crooned. "I can already see Pete spoiling
his little girl. He's so in love with her already."

"He couldn't be a prouder daddy-to-be. He already finished her room five months ago," she giggled.

While Susi, her maiden of honor, fussed with her dress, she admired the work Amanda had done to her hair. "I don't know how many times I've told you already, but you really have a gift, Mandy."

"Thank you, I love being creative," she replied, while fixing a stubborn twig of baby's breath.

"You know," Andi hesitated, "actually, I should be the one to thank you."

"What do you mean?"

"I want to thank you for trusting us with the book. If you hadn't given us the book for Pete to transcribe, and most importantly, hadn't volunteered to perform the spell, Volker and I would still be in big trouble." She shuddered with that thought.

"I'm just glad to help."

"Amelie would've been proud of you," Andi added and gave her a big hug.

Someone honked downstairs.

Susi peeked out of the window. "It's Fred. Are you ready?"

Andi nodded. "As ready as I'll ever be." Since Volker had his talk with a Fred after his unfortunate accident with his new car, he had become more of a staple in the Morgan/Metz household. He had helped Volker to get into an apprenticeship program with one of his contractors to become a modern mason. In fact, word about Volker's skills had spread around town and folks were standing in line to get some custom work done in the little free time he had. It turned out that Fred was more of a blessing than a curse in the big picture, if one could overlook his occasional bad attitude.

The girls got into his new, shiny luxury class BMW.

"Andi, you look very beautiful today," he said.

"Well, thank you, Fred."

"But the flowers on my hood have to come off before I take you to the airport!"

The girls laughed. Andi knew that they were pushing it by decorating his car with ribbons and a big flower bouquet on the hood.

Fred gently pressed on the gas pedal. "Let's get this wedding over with," he grumbled and drove them to the castle, where the guys were already waiting close to the chapel.

*F*red opened the door for Andi and helped her out of the car. Immediately, Ralf positioned himself to take some pictures of her and the girls next to the nice vehicle.

The girls hooked into one another's arms. "I think between the four of us, we can make it to the chapel in high heels on cobble stone," Andi giggled, suddenly feeling very giddy.

As they stumbled ungracefully toward the chapel in the courtyard, Markus greeted, or rather, laughed at them, from a spot where tourists couldn't see his slightly glowing and translucent form.

Andi reproached him, "Just wait. Your time will come, and we'll be the ones rolling on the floor laughing. By the way, that's a nice outfit you're wearing." She referred to his 17th century suit, if that's what you could call it.

"Well, thank you, my lady. I conjured it just before I arrived here, although, I did take care of choosing the most appropriate garments to wear for this special occasion. I'm glad it suits your taste."

Markus made himself invisible and walked with them

toward the chapel. He was going to be Volker's best man, but they didn't want to scare the priest to death before the ceremony. Instead, Pete agreed to stand in for Markus.

The wedding music started to play and, with Susi by her side, Andi walked with wobbly knees down the aisle. The second she saw Volker standing at the altar, she focused on him. Do not faint! Do not faint! Do NOT faint! Breathe…

"Are you okay," Susi asked half way down the aisle. "You look a little pale."

Andi was going for a reassuring smile but failed miserably. "I think I can make it."

"You can do this, kiddo. We're almost there."

When Andi began to wobble dangerously, Susi grabbed her by the arm and Volker came to the rescue.

Worried, they sat her down on a church pew for a few minutes and gave her some water to drink.

"I already feel better," she said.

"Are you sure," Volker asked concerned.

Andi nodded. "I'm ready." Or at least she hoped.

They proceeded to the altar, and after what seemed an eternity of preaching by the priest, finally exchanged their vows.

"I now pronounce you husband and wife," the priest announced. "You may kiss the bride."

Volker didn't waste a minute to draw Andi into his arms and kissed her like there was no tomorrow.

If there's a heaven, she thought, I'm in it. She didn't want him to stop, but when the priest cleared his throat, she smooched him on the lips one final time. "Ready?"

"Whenever you are, Frau Metz."

The guests clapped and cheered. As the newlywed couple left the chapel, they were showered with rice and rose petals.

"Meet us at the pub," Andi yelled over her shoulder after she took her shoes off and ran with Volker to the waiting car, with a bunch of cans in tow, and a 'Just Married' sign in the back window. Fred had made it clear all week that no one could write on his car.

*T*he Metz's arrived at the pub and Andi was beyond surprised how Amanda and Shai had decorated the place.

"Actually, the pub had become more popular than ever, thanks to Mandy's creativity," Kyla said, as she helped Andi arrange her gown as she tried to sit at the table.

Andi grinned. Maybe it was a hint of magic that attracted people to the pub.

A few minutes later, the guests trickled in and the celebration kicked into gear.

Even Markus attended with a quite bright glow around him. "I'm not going to miss out on this party," he had told Volker.

"And I wouldn't want you to," he had replied. "Besides, all our friends are accustomed to the paranormal by now."

Susi sat next to Andi at the table. "So, Frau Metz, how does it feel to be a newlywed?"

"I love it! Maybe we'll have another wedding in the family soon?" Andi couldn't help it.

"No, not this fast. Moving in with Ralf is already a big step for me. I've lived alone for so long. I want to take things slow."

Andi made a pouty face. "I still can't believe that you are leaving Volker and me alone in the house. Who am I going to eat breakfast with on the weekends?" She really was going to miss having Susi around as often.

She gave her a blank look. "Uh, you have a husband, remember?"

"But what if we have our first big argument and I need someone to be on my side?"

"Andi, relax. I'm just a phone call and 15 minutes away from you. Besides, you two will need the space, when you eventually start your family." Susi grinned.

Andi sure was thinking about babies a lot. Of course, it was all Belinda's fault for running around with her big belly. However, they decided that they wanted to become more financially stable before bringing a baby into this world.

"Single ladies! Come on over to the dance floor," Belinda called out. "Guess what time it is!"

Susi, Amanda, and Kyla timidly made their way to the open space.

"Yes, that's right! One of you will catch Andi's bouquet. Let's see who is next in line to get hitched! Andi, are you ready?"

The men lined up opposite of Andi, who had turned her back to the three ladies. Shai crossed himself then searched his pocket for his lucky coin.

Andi truly enjoyed this part. She began to count. "Ooooone, twooooo, aaaaand threeee!"

She tossed the bouquet high into the air and hit a chandelier. One of the ribbons caught on one of the pointy parts and slowly slid down as the ribbon gave.

Everyone's eyes were on the bouquet, including the men. Suddenly, it broke free and fell into the waiting group of girls below. The mad scrambling began and a few moments later, Amanda called out in surprise. "Oh my gosh, I got it!"

All the men stared at Shai. "Sorry dude!"

Shai walked over to Mandy, drew her into his arms and

gave her a big, fat smooch on her lips. "Well, Baby, I guess it's time to make plans," he announced as soon as he let go of her.

Andi and Volker laughed. "They do make a great couple," Volker remarked.

"I think so, too. Maybe we'll attend their wedding next."

*L*ater that afternoon, Andi and Volker just finished yet another dance. She gave him the most pleading look that she could manage.

"Should we get out of here?"

She nodded with a big grin.

He grabbed her by the hand, and together, they ran toward the front door. Fred came running after them, almost missing his cue.

The guests hooted and hollered as they left, when Volker poked his head back in the door one last time. "Have a great time and don't call us for two weeks!"

They climbed into the car, which was quite a task with Andi's wedding gown, and rushed off with Fred chauffeuring them to the Frankfurt Airport.

"I always wanted to stay at Chris de Burgh's castle. I'm so glad we're going there for our honeymoon," Andi sighed as she cuddled up to her husband on the backseat.

"Schatz?"

"Yes?" Andi looked up to him.

"You look happy," he said, flashing his irresistible smile at here. "That wouldn't happen to have anything to do with me, would it?"

"You're so full of it, Volker Metz." She punched him in the arm. "And yes, you have something to do with it."

Still smiling, she rested her head on his shoulder again.

Yes, she was truly happy. She finally found a man who loved her unconditionally. A man, who would spend the rest of his life with her. She had found her soul mate, the real-live hero of her novel. She was his princess.

~~~ THE END ~~~

Thank you so much for reading The Heidelberg Ghost. This really means the world to me!!!

I hope you enjoyed it as much as I did writing it, and I'd love it if you could rate it or even leave a quick 1 or 2-line review. This helps other readers decide if this story is something they would like as well.

If you fell in love with the charming characters of The Heidelberg Ghost and want to read more, grab a copy of The Shadow of His Past:

Remember Kyla, the bubbly waitress in the Irish pub? In this next story, she moves into her own apartment in an old family home. Soon, the excitement of her new-found independence wanes. Appliances seem to have a mind of their own, and her moody landlord accuses her of breaking things on purpose. Only when tragedy strikes, he believes her, and together they try to get to the bottom of these strange occurrences. However, the more time they spend together and grow fond of each other, the paranormal activity escalates, as if something or someone wants to keep them apart. Can they restore peace in the old family home and finally be free to fall in love with each other?

Read Kyla's and Chris's story in The Shadow of His Past.

Or if you're in the mood for another holiday story and want to meet many of the characters of the Heidelberg Ghost again, read Her Christmas Angel next. It's Julia & Tony's Christmas Story.

Finally, you can also join Nickie's mailing list and read Pete & Belinda's bonus story for free at https://bit.ly/30EL29h.

Until we meet again,
Nickie

ABOUT THE AUTHOR

Nickie was born and raised in Heidelberg, Germany. Many moons ago, she married her Soldier and spent 20 years as an Army wife attending university and raising their three kids, which are now grown. Nickie now lives with her hubby and her not-so-new kids of the furry kind smack-dab in the middle of Alabama. She works on an Air Force base during the day and dreams up stories at night.

Join Nickie's Mailing List and read Pete & Belinda's story for free at https://bit.ly/30EL29h.

Visit her website at nickie-cochran.com

Made in the USA
Monee, IL
16 April 2023

31944692R00154